WITHDRAWN FOR SALE

Murder in Petticoat Square

The body of Alan Chisnall, financial journalist and gambler, was sprawled on the floor of his parlour; his face had been battered into a bloody pulp. Beside him lay a heavy poker, its blackened end stained with blood.

This was Jack the Ripper country, but to Detective Sergeant Joseph Bragg and Detective Constable James Morton, of the City of London police, it was no opportunist murder.

A strong-box retrieved from the vaults of the Bank of Montreal revealed an embarrassing link with the aristocratic family of Constable Morton himself. Evidence was unearthed that Chisnall had been blackmailing prominent City figures.

The whole of the financial community held its breath when a posthumous play of Chisnall's promised to put the cat among the pigeons, and expose a widespread corruption. As the stock market dropped like a stone, Gatti's Music Hall, where the play was due to open to an invited audience, went up in smoke; further obscuring the two detectives' tortuous path to a solution of a brutal murder.

Ray Harrison's gift for introducing his readers to the elegant drawing-rooms, the offices of officialdom and the teeming by-ways of turn-of-the-century London is once more displayed with characteristic verve and conviction.

Books by Ray Harrison

French ordinary murder (1983)
Death of an Honourable Member (1984)
Deathwatch (1985)
Death of a dancing lady (1985)
Counterfeit of murder (1986)
A season for death (1987)
Harvest of death (1988)
Tincture of death (1989)
Sphere of death (1990)
Patently murder (1991)
Akin to murder (1992)

MURDER IN PETTICOAT SQUARE

Ray Harrison

Constable · London

First published in Great Britain 1993
by Constable & Company Ltd
3 The Lanchesters, 162 Fulham Palace Road
London W6 9ER
Copyright © 1993 by Ray Harrison
ISBN 0 09 472010 X
The right of Ray Harrison to be
identified as the author of this work
has been asserted by him in accordance
with the Copyright, Designs and Patents Act 1988
Set in Linotron Palatino
and printed in Great Britain by
Redwood Press, Melksham, Wiltshire

A CIP catalogue record for this book
is available from the British Library

To My Wife Gwyneth

1

Detective Sergeant Joseph Bragg and Detective Constable James Morton, of the City of London police force, were strolling along St Mary Axe towards the sixth division station in Bishopsgate. The previous night's thunderstorm had washed away the stickiness of the last few days, but already the July sun was sucking up the moisture again. They checked as a two-horse brewer's dray swung across their path into the yard of the Swan, then resumed their walk. Bragg glanced sourly at Morton. Although at first sight you would take him for a young clerk, he didn't stint himself. No putting up with winter worsteds all year for him. The frock coat he was wearing was made of a lightweight vicuna, his waistcoat of hopsack. And why not? He was made of money. With a titled family and a university degree in languages, he could have been a diplomat; ended up an ambassador. Well, if he wanted to waste his time playing at policemen, that was his look-out. . .

Bragg felt a trickle of sweat wriggling down his spine. It was his own fault. Mrs Jenks, his landlady, was always telling him to get some summer clothes; but it never seemed worth it. If you had a couple of weeks' real summer weather you were lucky. And this year had been no different. . . The new celluloid collar he was trying didn't help either. They were supposed to look smart, last longer. But there was no give in them. It was like having an iron band round your neck; being on a chain-gang. And Dora Jenks had not been all that pleased when he bought them. She had got on her high horse, saying that if he wasn't satisfied with the way she starched his collars he should send them to a laundry. Blast it! He was almost wanting the autumn to come. Wishing his life away. . .

He cleared his throat. 'I got a bit of a poser in this morning's post, lad,' he said gruffly.

Morton smiled. 'Ah! Could it be that the beautiful Miss Hildred has joined forces with her mother, to lure you back to Dorset?' he chaffed him. 'I can imagine that, on a morning such as this, the prospect of managing a Dorchester brewery – to say nothing of the charms of Miss Fanny herself – would seem infinitely preferable to plodding round the City of London, upholding the majesty of the law.'

Bragg refused to rise to the bait. 'No, I know where I am with the Bere Regis lot – they are my own kind,' he said gloomily. 'This is a deal trickier; and I expect you are the last person I should mention it to.'

'Then I must clearly respect your diffidence, sir, and change the subject.'

'Don't be stupid! Why do you think I brought it up? No. . .' His bushy eyebrows met in a frown. 'This morning I got an invitation to your sister's wedding.'

Morton grinned broadly. 'Why should that surprise you?' he asked. 'You know that Emily has always said she would never marry unless you approved!'

'That was only fun, as you well know. . . Anyway, Reuben Smith is a fine young chap, from what little I know of him.'

'Well then?'

Bragg walked on in silence for some moments. 'You know damn well what it is,' he said eventually. 'I don't belong there.'

'Rubbish!'

'No, it is not rubbish. I am an ordinary working-class chap, with no education to speak of and manners to match. It is only because you chose to waste your young manhood in the police that I have met your family at all. Blast it! Emily is the daughter of a baronet. The wedding is going to be at your family's estate in Kent. Half the nobs of England will be there.'

'But you know that such things are of no consequence to us. After all, the bridegroom has no title, nor any prospect of one.'

'He is the only son of a banking family. I do know that.'

Morton laughed. 'Then my sister is marrying a tradesman; and snobbery – inverted or otherwise – is inappropriate.'

'I don't know, lad. . .'

They checked as they reached Houndsditch, and waited for a gap in the traffic. Looking up a side-street opposite them, they could see a boy weaving his way towards the main street. He was pushing rudely along the pavement. When the press of pedestrians impeded him, he would skip out into the roadway, among the hansom cabs and carts. A cab driver reached for his whip as the youth darted out and caused the horse to rear. It was madness to run through the traffic like that, Bragg thought. . . Was he being chased? He reached Houndsditch and plunged into the knot of pedestrians waiting to cross. There were shouts of outrage, a woman's cry of 'Police!' The boy broke through them and dashed into the middle of the street. The driver of an omnibus swore fiercely at him when he ducked under the noses of his horses. As he gained the pavement, Bragg grabbed him and twisted his arm behind his back.

'Well now, young man,' he said gruffly, 'what are you up to?'

'Get off!' the lad gasped, wriggling in Bragg's grasp. 'I'm going for the police. There's been a murder!'

'A murder, eh?' Bragg said sceptically. 'When was that?'

'I dunno. . . Last night I 'spect. He was cold they said, and battered somethin' 'orrible.'

'We are police officers,' Bragg said sternly. 'Whereabouts was this murder?'

'Next door. My mum said she might have heard somethin', but thought nothin' of it.'

'I see. How old are you, son?'

'Twelve.'

'And where do you live?'

'Eight, Petticoat Square.'

Bragg turned to Morton. 'That's just inside the City boundary. . . Right. You go along and alert the coroner. Get Sir Rufus to appoint me his officer for this one. We could do with something to get our teeth into. Tell him I have already gone to the scene. And get the pathologist down there as soon as he can.'

'Very good, sir.' Morton turned briskly away.

Bragg took hold of the lad's wrist. 'Now, son, take me there,' he growled. 'And if you have been bulling me, I will tan you within an inch of your life.'

The boy went quietly enough. A withdrawn look had come over his face; he said nothing as he picked his way through the narrow alleys. Bragg began to wonder just what he could do to

9

him, if it were merely a jape. Then the boy looked up, and he saw fear in his eyes.

'Who was it that was killed?' he asked.

'Mr. Chisnall, at number seven on the corner.'

'When was he found?'

'His cleanin' woman saw it, when she got there this mornin'.'

'I see. Live alone, did he?'

'Yes.'

Bragg looked at the boy speculatively. 'Did you see him?' he asked.

'I peeped from the hall, when nobody was lookin'.'

'You shouldn't have done that,' Bragg said in a fatherly voice. 'There are some things that are best left alone. . . How much further?'

'We turn right here, down Nightingale Place.'

It was a long time since nightingales had sung in this neighbourhood, Bragg thought. It was an area of mean houses; built in the eighteenth century for the grooms and street sweepers, the skivvies and servants that made a life of luxury possible in the fine houses at the centre of the City. Now the pavements were uneven, the surface of the road rutted. Slates were missing from the roofs, paint peeling from the doors. And over all loomed the menacing bulk of the East India trade warehouses. The contrast with somewhere like Grosvenor Square could hardly be more marked, Bragg thought. No gracious houses, no lawns and trees where the residents could relax in the sun. In fact Petticoat Square consisted of a block of twelve terraced houses, back to back. They stared out grimly over the narrow streets that surrounded them, like a square of infantry at a hostile force. Before the main sewer was put in, Bragg thought, the alley running through the centre of them, behind the privies, must have been little more than a fetid drain.

Bragg approached a knot of people standing in front of a corner house. 'City police,' he said. 'Is this where the body is?'

A burly man in a collarless shirt stepped forward. 'Yes,' he said. 'Mrs Plumb found him, when she came to clean this morning.'

'Is she here?'

'No. She went home. She was all of a shake.'

'Where is home?'
'Nightingale Place – five, I think.'
'Just down the street there?'
'Yes.'
Bragg turned to the house. 'Is this door open?' he asked.
'Yes.'
The man followed Bragg into the narrow hall, then checked. 'He's in there,' he said, pointing to a doorway at the rear of the house.
'Aren't you going to show me?' Bragg asked drily.
'Not bloody likely! Once was enough.'
Bragg walked to the far end of the hallway. Straight ahead was a small kitchen, with a glazed sink and a newish gas cooker; to the left was a half-open door. He pushed into the room. The body of a man was sprawled on the floor; the face had been battered into a bloody pulp. On the carpet beside it lay a heavy poker, its blackened end stained with blood.

Bragg looked around the room. A small dining table was under the window, with two coffee cups and a half-full jug of milk on it. He sniffed the milk; it was still fresh. On either side of the empty fireplace were armchairs, their chintz covers grubby and worn. A small bamboo table stood in the alcove near the window. On it was a spindly plant, the soil in its pot hard and dry. The room itself was superficially clean and tidy, but it had not been cleaned thoroughly for a long time. Black dirt had accumulated in the corners of the window panes. A cobweb, hanging from the ceiling, stirred gently in the draught from the open door.

He went back to the hall and up the stairs. The door to the front bedroom refused to open. He put his shoulder to it, and stumbled into a room cluttered with dingy furniture. The bed had no mattress; its springs were rusting in the all-pervasive dampness. Every surface was covered with dust, the air stale. He closed the door and went into the bedroom at the back. Here the top window was open a foot and the bed had been properly made. Bragg opened the door of a large wardrobe. It contained jackets and trousers, overcoats and waistcoats of reasonable quality. On the top shelf was an assortment of hats – all men's. In the whole house he had not seen a sign of a woman's presence.

Bragg went downstairs again, and into the room at the front. On the window side of the chimney breast was an open roll-top desk. Papers were strewn untidily over its surface. The drawers had been pulled out of the pedestals and their contents tipped on to the floor. In the other alcove stood a bookcase. Its volumes had been scooped from the shelves, and they lay scattered over the carpet. Apart from a swivel chair and the pictures on the walls, there was no more furniture in the room. Most of the floor area was taken up by cardboard whisky cartons and wooden wine boxes; upended all of them. They had been thrown haphazardly on scattered heaps of the papers they had once contained. It looked like a burglary. But what burglar would stay to read old newspapers? Anyway, there were the two cups in the living-room. . .

Bragg went out into the street and pulled the door closed behind him. He enjoined a neighbour not to let anyone but the police into the house, then walked back to Nightingale Place. He found Mrs Plumb's house. She was red-eyed and dazed.

'I gather that you found Mr Chisnall's body,' Bragg said quietly.

'Yes. . . I'd been in the house half an hour already,' she said dully. 'I'd done the washing up and cleaned the kitchen . . . and all the time he was lying there. . . It don't seem right. . .' She blew her nose in her damp handerkchief.

'You thought a lot of him, then?' Bragg remarked gently.

She looked up. 'No, not specially. He was all right for a man. A bit funny in his ways. . . But to go like that. . .'

'How long have you worked for him, Mrs Plumb?'

'It'll be three years, come October. Before me, Mrs Murphy from Bull Court did for him.'

'I see. Did he live on his own? No wife, no children?'

'I never seen no sign of any. Not that I pried, mind you! A body has a right to live their own life.'

'Indeed. Did he go out to work?'

'He said he worked from home. And he was as often as not there when I went.'

'What did he do?'

'He was a journalist – at least that's what he said. But my sister's girl lives next door to a journalist, and he's never at home!'

'So you had your doubts?'

'No, not me!' She looked up sharply. 'People have a right to do what they wants, haven't they?'

'What time did you arrive at his house this morning?'

'Nine o'clock. I'd rather start at half–past eight myself, but he wouldn't have it. It's a tight squeeze for me to get my three hours in, and go over to Gravel Lane to pick up our Edna's little girl from school.'

'I understand. . . How often did you clean for him?'

'Just the Monday mornings. He used to say the place was all clean and tidy to start the week.' She blew her nose again.

Bragg pondered. 'What kind of man was he?' he asked.

'Well. . .' She hesitated. 'I've heard it said he sometimes had a drop too much to drink. But he was always all right with me.'

'Hmn. . . It looks as if he managed to get into someone's bad books, all the same. Have you ever seen anyone at the house while you were there?'

'No. But then, Monday morning isn't much of a time for visiting, is it?'

'You have your own key to the front door?'

'Yes.'

'Would you mind if I take it? I don't think you will be doing much more cleaning there.'

She sniffed. 'No, I don't suppose I shall.' She took a latchkey from her handbag and passed it over. 'Do you know when the funeral will be?' she asked. 'I'd like to pay my last respects.'

'No. I expect his next-door neighbours will know, in a day or two. Who are they?'

'That's Ernie Johnson. His wife is Alice. It was her got me the job in the first place.'

Bragg stood up. 'Well, thank you, Mrs Plumb. If you think of anything else, let us know at the police headquarters in Old Jewry. If you cannot get there, a message in any City police station will get to me.'

He arrived back at the house just as a hansom cab drew up. Morton jumped down, followed by the portly figure of Dr Burney, the chief police-surgeon. He was also the professor of pathology at St Bartholomew's teaching hospital, and an acknowledged authority in his field. He had a round cherubic face, and a wide flaccid mouth which was liable to break into a Cheshire-cat grin at the most inauspicious moments.

'Ah, Sergeant Bragg,' he beamed. 'I gather that there is something speculative about this summons. It is unusual for you to act on an unsupported report from a child. I trust that my journey will not have been in vain. I ought to be conducting a tutorial at this very moment!'

'There is nothing speculative about the poor sod in the back room,' Bragg said gruffly. 'He knows what it's all about by now.'

'Good! Then let us to work.'

Burney marched down the hallway, with the policemen following. Bragg heard Morton's sudden intake of breath as he saw the corpse.

The pathologist put down his bag, and waved his hands to clear away the flies that had settled on the wounds. 'Ah yes,' he said musingly. 'A domestic quarrel? A little tap from the nearest and dearest?'

'I gather that he lived alone,' Bragg said.

'Hmm. . . Well, I am of the opinion that you need look no further for the murder weapon.' He picked up the poker and fitted it to one of the bloody weals on Chisnall's head. 'Yes. . . I would like to take that away with me, all the same. In such a frenzied attack, it is entirely possible that a second weapon could have been used, and its marks have been obliterated by the poker.'

'A second weapon and a second attacker, you mean?' Bragg asked.

'That could follow, certainly.'

'We gather that the neighbours heard some sort of disturbance last evening. Could that fit in?'

Burney stooped and took hold of an arm. 'It could well be so. Rigor mortis is fully established, certainly. I will be able to tell more precisely when I have taken the rectal temperature. Can you get the body over to the mortuary within the hour?'

'Almost certainly,' Morton broke in. 'I alerted Noakes, when I called there to look for you.'

'Excellent! Then I shall be able to make amends to my students, by summoning them to a practical demonstration of the autoptic art. If you would like to join us, constable, you might find it of interest.'

'No thank you, sir,' Morton said hurriedly. 'I am sure that there are more pressing things to occupy me.'

There came the sound of an altercation in the hallway, then a tall figure with a mane of grey hair appeared in the doorway.

'Ah, Burney! You have anticipated me.' Sir Rufus Stone QC, the coroner for the City of London, glanced at Bragg then crossed to the body and stared down at it. 'Assault and battery on a grand scale, eh?' he remarked.

The pathologist's mouth sagged open in a shamefaced grin. 'That is the superficial impression, Sir Rufus,' he said.

'I would have thought it was beyond a peradventure. . . Ah, you are punning,' the coroner exclaimed in a disapproving tone. 'Indentations on the surface of the body. . . I find that in rather bad taste, Burney. Anyway, you ought to have grown out of punning at your prep school.'

Burney gave a loose smile. 'I thought that you might appreciate it, since you dabbled in medicine in your youth.'

Sir Rufus glared at him. 'Dabbled? I will have you know, Burney, that I studied for three whole years at St Thomas's, before realising that your trade is little better than butchery and turning to the law.'

Bragg intervened. 'Can I take it that you have appointed me your officer for this one, sir?' he asked.

Sir Rufus swung round disagreeably. 'You may, Bragg. Though I am less than pleased at being presented with a virtual *fait accompli*.'

'Thank you, sir,' Bragg said meekly.

The coroner surveyed the room. 'Well, what have you discovered?' he demanded.

'The dead man was a journalist by profession, sir.'

'Profession?' Sir Rufus looked coldly at him. 'Since when has a scribbler aspired to such eminence? I will have you know, Bragg, that "profession" applies to only three areas of human activity – the law, medicine and some branches of teaching!'

'Yes, sir.'

'What kind of journalist was he?'

'Not much of one, from what his cleaning woman says.'

Sir Rufus wrinkled his nose in distaste. 'Gossiping with the servants again, Bragg? I would have thought that you could have been better employed in examining the scene of the crime! For instance, it is noteworthy that there are two empty cups on the table, suggesting that there was some social relationship between the deceased and his murderer; perhaps that they met by appointment.'

'I had noticed that, sir,' Bragg said shortly.

'I would hope so! Well, now, I will open the inquest on Thursday the fifth, at ten o'clock in the morning. That is in two days' time. I will take evidence of identity and discovery, then adjourn. I take it that you will make the necessary arrangements, Bragg.'

'From some bills in his desk, sir, the man's name was Alan Chisnall. I will get the next-door neighbour to give evidence of identity.'

'Who discovered the body?'

'A Mrs Plumb who comes to clean for him. She is very upset about it, as you can imagine.'

'Since when has that been relevant?' the coroner said sharply. 'See that she is present.' He turned and strode out of the room.

Burney smiled beatifically. 'If only Sir Rufus had spared us five minutes more,' he remarked, 'he could have solved the case by the sheer power of his intellect! Well, now, a van should be here shortly to collect the remains. If you care to pop in around five o'clock, I shall be able to tell you what will be in my post-mortem report.' He picked up his bag and sauntered out.

Bragg turned to Morton. 'You stay here until the body has been taken away, lad, while I pop next door. Go into the front room and see what you make of the mess there. Anything you think we should take back with us, pack in the boxes.'

There was still a knot of people standing on the pavement when Bragg emerged. Fortunately the press had not yet got wind of the murder, or they would have been down in a pack. It was surprising, he thought, that scarcely any reporters got themselves knocked off, considering the trouble they stirred up. He rapped on the door of the adjoining house. It was opened by the burly man who had shown him into Chisnall's house.

'Mr Ernest Johnson?' Bragg enquired formally.

A look of alarm flitted across the man's face, and was gone. 'That's right,' he said.

'May I come in?'

He hesitated for a moment, then beckoned. He ushered Bragg into a parlour at the front. 'I will fetch the wife,' he said.

The room was equivalent to the office next door. It was furnished with old, shabby pieces, but was scrupulously clean. In layout this was the mirror image of Chisnall's house. Between this room and the journalist's office were the two hallways; so the two kitchens would separate the Johnsons' living-room from the place where Chisnall had been murdered. One would be lucky to hear much across that distance.

Johnson came back followed by a plump, motherly woman. Bragg had seen her on the pavement when he first arrived. Johnson motioned him to a chair and sat down opposite him. Mrs Johnson perched on the arm of her husband's chair.

'First of all,' Bragg said amiably, 'let me say what a fine young fellow your son is. If there were more like him around, it would make our lives a sight easier.' He took out his notebook. 'Now then, Mrs Johnson, can I have your first name – just for the record?'

She glanced uncertainly at her husband. 'Alice,' she said.

'Now, I gathered from your son that you might have heard a commotion next door.'

She bit her lip for a moment. 'Well, I did. But how was I to know the poor man was being murdered?'

'What exactly did you hear?'

'I was just going to go upstairs, when I heard some bangs at the front. I didn't think anything of it at the time.'

'When was this?'

'About six o'clock. I was on the lookout for Ernie; he's usually home around then.'

'How long did these bangs go on for?'

'Not long. . . You see, Mr. Chisnall would sometimes get the worse for drink, and then he would throw things.'

'Strange that Mrs Plumb didn't mention that,' Bragg murmured.

'Well, she'd tidied up after him enough times, in all conscience!' she exclaimed.

'Do you think these bumps could have been caused by the desk drawers being pulled out and the boxes being thrown about?'

'That's what we thought, isn't it, Ernie?'

Her husband nodded unwillingly.

'But now you think it wasn't Mr Chisnall making the racket, but his murderer.'

'Well . . . yes.'

'He would have been taking a big risk, wouldn't he? After all, it was broad daylight at that time. There would have been people in the street, children playing.'

'I've asked around,' Johnson broke in. 'Nobody saw him, from what they say.'

'All right, leave that for the moment. . . Tell me, what kind of a neighbour was Mr Chisnall?'

The Johnsons exchanged glances. 'Well,' the wife began, 'he wasn't a neighbour really; not a proper neighbour. If you ask me, he felt he was too good for the likes of us!'

'Too good for you?' Bragg asked in a surprised tone.

'It's true enough,' Ernie interposed. 'He was too good for round here. He'd been a nob in his time. Once, when he was a bit worse for drink, he told me he'd been to the City of London School, and after that he'd been a stockbroker.'

'Did you believe him?'

'Yes . . . yes, I did.'

'So he had come down in the world?'

'I reckon so.'

Bragg mused for some moments then: 'Did he have many visitors?' he asked.

Mrs Johnson furrowed her brow. 'Not many really,' she said.

'Any regular visitors?'

'Well, I've more to do than keep watch on next door . . . but I would say he had hardly any visitors.'

Bragg rose to his feet. 'Well, thank you for your help.' He turned to go, then swung back. 'By the way, do you hold a spare key to his house?'

The Johnsons glanced quickly at each other. 'No,' they said almost in unison.

Bragg gave them a long stare, then marched out into the street. He found Morton in Chisnall's office, staring glumly at a stack of boxes. 'You seem to have packed everything up for us to take,' Bragg remarked.

Morton pulled a wry face. 'I am afraid so. It seemed simpler. Most of them are financial circulars and newspapers. I find it impossible to say with any certainty that they have no relevance to his death.'

'What about the books? I see you have put them back.'

'Yes. They seem to be innocuous novels, travel books and so forth. I shook each one to make sure that there were no secret papers hidden in them!'

'Well, we shall not get this lot in a cab – even a growler. Has the body been collected?'

'A few moments ago.'

'Good. Have you got the bunch of keys?'

'Yes. Here they are.'

'Then we will lock up for now, and you can come back for the boxes after we've had a spot of lunch.'

'Very well... Oh, there is one rather odd thing, sir.'

'What is that?'

'The fireplace. It is full of ash – not the residue of a coal fire, rather the remains of papers.'

Bragg went over and squatted down by the grate. 'Hmn... it almost looks as if they have been deliberately beaten to dust. It is certainly paper but, left to itself, burnt paper stays in big pieces – sometimes you can even see what was printed on it.'

'You think that the residue was pounded into dust so that no one could identify the documents?'

'It seems that way to me.' Bragg pulled back the fret and lifted out the grate, then scooped out the ashes that filled the hearth. He sifted them carefully through his fingers.

'Nothing,' he said, looking at his blackened hands with irritation. 'Right, it's your turn, lad.'

'How do you mean?'

'Come on! Surely you have seen burning fragments of paper wafted up into the chimney? They don't always burn through, you know.'

'Perhaps. However, since it is your theory, sir, I am content that you should put it to the test.'

'Ah, but it needs a delicate touch. Your sensitive hands are just the thing!'

Morton reluctantly took off his coat and rolled up the sleeves of his white shirt, then placing a newspaper to kneel on he pushed his arm up the chimney. 'There seems to be a great deal of soot here,' he said. 'I cannot think that this chimney has been swept for a year!'

'Then, scoop out all you can reach and let it fall in the grate.'

Morton gave a grimace and, reaching up into the flue, began to scrape down the soot with his hand. Immediately there was an avalanche; soot billowed out in a cloud, enveloping the constable, filling the room, settling on every surface. Bragg retreated to the door as Morton worked in a frenzy. Then he got to his feet and made a dash for the window. He leaned out for some minutes, coughing and wheezing. Then he turned back; his eyes were red-rimmed and streaming, his shoes and clothes smothered with soot.

'Hmm,' Bragg said slowly. 'I think you had better stay in the police, lad. You wouldn't make much of a living as a chimney-sweep.'

Morton gave him a baleful glare. 'Well, you might at least find out if my efforts have borne any fruit.'

'I wouldn't deny you your triumph. Especially as you look like a collier already!'

Morton snorted and turned back to the fireplace. He squatted down and began to pass the mound of soot through his fingers. Finally he stood up,.

'That is all I can find,' he said, placing a singed scrap of paper on the desk. It bore four letters written in black ink.

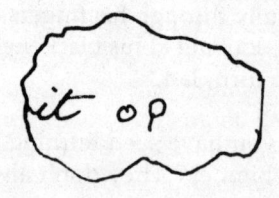

it o p

Bragg stared at it. 'Does that mean anything to you?' he asked.

'Not at the moment. The "i" and the "t" seem to be in cursive script. I suppose it is possible that the "o" and the "p" are in lower case, but equally they might be capitals.'

'Hmn... Well, we will keep it anyway.'

'I suppose', Morton said acidly, 'you have already discarded the possibility that this fragment could have been in the chimney for months, and has no connection whatever with the ashes in the grate.'

'Well, there is that,' Bragg said solemnly. 'But if we thought that way, you would have got filthy for nothing! No, we will keep it... Now, go home and have a bath, then come back here and do two things.'

'What are they?'

'Firstly go round all the neighbourhood, and find out if anyone saw a man – or a woman, for that matter – coming into this house or leaving it, between four and seven yesterday evening.'

'Right. And the second thing?'

'Why, I think you might call on Mrs Plumb, and apologise for the mess we've made in her nice clean room! Slip her half a crown, and she might agree to clean up after us!'

Bragg went back to Old Jewry, to arrange for a van to go to Petticoat Square, then had a leisurely lunch in a pub. At half-past two he strolled back to Chisnall's house and let himself in with Mrs Plumb's key. He went from room to room trying to absorb the atmosphere, gauge the character of the man. He had once been a nob, according to his neighbour. Well, there was no evidence of it that he could see. No fine ornaments, no silver teapots – no photographs even. But it wasn't that Chisnall was an ascetic, despising the things of the flesh. He indulged his liking for drink all right... Yet to judge from the boxes in the office, it was mainly quantity not quality that he was interested in. Of course Chisnall could have been lying to Johnson about his past; trying to set himself high in the estimation of his neighbours. It was natural enough. He must have had a lot more education than anyone round here, to have become any kind of journalist. He might have invented an upper-crust past to keep his distance.

There came a banging on the front door, and Bragg went to help the carrier load the boxes of papers into his van. As they were finishing Morton sauntered into the hallway, a broad grin on his handsome face.

'Ah, I see that I am just too late to help,' he said innocently.

'I bet you bloody made sure,' Bragg growled.

'Where do you want this lot taken, squire?' the driver asked.

'The police headquarters, in Old Jewry.'

'There's a bit of a courtyard there I can drive into, isn't there?'

'That's the one. The desk sergeant will tell you where to put the stuff.'

'Right, I'll be off.'

Bragg and Morton made a final tour of the house. Now that the boxes had gone, the office seemed empty and cheerless. Somehow it irritated Bragg. There was scarcely a jot of comfort in the whole house. What kind of man would live like this? Bragg and his wife had occupied a police quarter for a couple of years, before she had died in childbirth. It was nothing like as spacious as this place, but she had made it feel like a home. . . And there was all that furniture stored in the front bedroom. The place could have been made decent without much effort. . . Perhaps it had been once.

'According to the Johnsons,' he remarked. 'Chisnall told them he had been a stockbroker once, and had been educated at the City of London School – for what that's worth.'

Morton raised his eyebrows. 'That is the one on the north of Cheapside,' he said. 'It has an excellent reputation, I believe.'

'A grammar school, is it?'

'Yes. Day-boys only, I think.'

'Well, Chisnall is not much of an advert for them. . . How did you get on with the neighbours, lad?'

'No one would admit to having seen anyone going into, or coming out of this house for days.'

'I see. Were they lying, do you think?'

'I would say that it was no more than the instinctive non-co-operation that we find in areas such as this.'

'We might as well get back, then, and sort out those boxes of yours.'

'Why are they suddenly mine?' Morton asked.

'Well, I know you never went to school, but you did go to Cambridge – so you must be the one with the brains. It's the only reason I put up with you!'

Morton grinned. 'Since the newspapers are largely copies of the *Financial News*, I fear that my education in the liberal arts will be of little advantage.'

'Ah, but you understand money, having so much of your own. Come on, and make sure you lock the door behind you.'

They made their way back to Old Jewry, and spent a long time sorting out the contents of the various boxes. When Bragg's room was reasonably orderly again they went to Golden Lane, on the north side of the City, where the mortuary was situated. They entered a large room with a glass roof. Ranged around its sides were heavy slate slabs. On some of them they could see recumbent figures covered with twill sheets. Noakes, the mortuary assistant, was sitting in the current of air by the door, reading a copy of *Tit Bits*.

'Is Professor Burney in?' Bragg asked.

'Yes. His students have just gone,' Noakes said cheerfully. 'You can go in. He is expecting you.'

They went through a door in the corner, into the examination room. A window ran the whole length of one wall. Under it was a laboratory bench, with a glazed sink at one end. The centre of the room was taken up by a mortuary slab, on which Chisnall's body lay. At least, Morton presumed it was his body. It looked more like a biological specimen laid out for display.

'Ah, there you are, gentlemen!' Burney wiped his hands on the bloodied apron round his middle. 'My students are, I am sure, very grateful to you. It was an extremely interesting subject.'

'Thank you, sir,' Bragg said drily. 'Have you anything for us?'

'Why yes.' The pathologist's loose smile became oddly bashful. 'But before we become too immersed in the detail, I must tell you that I would have been surprised if the subject had survived very much longer, in the natural course. When I dissected out the heart, I encountered considerable fatty degeneration of the muscle tissue.'

'But he didn't die of that, did he?'

'No, sergeant. Have no fear!'

'That's all right then.'

'Death was undoubtedly brought about by extensive laceration of the brain, resulting from the fracturing of the skull by means of a blunt instrument.'

'The poker?'

'Yes. And in my opinion only the poker.'

'I see. . . Just one murderer then?'

Burney's eyes gleamed in anticipation. 'It is far beyond my duty to engage in hypothesizing,' he said. 'Nevertheless the circumstances of this case tempt me to do so.'

'I would rather you gave it to us straight first, sir.'

'Certainly, sergeant. Then I must tell you that the bones of the subject's skull were unusually thin. I found splinters of bone driven deep into the brain tissue.'

'I thought that skulls were all the same,' Bragg said.

'By no means! I have known death to supervene where such a subject has slipped on wet linoleum, and the head has been banged on the corner of a table.'

'So where does that leave us?'

'If you would half roll him over. . . Just lift the shoulder. . . That's the ticket! Now, I think that the first blow was delivered to the back of the head, fracturing the parietal bone. . . You see? Along this line.'

Bragg glanced at the nauseating pulp indicated by the probe and looked away.

'Since fragments of bone were propelled into the brain,' Burney said with relish, 'it is probably legitimate to assume that the first blow was fatal.'

'Right.'

Burney's grin became positively ghoulish. 'You see what I am driving at, sergeant?'

'No, sir.'

'Very well, roll him on his back again. . . You see the lacerations on the face?'

'There is not much face left,' Bragg grunted.

'Exactly. And yet, because of the comparative lack of haemorrhaging associated with these wounds, I am of the opinion that they were delivered when the subject was already dead.'

'How long after?'

Burney shrugged. 'Up to an hour perhaps. I cannot be exact.'

'So why come and smash his face in? Did they want to stop him being recognised? . . . It would hardly make sense in his own house.'

'Agreed. But it could do so if we were to alter our line of reasoning. As I have said, the subject's skull was abnormally fragile. The person delivering the blow to the back of the head might have been totally unaware that it had proved fatal. The subject would certainly appear to be unconscious. But the assailant might reasonably feel, from past experience perhaps, that the force of the blow had not been great enough to kill.'

'I see. So, after he had turned the place upside down, and maybe found what he wanted, he came back and finished the job properly.'

'Exactly – except that the subject was, in fact, already dead.'

'They don't come much more cold-blooded than that,' Bragg muttered. 'So what sort of a man are we looking for? Tall, medium height?'

'If the subject had been seated when the first blow was struck, it could have been almost anyone . . . a well-built child even.'

Bragg tugged at the corner of his untidy moustache. 'You are not suggesting it could have been done by a woman, are you, sir?'

'Oh yes! Most certainly.'

'Christ! And I told the coroner I wanted this case. What a sodding mess!. . . And when do you reckon it was done, sir?'

Burney pursed his flaccid mouth. 'The internal temperature was consistent with the indications from lividity and rigor. 'I would say that death occurred around six o'clock last evening.'

Harriet Marsden closed her novel with a sigh of contentment. All the difficulties and misunderstandings had been resolved, the villain despatched, the lovers reunited in blissful contentment. If only real life could be like that. . . She looked across at her daughter Catherine, who was writing notes for a newspaper article in the cool air from the french windows. In some ways it was like old times. Since William was away in the country, painting an exceptionally remunerative portrait, she and Catherine had taken a light supper on the balcony overlooking Park Lane. When they first came to London from Winchester, her husband had been prepared to travel anywhere – stay away for a week at a time. But once he had made his way, and more particularly after he had been elected to the Royal Academy, his subjects had clamoured to come to him. He had been able to demand a thousand guineas for a portrait, and still have more commissions than he could comfortably execute. She was surprised that he had accepted this one, since it involved a journey to the inhospitable north country. The fact that the subject was a duchess would not normally have caused him to bend to pressure. But he had said that he was bored with the unending succession of débutantes and society beauties. The duchess was old, her face full of character, he said; she was interesting. She ought to find that reassuring. . . But he had said he would never leave his studio again, not even for Queen Victoria herself. . .

'Why are you sighing so, Mamma?' Catherine asked from the window.

'Sighing?' Harriet echoed irritably. 'Would you not sigh, if you had an only child who was as headstrong as you are?'

'Headstrong? I could hardly accept that description, Mamma,' Catherine said mildly. 'Determined, resolute perhaps. But hardly self-willed!'

'But that exactly describes you. Here you are, twenty-four next birthday, and still not married! I do not understand you! You have had suitor after suitor, from the best families in the land, and you have scorned them. I sometimes think. . .' She checked.

'What is it that you sometimes think, Mamma?' Catherine asked with a smile. 'Come along, tell me the truth!'

'I. . . Well, I sometimes wonder if, for all your vivacity and charm when you are with them, whether you. . .'

'Go on, Mamma! It will be instructive to have such a keen parental insight into my character!'

Harriet paused, irresolute. 'I do not want you to get all cross and self-righteous, but . . . well, there are women who . . . who do not really like men at all . . . not really. . .'

Catherine laughed. 'Oh, Mamma! You think that because I prefer the satisfaction of a real job to fawning on men and spawning an endless succession of progeny, that I must be lesbian! I assure you that I am perfectly normal, that the company of certain men delights me and that, given the right combination of circumstances, I would certainly marry and have children!'

'Well then!'

'Well what?'

Harriet frowned. 'You are being deliberately obtuse, child,' she said irritably. 'You are well aware that your post as a reporter on the *City Press* does not stretch you. The articles you write, while interesting in themselves, and culturally informative, are not concerned with the real issues that affect the people of this country. You may be the best-known female journalist in London, but your job is little more than a concession to the women's movement. You are ruining your life for the sake of something which will come about in its own good time, if it is to come about at all.'

Catherine flushed angrily. 'If you wished me to be no more than a posturing ninny, Mamma, you should not have abrogated your parental responsibility by sending me to boarding-school. I cannot now betray my education, and pretend to be ignorant and shallow just to get a husband! I am what you made me, and you will have to put up with it!' She hurried out of the room and banged the door behind her.

Her mother sighed, then reached out for a bon-bon to console herself. It was really all William's fault. If only he were at home, he would be able to talk to her. Somehow he could convey his pride in her and her achievements. It made it easier for her to listen to him. . . Not that she would always do what he said – far from it – but it did not all end in a row. He could handle her. . . She tried to imagine what her husband would be doing at that moment. No doubt in such a palatial establishment they would still be at dinner. . . She found herself wondering if the duke was at home, if the duchess was really as old as William had said. He had seemed a little too emphatic. . .

There was a knock on the door and the maid appeared. She dropped a perfunctory curtsy. 'There's that nice young policeman at the door, mum. I told him it was a bit late for calling, but he still asked if you would see him. . . I expect it's

Miss Catherine he wants really, though.'

Harriet bit her tongue at the girl's impudence. 'By all means show him up, Joan. And you may let Miss Catherine know he is here.' She glanced round the room to see that it was tidy, then got up to close the french windows.

'Good evening, ma'am.' James Morton was standing in the doorway, tall, athletic and handsome. Such a fine young man she thought; and she was sure that her daughter was attracted to him.

'Good evening, James,' she said. 'I am afraid that my husband is away at the moment, but Catherine may join us in a few moments. I believe that she has been working in her room.' Harriet was sure that her face had betrayed her lie. Oh dear! Human relationships were so fraught with difficulty.

'I have to confess', he said lightly, 'that not only would I enjoy her company immensely, but that I have actually come to seek it.'

'So this is not merely a social call?'

'I am afraid not, ma'am. I have come to ask for her assistance.'

'That does not at all surprise me,' Harriet said with an edge to her tone. 'Young people seem to pay less and less attention to the social niceties nowadays.'

'I can only tender my apologies,' Morton said contritely. 'Life is so hectic. . . I suppose that I ought to have delayed until tomorrow, and come at a more seemly hour. But as Miss Marsden is herself in employment. . .'

'James! What a pleasant surprise!' Catherine was standing in the doorway, a delighted smile on her face. She went towards him and taking his hand steered him towards the settee.

Morton looked at her teasingly. 'I am conscious that this is much too late for a social call,' he said. 'But then, this can hardly be so described.'

Catherine's brow wrinkled in resignation. 'So you are about to impose on my goodwill yet again,' she said wryly. 'What is it this time?'

'A man has been murdered in a particularly grisly way. Apparently, he had told his next-door neighbour that he was a journalist, and had once been a stockbroker.'

'Do you know his name?'

'Alan Chisnall.'

Catherine frowned. 'I cannot say that I have heard of him,' she said. 'However, that is hardly surprising. If he went into journalism from stockbroking, he probably became a financial journalist.'

'That would narrow the field considerably,' Morton said.

'Not so much as you would think. The *Financial News* is pre-eminently the financial newspaper, but there is also the *Economist*. And every serious newspaper has a financial section also. . . I will ask at the *City Press*; though their interests are limited to things like government stocks and cotton futures. And, of course, I do know the City editor of the *Star*. As I write my occasional column for the paper, I am sure that they would be willing to help.'

'I am most grateful.'

Catherine smiled. 'And in return I will exact a service from you.'

'Gladly! What is it?'

'As you undoubtedly remember every waking second, there is a rehearsal on Saturday for Emily's wedding.'

'Oh, Lord!' Morton groaned. 'I could well do without it.'

'But they cannot well do without you,' Catherine said severely. 'As you are a groomsman and I am to be a bridesmaid, it is essential that we should know what is expected of us.'

'Ah well! I suppose it is my own fault, for introducing her to Reuben in the first place! Anyway, I have already been given leave of absence for Saturday morning. May I have the pleasure of escorting you down? I propose to take the ten o'clock train. Would that be convenient to you?'

Catherine smiled warmly at finding her request anticipated. 'It would give me the greatest pleasure,' she said.

'Good. Now, what was the favour you require of me?'

'Do you know, I have utterly forgotten!' she said lightly. 'It has totally slipped my mind. But I am sure that it will come back to me in time.'

2

Next morning Morton was at Old Jewry by eight o'clock. He was conscious that Saturday was all too near. If the routine work were still incomplete, he could be under pressure from Bragg to forgo his leave. He would find it difficult to resist for the sake of a mere rehearsal. But Catherine would be less than pleased. . . He had sorted most of the documents into chronological order, and was beginning on the newspapers when Bragg marched in.

'Right, lad, where are we?' he asked breezily.

'The documents are in proper order, sir, but I am hoping that we will be able to jettison most of the newspapers.'

'Jettison them? Why did we bring them here in the first place?'

Morton smiled. 'I am afraid that our venerated language is sometimes insufficiently precise!' he said.

'And what is that supposed to mean?'

'About three-quarters of the newspapers here are old copies of the *Financial News*. In fact they cover the years from 1873 to 1885. I assume that those were the years when Chisnall was employed by that journal.'

'How do you get as far as that?' Bragg asked sceptically.

'Firstly, there is not a copy of every issue of the paper for those years. Secondly, in every copy we have there is an article that has been marked with a pencilled cross. I am wondering if we may safely keep only those articles.'

'You think he wrote them, eh? It could be. What kind of articles are they?'

Morton wrinkled his brow. 'From a very superficial examination of no more than a dozen, they seem to be exercises in assessing the value of various companies, and forecasting their prospects as investments.'

'Companies quoted on the Stock Exchange, you mean?'

'Yes.'

'I see. Well, it would make sense if he had started out as a stockbroker. . . And what about that pile of the *Sporting Life* over there? At least they seem to be recent.'

Morton grinned. 'It was a most instructive exercise! I am not a gambler; but even if I were, my addiction would scarcely survive the examination of those papers!'

'What the hell are you on about?' Bragg asked grumpily.

'Chisnall has marked a horse in virtually every race. One must assume that he was trying to pick the winner. There is an unbroken sequence over several months. So for each day's runners, the following day's edition gives the winners. It is thus possible to demonstrate that virtually every horse he selected did not even finish in the first three!'

'But he might not have actually had a bet on every one – or any at all.'

'True. But in that event, it would have been a rather whimsical exercise to maintain for such a long period.'

'So you think that he was a racing man?'

'Yes. Probably nothing so exalted as a racehorse owner, but a punter certainly.'

Bragg frowned. 'Racing is a mug's game through and through, lad. Only folk who have more money than sense get involved in it. . . Still, it would be interesting to know if Chisnall was a gambler.' He swung round as the door opened and the Commissioner wandered in.

Lieutenant-Colonel Sir William Sumner KCB had been appointed in the days before the Gordon riots, when experience of military command was still seen as an essential prerequisite to taking charge of a police force. He was a short, stiff man, with a pronounced resemblance to the Prince of Wales – which his detractors said was carefully cultivated. It was to his credit that he tried not to be a remote figurehead. Indeed, with fewer than eight hundred men in the force, and with an area of a mere square mile to cover, he was a familiar sight to most of his men. His weakness was that he was too paternalistic. He would try to get close to the poor bloody infantry; would find himself discussing a case with the detective on the ground, making suggestions, appearing to authorise action that sometimes ran counter to the tactics of the inspector in charge of the investigation. After a few brushes with the senior officers of the force, he had agreed to desist. But as part of his capitulation it had been agreed that, subject to the nominal control of Inspector Cotton, he should have general oversight of one detective team. The superintendent of the detective division had been quite content to abandon Bragg and Morton to him. Bragg was an individualist; unorthodox in method, impatient of authority, scornful of advancement. Only his flair for solving the most intractable of cases had prevented him from being thrown to the wolves long ago. As for Morton, he was a misfit. It was said that the Commissioner had met him at a dinner party; challenged him to eschew the life of self-indulgent idleness pursued by most of his class, join the force and work his way up from the bottom. There had been a rumour that he was being groomed to become Sir William's successor. But once Morton had been picked to play cricket for England, and spent months at a time on overseas tours, that notion had begun to fade.

The Commissioner came across to the desk. 'Ah, Bragg,' he said. 'I understand that you have been appointed coroner's officer for the murder in Petticoat Square.'

'Yes, sir.'

'I take it that all this. . .' He waved his hand at the boxes overflowing with papers. 'All these documents are connected with the investigation.'

'That is correct, sir.'

'Hmn. . . And what do you expect to gain from their examination?'

Bragg suppressed his irritation and decided to humour him. 'The victim was an educated man, sir, for all that he lived in such a run-down area. He seems to have been trained as a stockbroker, and then became a financial journalist. So far, we know very little about him. We have brought every bit of paper that we could find back here, to see if they will shed some light on why he was killed.'

'I see. . . You think that the motive lay in his business life, rather than his personal life?'

'We have an open mind, of course,' Bragg said respectfully. 'But we don't think he had much of a personal life. Women don't seem to figure in it, anyway. He seems never to have married, and he was a bit old to be tickling up other men's wives.'

'Ah, yes. . .' Sir William cleared his throat in embarrassment. 'But he was connected with the financial side of the City, you think.'

'So it seems, sir. Though to what extent, it is too early to say.'

'Hmm. . . Well, I am sure that you will proceed with the utmost caution, Bragg,' the Commissioner said plaintively. 'You know how sensitive the markets are to the slightest rumour. I do not want the Governor of the Bank of England coming down on me for no good reason.'

'I appreciate that, sir,' Bragg said deferentially. 'Perhaps you would rather we kept the details from you. It would be easier for you to disown us then.'

The Commissioner looked up suspiciously. 'No, Bragg. While such a course might have its advantages, it could hardly deflect the displeasure of the authorities, should things go wrong.'

Bragg smiled warmly. 'Very good, sir. It is helpful for us to know that we have express authority of the head of the force behind us. These powerful City folk do not always want to co-operate with the police as fully as they should. With your personal backing, no one will dare deny us.'

Sir William flinched. 'I do hope, Bragg,' he said, 'that you will handle this investigation with the utmost discretion. Whilst we must inevitably subscribe to the notion that justice must be seen to be done in every case, there are those in the City who feel that one can pay too high a price for it. I rely on you to proceed with the utmost circumspection.'

'Very good, sir.'

The Commissioner hovered irresolutely, then departed without adding to his homily.

Bragg sighed in exasperation. 'God knows how anybody thought him fit to run an officers' mess, never mind an infantry regiment,' he said. 'Now, where were we?'

'I was expatiating on my theory that Chisnall was a gambler,' Morton said lightly.

'Right. Anything more on that subject?'

'No.'

'Then we will bear it in mind. . . Now then, I think I have come up with a bit of a conundrum.' Bragg dived into his pocket and produced a bunch of keys. 'I went back to Petticoat

Square and found these in one of Chisnall's coat pockets. Then I went round the house trying them in locks. I found a lock for every key except this one.'

Morton took the bunch and examined it. 'It is of a size that one would expect to fit the lock of a piece of furniture, such as a bureau.'

'Yes, but the desk key is next but one to it.'

'I see. . . In fact, on reflection, it seems much too elaborate for an ordinary lock. I have only seen keys like this in use for strong-boxes and the like.'

'A strong-box, eh?' Bragg mused. 'There was nothing like that in the house. Do you think the murderer took it?'

'It is hardly likely. Surely even the most obtuse observer would have seen him carrying it. It was, after all, fully daylight – and at a time in the evening when many people were coming home from work.'

'Hmn. . . So, unless the box was nicked by a neighbour, after the murder, it must be in a bank. . . But which? Have you come across any bank-books, lad?'

'Yes. A current account only . . . where on earth can it be?. . . It was in a Buchanan's Red Seal whisky carton, I think.' He rummaged around in several boxes, then straightened up triumphantly. 'Here we are! An account with Derenburg & Co.'s bank, in Drapers' Gardens.'

Bragg took the little bundle of books and slid off the elastic band that held them. 'Drapers' Gardens is off Throgmorton Avenue, isn't it?' he asked. 'Close to the Stock Exchange.'

'Yes indeed.'

Bragg flipped through the books. 'Not much of an account,' he said. 'Opened in October eighteen fifty-eight. . . Difficult to work out how old he was then, from the look of him yesterday!'

'It could be that he opened it when he began his career as a stockbroker,' Morton suggested.

'Well, that's what it seems, anyway. But it has hardly been what you would call an active account.' He flipped through one pass-book after another. 'For the last few years it has hardly been worth keeping open. . . Do you think journalists get paid in cash, lad?'

Morton smiled. 'I am sure it could be arranged,' he said.

'And are these the only bank-books you found?'

'Yes, sir.'

'Why then, we don't seem to have much option but to call on Derenburg's, do we? I suppose you do not happen to have any of your millions with them?'

Morton laughed. 'Neither I nor my trustees, I think!'

'Pity. What you should do, lad, is drop a few hundred thousand with every bank in London. We could lean on any one of them then!'

They walked through the humid air along Lothbury, then through great iron gates, and down a gracious avenue of Georgian houses that were rapidly being engulfed by the tide of commerce. The premises of Derenburg & Co. were marked by a discreet brass plate. Not a bank for the *hoi polloi* then. Bragg showed his warrant-card to a grizzled clerk, and they were led down a carpeted corridor to the manager's office. He turned out to be a man in his early forties, meticulously dressed in a silk-faced frock coat and double-breasted waistcoat.

'Two gentlemen from the police to see you, sir,' the clerk said and withdrew.

The manager rose and held out his hand. 'I trust that our sins have not yet found us out!' he said with cautious affability. 'Do sit down.'

'You have a client named Alan Chisnall, I understand,' Bragg began.

'I believe that to be the case,' the manager said guardedly.

'I do not suppose that you are yet aware of it, but he was murdered the evening before last.'

'Murdered?' His eyebrows rose in distaste. 'I see. . . Then you have no doubt come in that connection.'

'That is so, sir. We have his bank-books for the account with you. We just wondered if you could put some flesh on their bare bones, so to speak.'

'I see.' The manager pondered briefly. 'Well, since you already have details of the transactions themselves, I cannot see that there would be any serious breach of confidentiality. . . Indeed, since you are presumably concerned to capture the perpetrator of this crime, I may safely assume that our late client would have wished me to co-operate in this matter. . . Yes. One moment.'

He went out, and returned shortly with a manila folder. Behind him came a clerk bearing an immense ledger. He placed it gravely on the manager's desk and withdrew.

'I take it', the manager said, resuming his seat, 'that your main interest is in any background information we may hold. After all, you have got the transactions of the account in your possession.'

'That's right, sir,' Bragg said earnestly. 'To be honest, we have very little to go on. His neighbours appear to know next to nothing about him, even though we understand he worked from home. Nobody seems to have been close to him. Anything at all you can tell us, might hold the key to the puzzle.'

The manager opened the file and leafed through its meagre contents. 'Well, let us begin at the beginning,' he said. 'Alan Chisnall was introduced to us by his father. Now, quite fortuitously, I can tell you about Chisnall *père*. We have recently been involved in a public flotation of the company by which he was employed. Would such information have relevance to your enquiries?'

'It might,' Bragg said.

'Very well.' The manager leaned back in his chair and clasped his hands behind his head. 'Samuel Chisnall was a shareholder in, and director of, a limited company trading as Rafferty Thornton & Co. It had, indeed still has, its registered office in Old Broad Street. Although Mr Chisnall senior had a significant shareholding in the company, he by no means controlled it. Nevertheless he was a man of considerable standing in the City; upright, honourable, trustworthy. My predecessor, in eighteen fifty-seven, had no qualms about accepting the son as a client on his recommendation. . . I should tell you that Rafferty Thornton & Co. were timber importers; bringing softwoods from Sweden into Crown Wharf, Canning Town. When the construction of the Victoria Dock began, it became obvious to the directors of the company that their operations would not be able to continue from that location. They therefore embarked on a bold strategy. Instead of transferring their operations to another wharf on the river Thames, they relocated the entire business in Bristol, on the other side of the country. I gather that, at the time, it was seen as a somewhat risky proceeding. But the timber was needed in the expanding cities of the Midlands;

and that market could be supplied just as well from Bristol. In the event, the directors' judgement was vindicated. For a few years the business was wholly directed from London. Then, in eighteen fifty-seven, Samuel Chisnall took up residence in Bristol. It must have been out of that transfer of residence that the necessity arose for Alan Chisnall to have a bank account in his own name.'

'I take it that you asked for character references,' Bragg said.

'Of course. Both the headmaster of the City of London School and the rector of St James's Church, Islington, spoke most warmly of Alan Chisnall.'

'They would, wouldn't they?' Bragg said sardonically. 'So what happened to the son?'

'From Samuel's letter of introduction, it appears that it was his intention to go into stockbroking.'

'Right. What address do you have for him, at that stage?'

The manager looked back through his file. 'The earliest address I have is twenty-one Monkwell Street.'

'Ah, yes. Behind the Barbers' Hall. And did Alan live up to all these recommendations?'

The manager pulled the ledger towards him, opened it and scrutinised the page intently.

'I would say so,' he remarked. 'You can see from the passbooks that, in the early years, the account was conducted with satisfactory restraint. What I take to be his monthly salary cheques are paid in, and drawn on for his living expenses. . . You will see also the occasional deposit outside that pattern. For instance, on the twelfth of December eighteen sixty-four. . . You have it? The deposit of two hundred pounds?'

'Yes, here it is.'

'I have a pencil annotation in the ledger to the effect that this deposit was made by Samuel, via his bank in Bristol. No doubt it was prompted by the imminence of Christmas.'

'No doubt. . . But later on he started going off the rails, didn't he? If you look at June eighteen seventy, he went overdrawn on the fourth, and he has been in and out of credit ever since.'

'Yes.' The manager flipped through the file. 'I see that the then incumbent of this office interviewed him, and found him somewhat unsatisfactory. I imagine that he either managed his affairs mainly in cash thereafter, or he opened an account with another bank.'

'Have you a reference in your file to any other bank?' Bragg asked.

'No, none.'

'Why did he keep this account open, if you think he had one elsewhere?'

'That is easily answered, sergeant. Following the death of his father, he became entitled to an annuity out of the estate. As you have no doubt noted, it is paid, in monthly instalments, to this account.'

'Is it being paid still?'

'Oh yes.'

'When did old Samuel die?'

'In March eighteen seventy-three.'

Bragg pondered. 'That all seems very odd to me,' he said. 'Why has the estate not been distributed, in twenty years?'

A solemn look came over the bank manager's face. 'I see from the notes that there was some suggestion of a mentally deranged sister. No doubt the estate was kept in trust against her death.'

'But Chisnall got himself killed first, is that it?'

'So it would appear.'

'And I suppose the trustees would not know if he had another bank, any more than you would?'

'That would seem to follow, sergeant.'

'I see. . . Tell me, sir, have you got a strong-box in his name?'

The manager's head jerked up in surprise. 'No, we have not,' he said firmly.

'Have you ever had?'

'No. There would have been a prominent note inside the cover of the file, had that been the case.'

On leaving Derenburg's, Bragg decided that they should divide their efforts. He sent Morton to the *Sporting Life*, while himself embarking on a round of visits to likely banks.

Morton found the office of the *Sporting Life* at the bottom of Fleet Street. He was surprised to find a cheerful young woman in the enquiry-room. She wore a demure white blouse, but her hair was swept up stylishly into perky curls on her head. She seemed somehow out of place; Morton had always thought of racing and gambling as a male preserve. When he showed his warrant-card, her eyes opened wide in concern.

'I really need some general information,' he said. 'I am investigating a rather brutal killing. In the house of the murdered man was a bundle of recent copies of your paper. As he had been a journalist, I wondered if he had any acquaintances here.'

'Ah, you are not chasing us, then?' she said brightly. 'What is the name of your man?'

'Chisnall – Alan Chisnall.'

She knitted her brows. 'It is not a name that I recognise,' she said. 'I can ask, if you like.'

Morton smiled warmly at her. 'I would be most grateful,' he said. 'I imagine that he would be known by your own journalists, if at all.'

She went out, and he was left to kick his heels for a quarter of an hour. Then she reappeared. 'Our Mr Jimson says he knows him,' she said. 'Let me take you to him.'

Morton followed her slim ankles up a succession of steep staircases, to an attic room at the back of the building. It was crammed with desks and tables, their edges marked with the furrows of cigarette burns. From the ceiling, electric lamps hung low. The air was thick with tobacco smoke.

'Over there,' said the girl, pointing to a bald-headed man in shirt-sleeves.

Morton went over. 'Mr Jimson?' he asked.

The man looked up. 'Ah. You the copper?' he asked abruptly. 'How do you think I can help you?'

'I gather that you may have known the man whose death I am enquiring into.'

'Alan Chisnall, she said. Is that right?'

'That is so. He was found battered to death in his house, yesterday morning.'

'Well, I plead not guilty, milud!' He leaned back in his chair, took a half-smoked cigarette from behind his ear and lit it. He exhaled a lungful of smoke in Morton's face as he spoke. 'I did know him, yes. Bloody nuisance he was an' all.'

'You knew him as a fellow journalist?'

Jimson reflected for a moment. 'In a sense, I suppose. I met him at a pub where newspaper folk hang out. But I knew him as a punter. Moaning bugger he was. If a horse I'd mentioned didn't finish in the first three, he was on to me as if I was in a conspiracy against him.'

'Was he a poor loser?' Morton asked.

'If he wasn't he gave a good imitation of one! But I could be misleading you. I have no actual knowledge of whether he backed horses, or to what extent if he did. I am just assuming; like you, I suppose. What I do in my column is to sort out the form of the various horses, discuss their pedigree. I am not a tipster. I just try to give our readers a chance to make an informed guess about which runners will come up trumps. But if every horse ran to the form book, I would be sunning myself in Biarritz and the bookies would all be broke.'

'From what you say, one might nevertheless suppose that Chisnall was a habitual gambler, and took it very seriously.'

Jimson spat out a fragment of tobacco. 'Two sides of the same coin,' he said. 'You see it time and time again. . . They all lose in the end. It's just that some start with more money, so it takes them longer.'

Morton grinned. 'With such a philosophy, I wonder that you can be part of the racing scene at all,' he said.

'I make a living. And everybody is entitled to find their own way to their own particular perdition.'

'I doubt if Chisnall had quite that mode of exit in mind!'

Jimson cocked an eyebrow. 'I suppose you are thinking that he might have been killed because he had not paid his gambling debts.'

'I must confess that it had not crossed my mind in those particular terms.'

'Well, it should. Betting on the horses is not a nursery game.'

Morton considered for a moment. 'Not being interested in gambling myself,' he said, 'I am at something of a loss as to how to proceed. I cannot even satisfy myself that he did make wagers on the various horses he marked in your illustrious newspaper!'

Jimson ground out the stub of his cigarette in the ashtray. 'I don't know that I feel like helping you either,' he said. 'With gambling being pilloried by society, the way it is, anyone connected with racing is liable to be tarred with the same brush – including people like me.'

'I can understand that,' Morton said quietly. 'Nevertheless, the law which I am engaged in upholding goes back to the sixth commandment. "Thou shalt do no murder." Against that, the vagaries of our domestic law are surely immaterial?'

'I suppose so.' Jimson looked up. 'There is a race meeting at Sandown Park this afternoon,' he said. 'If I were you, I would get down there, and talk to the bookmakers in the Tattersalls enclosure. If you have a few bets with them – and lose, of course – they might tell you something.'

Bragg sipped disconsolately at his glass of tepid beer. They must have been getting near the bottom of the barrel, he decided. Its contents were slightly muddy, and tasted stale. And the pork pie he had eaten had been more gristle than meat. . . But it was his own fault. He should have gone back to Cheapside for his lunch, instead of settling for a place like this. He wondered if he had time to unlace his boots – ease his feet a bit. There was always another day. He did not have to go round every bank in London before nightfall. . . Not that he had that sort of time. The blasted banks only opened from half-past nine in the morning to three o'clock in the afternoon. And their managers all seemed to be out at lunch from half-past twelve till two! He had damn near worn holes in his socks, rattling about from one to another.

'Have you got a Mr Alan Chisnall as a customer, please?'

'Just a moment, sir, I shall have to ask the manager to deal with your enquiry.'

He had heard that exchange, or something like it, scores of times already. He had gone round the financial district like a demented whippet, in a widening circle around the Bank of England and the Stock Exchange. He was certain that a City man would never go outside it. He would feel it would be losing caste. Even a one-time stockbroker would not venture outside the Square Mile. Bragg checked the angry rush of his thoughts. Chisnall had been a journalist after he had been a stockbroker. When the change had come, he did not know. But suppose

Chisnall was already working for the financial press when he felt the need of another bank account. . . Bragg got to his feet, took a final sip of his disgusting brew and went off in search of a hansom cab.

Having found one, he was assured by the driver that the office of the *Financial News* was nowhere near Fleet Street, where the rest of the newspaper world was congregated. It was in the City, in Abchurch Lane, he said. Bragg's heart sank. If so, it was within the circle he had traversed most of the morning. And he had never heard of a bank in Abchurch Lane. It looked as if this bright idea was going to be sterile too. As they turned into Abchurch Lane he saw that it was blocked by a huge van unloading rolls of newsprint. He stopped the cabby and paid him off, then strolled down its narrow length. It felt almost cool here. The tall buildings kept the lane shaded from the sun, and their height seemed to create a draught of air along it. If he found nothing else, he would at least have stopped sweating for a bit. Now he had almost reached the van drawn up by the warehouse. Beyond it was the office of the newspaper itself. That would bear a visit before long. . . A fly detached itself from the swarm by the horses and began to circle around Bragg's head. It settled on his forehead. He waved his hand, and it resumed its buzzing around him. It was the sweat that was attracting it, of course. He took off his bowler and lashed out at it. Still it came back, round and round his head. He let it settle then, with the flat of his hand, whacked against his forehead. That should have got rid of the blasted thing! His head smarted enough. . . But no. It was buzzing round him again as if he were a rotting corpse. He swung round to try to snatch it out of the air, and became aware of a small, somewhat tarnished brass plate. It was mounted beside an unpretentious doorway; it looked like the entrance to a dentist's surgery. He crossed over, and was seized with sudden elation.

THE BANK OF MONTREAL
Ashworth Caldwell
Manager

Bragg pulled out his battered gunmetal watch. A quarter to three. With any luck Mr Ashworth Caldwell ought to be back from his lunch. As he went up the steps, he became more and more convinced that he had struck gold this time. A foreign bank would not be as anxious to swap information as a British bank. It was outside the charmed circle – not a member of the club. He marched up to the enquiry desk and laid his warrant-card before the startled clerk.

'Sergeant Bragg, City of London police,' he said. 'Is Mr Caldwell in?'

The young man's eyes widened. 'I . . . yes, I think he is.'

'Good. Tell him I want to see him,' Bragg said brusquely.

'What is it you wish –'

'Tell him!' Bragg interrupted.

With a backward look of alarm, the clerk hurried through a door on the other side of the room. He soon returned, followed by a tall, balding man with a look of incredulity tempered by uncertainty on his face. At last, thought Bragg, he knew what Keats's phrase 'wild surmise' meant.

'What do you want, officer?' The accent was upper-class English, but lacked the dogmatic, God-given confidence of the type.

'Just a chat, sir,' Bragg said smoothly. 'In confidence.'

Caldwell hesitated. 'Er . . . yes. . . You had better come to my office.'

Bragg followed him to a room looking on to the well of the block of buildings. Precious little daylight would penetrate down here at the best of times. But, to improve the outlook, or rather to blot it out, a white net curtain had been hung across the window. The Bank of Montreal was not of much consequence, if it had to settle for premises like this in the city that was the heart of the empire, the commercial hub of the world. Nevertheless, the rest of the room was furnished impressively enough. Bragg sat down at the wide mahogany desk. After a moment of indecision, Caldwell took his own seat opposite him.

'Would you be good enough to give me your name?' he asked uncertainly.

'Sergeant Bragg, City of London police,' Bragg said evenly. 'I understand that you have as a client a certain Mr Alan Chisnall.'

'Er. . . I do seem to recognise the name.'

'Would you please confirm the fact, sir, before we go any further?'

Caldwell pulled open a drawer in his desk. He took from it a register-book and turned the pages.

'Yes . . . yes, my recollection was correct.'

'He doesn't sound like a very substantial client, if you couldn't be certain straight off.'

The manager shrugged. 'Most of our clients are companies and other foreign banks.'

'Are they? Then why would Mr Chisnall choose you to bank with?'

Caldwell's self-assurance was returning. 'That is a question you will have to put to him, sergeant,' he said.

'That's fair, sir. The trouble is, the only time I saw him he was lying on the floor with his head beaten in.'

A look of revulsion crossed Caldwell's face. 'I assure you, sergeant, that the bank has no information which could possibly impinge on such a tragic happening.'

Bragg smiled. 'Well, we'll see, shall we? Can I have a look at his account? We did not find any pass-books for it in his desk.'

'Nor would you, sergeant. The Bank of Montreal does not offer a current account service to its clients. As we are not a part of the central clearing system for cheques, to do so would be unacceptably cumbersome.'

'What sort of a client was he, then?'

Caldwell got to his feet and went over to a wooden press in the corner. From it he extracted a slim file and brought it to his desk.

'I see that he became a client in October of eighteen seventy-two, which was a little before my time as manager!' He gave a condescending smile, but Bragg ignored it.

'Did he open a deposit account, or something?' he asked.

'No. He merely placed in our keeping one strong-box.'

'Ah! I would like to see it, please.'

A wooden look came over the manager's face. 'I am afraid that it would be impossible for me to make it available, sergeant. My head office in Montreal would never countenance such an action on my part.'

'Why not?'

'It would be an egregious breach of a client's confidence.'

Bragg snorted. 'Believe you me, he is not in much of a condition to have confidence in you or anybody else, at the moment.'

'Nevertheless, it is the clear policy of the bank.'

'But other banks have not taken that view.'

Caldwell's eyes narrowed. 'In this same case?'

'In this same case,' Bragg repeated firmly.

'I see. . . Nevertheless, I dare not depart from my instructions. They clearly state that information concerning a client's affairs can only be imparted to any other person or body after due legal process.'

Bragg frowned. 'We have not got that sort of time,' he growled. 'We have to catch the person who did it, before someone else gets the chop.'

The manager's face was implacable. 'I am not prepared to risk my position, in order to enable you to cut corners, sergeant,' he said.

Bragg took a deep breath. 'Look, sir,' he said in a reasonable voice, 'both you and I know that this box might contain material evidence concerning the battering to death of Alan Chisnall. All I have to do is go before a Justice of the Peace, swear as much, and I shall have a summons requiring you to produce it. But it would save us both a lot of time if I could have a quick look at it now.'

'No, sergeant!' the manager said harshly. 'I will not be put under pressure in this way! My duty of confidentiality to our late client can only be overridden by an order of the court. I shall in no way be influenced by your assertion that other banks have seen their duty in a different light. When you come back with a proper legal document, I will co-operate fully with you.'

Bragg paused in thought, then brought out Chisnall's bunch of keys. 'I don't suppose you would try this in the lock would you, sir? It could save us both a great deal of bother.'

Caldwell flushed with anger. 'No, I will not, sergeant! Are you utterly obtuse? I will do nothing without an official warrant!'

When Morton arrived at the Sandown Park racecourse, the horses were parading for the last race. He went down to the ring and watched the grooms leading them quietly round. He tried to make up his mind from pure observation as to which of them would be first past the winning-post. To judge from their glossy coats and aristocratic bearing, there was nothing to choose between them. Presumably therein lay the value of Jimson's observations on the blood-lines of the various runners. And yet, though Chisnall had appeared to use them in selecting horses, he seemed to have been invariably wrong. Pedigree was not everything, then. Indeed it seemed to count for little. . . One of the horses was getting restive, pulling against the reins, rearing up. Did that mean it was full of vigour, that it would leave all the others standing? Or was it headstrong and unmanageable, a certain loser? He noticed a froth of sweat under the saddle of a bay. He would not have wagered much on that horse's lasting a long race; but in such matters he was ignorant, an innocent.

He began to make his way to the Tattersalls enclosure, where the bookmakers had their stands. This was one of the few places where they could legally ply their trade. He stood by the entrance watching the public jostling to place their bets, the incomprehensible signals of the tick-tack men. The *savoir-faire* of the bookmakers was remarkable, as bets rained in on them. How could they possibly keep track of what they stood to win or lose? But perhaps the odds were set so that the public were competing against each other, with the bookies always clear winners.

'Good heavens! James Morton. I never thought to see you at a racecourse!' A florid young man with fair hair stood at his elbow. Morton desperately tried to remember his name.

'Ah, Lionel!' he exclaimed. 'This is a pleasant surprise! How is your beautiful wife? Well, I trust.'

The young man grinned. 'In great shape – quite literally! In pod at the moment. Another month and, with luck, we shall have an heir to the title.'

'Congratulations! Give her my warm regards. . . But why are you wasting your time here, when you could be feeding her with milk and honey?'

'Duty, James. Serious stuff! I have been made a steward of the Jockey Club. I am here to see fair play.'

'Then fortune favours me. I too am here on business.'

Lionel looked at him in surprise, then his face fell. 'Oh, I had forgotten that you joined the police. What on earth are you down here for?'

'I want a chat with the bookmakers, to see if they recognise someone involved in a case.'

Lionel pulled a disapproving face. 'Oh well, I suppose you now have no option but to dabble in the dirt. Is it any particular bookmaker you want?'

'No. I was told that my man was a habitual gambler, and that the bookies here would be likely to recognise his name.'

'That would surprise me. It is all cash betting here. Why would a bookie need to know his punters' names?'

'I have no idea. I am merely following a suggestion put to me by Jimson, of the *Sporting Life*.'

'Ah well. There is no harm in trying. It is almost time for the off. Then the bookies will have a few minutes' respite.'

The enclosure suddenly emptied, as the hands of the clock on the grandstand approached five o'clock. Lionel mounted one of the bookies' stands.

'Gentlemen,' he called, 'I wonder if you can help a friend of mine. I must tell you that he is a policeman – but for all that, he is a jolly good chap; plays cricket for England, and so on. Do what you can for him.' He got down and hurried away.

The bookies drifted over to where Morton was standing.

'A man has been beaten to death in London,' he began. 'So far as we know, he had no connection with the criminal classes. Now, we have reason to believe that he regularly attended race meetings in the Home Counties. Certainly he was a habitual gambler on horses. Jimson, of the *Sporting Life*, suggested that you might be able to help.'

There was a silence; someone called, 'What, us help the police?' A titter ran round the circle.

'Are you trying to identify him?' another asked.

'No. We know that his name was Alan Chisnall. He was about five foot eight inches in height, had brown hair and a darkish complexion.'

'Yeah. But what did he look like?'

Morton paused. 'I am afraid that he was so badly beaten as to make his face unrecognisable.'

'Blimey!'

There was an uncomfortable silence.

'He was well known to Jimson,' Morton added. 'Perhaps that was because he was a journalist also.'

'Wait a minute!' A man with raddled features and a fringe of white hair under his hat spoke up. 'I think I know that bloke. If it's the one I think, he started off as a stockbroker.'

'That certainly fits,' Morton said. 'We believe that he gravitated from that to financial journalism.'

There came a roar from the spectators that crescendoed, then fell away. A young man scuttled into the enclosure.

'Apogee, Gardener's Lad, Copernicus,' he shouted.

No sooner had the bookies got to their stands again than a clamorous flood of spectators engulfed them, waving betting slips, demanding their winnings. Morton strolled over to the raddled bookie, and waited until the pay-out had been completed. Then the man caught his eye and beckoned.

'This bloke of yours,' he said. 'Chisnall. I'm sure it is the same one. Lived in the City; placed bets with me regular. Should have stuck to gambling on the Stock Exchange, except he said it was too slow.'

'Would you say that he was a heavy gambler?' Morton asked.

'Nah! Not the way some of the nobs go at it! Steady, I'd say. He would have a pony on most races; hardly ever more.'

'Twenty-five pounds? That would add up to a considerable sum, if he went to most meetings in the season. Did he often win?'

The bookmaker lifted an eyebrow. 'Not enough to get me worried, and that's a fact! He always backed the fancied horses, the ones that should have won. But even when they did, the odds were so short that he made precious little. If he went on with other bookies the way he did with me, he must have lost a right packet over the years.'

3

Next morning, Bragg and Morton arrived at the coroner's court, in Golden Lane, in good time for the inquest on Chisnall. Sir Rufus Stone was erratic, to say the least. As a Queen's Counsel, he was a much sought-after leader in civil cases; and he had made it plain that his legal practice must come first. Three years earlier, the then coroner for the City of London had been guilty of a serious dereliction of duty. He had manipulated the legal process in connection with the sudden death of a friend. When the man proved to have been murdered, Dr Primrose's position became untenable and he resigned. As a result, the newspapers had got hold of the story. The cosy oligarchical government of the City had been attacked, the Fabians had tried to turn the incident into a national political issue. Charges of corruption, nepotism, venality were freely bandied about, and the reputation of the City's institutions had begun to suffer. It was said the Governor of the Bank of England had insisted that some public gesture must be made, which would demonstrate the determination of the City authorities to restore its position. Whether that was true or not, they had certainly gone outside the City for their new coroner. Sir Rufus Stone's eminence at the bar was undisputed, his scorn of political jobbery well-known, his independence of thought manifest. Although he had accepted the office reluctantly, he had set about his duties with a vigour and determination that would brook neither interference nor slackness. 'I have been brought in to cleanse the Augean stables,' he would declaim, 'and, by God, cleanse them I will!'

Sir Rufus's high-handed methods had frequently raised the hackles of self-important City personages. It was said that they were biding their time, that he had only to put a foot wrong and they would be rid of him. If he knew of the rumour, he disregarded it. The City fathers had come to plead with him to rescue them from opprobium, he would say, and he had set his own terms. These apparently included the indulgence of a lofty disregard for the convenience of everyone but himself.

On this particular morning he elected to arrive forty minutes after the set time. When he did so he hustled and harried the usher and the clerk, as if it was their fault that everybody had been kept waiting. He glared mistrustfully at Ernie Johnson, while he gave evidence of identity. When Mrs Plumb came to relate the circumstances of her discovery of the body, he blatantly put words in her mouth. Then he abruptly adjourned the proceedings *sine die*, and hurried away.

49

'At least he did not have time to give us the benefit of his advice,' Bragg said with a grin. 'Come on, we can just get to the police court before everything shuts down for lunch.'

'Do you really think that the answer to all our problems will be found in the strong-box?' Morton asked lightly.

Bragg frowned. 'To be honest lad, I don't know. There are bits of the puzzle that somehow don't fit.'

'Why is that, sir?'

'To start with, it was a hot evening when Chisnall was killed. People were bound to be around. Dammit, it was early enough for the children to be playing in the street. Why kill him then? Why not leave it till after nine o'clock, when it had gone dark?'

'Perhaps it was done on an impulse.'

'Maybe... But if you just lost your temper over something trivial, you would hardly reach for the poker and belt your host over the head.'

'Unless you were mentally unbalanced,' Morton suggested.

They walked some distance in silence, then. 'No, lad. It will not do. If Chisnall had been murdered on the spur of the moment, I cannot see the culprit hanging around to look through his papers.'

'Then perhaps it was a deliberate, calculated act, and the perpetrator was looking for something specific.'

'Do you think Chisnall had some hold over his killer?' Bragg mused. 'Some incriminating document? The murderer certainly took a risk in turning over the office.'

Morton laughed. 'So we are looking for a man with an iron nerve, who had been indiscreet and was being blackmailed by Chisnall!'

'Or some woman,' Bragg said laconically.

'But surely no woman could be so cold-blooded and methodical?' Morton protested.

'You will never learn, will you, lad? Women are not cuddly dolls, for men to hang clothes on and stuff. Not even in your class, where they are of no more use than pet spaniels. Women give life, and they are just as prepared to take it, if the need arises.'

'It would have to be an overwhelming need, surely?'

'And you don't think a woman could feel so vindictive as to kill?'

Morton considered for a moment. 'Certainly the pathologist made it clear that a woman could have killed him. . . I suppose that what sticks in my craw is the notion of a woman going back to his inert figure and deliberately setting about beating him to death.'

'I know it takes some swallowing, lad, but bear in mind that women have more to lose than men – particularly in the pampered classes. One breath of scandal and they could lose everything.'

'I think that your preconceptions, not to say prejudices, may be misleading you, sir,' Morton said with a smile. 'Among the circle of the Prince of Wales, infidelity is almost the norm. Once a young bride has borne her husband a son, she becomes fair game for anyone. Affairs are tolerated, provided that they are carried on with discretion. A man would not pillory his wife for taking a lover – even being seen with him – so long as the liaison was conducted circumspectly. After all, the husband would have mistresses in his turn.'

Bragg snorted. 'Sounds like a lot of randy chimpanzees – and not far out either. But I don't see where your argument gets us. Once there was a risk of open scandal, there would be no difference at all. And don't forget that somebody like Chisnall would not uphold their snobby code of secrecy. Why should he? He's on the outside looking in!'

They came to the Bank of England crossing, and picked their way between the carts and omnibuses to the Royal Exchange; then over Cornhill to the Mansion House. They ignored the imposing flight of steps leading to its columned portico, and went round to the rear of the building. There they entered a low doorway and went down a stone-flagged corridor to the office of the magistrates' clerk. They found an elderly assistant seated at a desk, looking gloomily at the pile of forms in front of him. He glanced up.

'Ah, Sergeant Bragg,' he said peevishly. 'I had not noticed that we have one of yours down this morning.'

'You haven't, sir,' Bragg said mildly.

'Then, what are you here for? Not asking for favours, I hope.'

'Favours? No! I was just wondering if there was a spare five minutes for a witness summons.'

'Oh?' the clerk said guardedly.

'I wouldn't trouble you normally, sir, as you well know. But it is a murder case – as brutal as they come.'

'What has that to do with anything?' the man asked sharply.

'Well, the victim had a strong-box with the Bank of Montreal. The manager is a bit coy, and won't let me look in it without a witness summons.'

The clerk looked at him with distaste. 'That is not being coy, Bragg; that is applying the law correctly. You know very well that cutting corners only brings problems in the end.'

'I expect you are right, sir,' Bragg said reasonably. 'Can you find me a few minutes for an application this morning?'

The clerk glanced through the court list and pursed his lips. 'Not possible!' he said.

'But surely. . .'

'The Lord Mayor has had to go off to a luncheon at the Guildhall. I only have Alderman Wright and Mr Ponsonby here, and they are hearing a robbery with violence. The best I can do is to put you on the list for tomorrow. I could squeeze you in at nine o'clock.'

Bragg sighed in exasperation. 'Very well. Thank you, sir.'

'What a bloody circus!' he exclaimed, when they reached the street. 'That is Inspector Cotton's case! It has been hanging about for weeks, while he polished his opening submission. He doesn't care whether he gets a committal to the assizes or not, as long as he cuts a dash and gets a mention in the newspapers!'

'We do have another string to our bow,' Morton said with a grin.

'If we have, I don't know of it!'

'Under Section six of the City of London Police Act, the Commissioner is empowered to act as a Justice of the Peace. Surely the power was given to be used?'

'By God, lad, I believe you are right. Let's get back, before he decides it is lunch-time.'

They hurried to Old Jewry. 'Is Sir William still in?' Bragg asked the desk sergeant breathlessly.

'As far as I know, Joe.'

Bragg led the way up the curving Georgian staircase, to the Commissioner's ante-room. No one was waiting there. He tapped on the door of his office.

'Come in!'

Bragg pushed open the door. They stood for some minutes by the desk, while Sir William finished reading a report. Then he raised his head.

'Ah, Bragg,' he said unenthusiastically. 'What can I do for you?'

'I am sorry to trouble you, sir,' Bragg said meekly. 'It will not take a moment. I just want a Section six summons, in the Chisnall case.'

'A what?'

'A Section six summons, sir.'

The Commissioner leaned back frowning. 'What on earth are you talking about? Have you gone off your head?'

'No, sir,' Bragg said genially. 'You remember the journalist who was murdered in Petticoat Square?'

'Of course.'

'Well, we have discovered that he deposited a strong-box with the Bank of Montreal. We think that was what the murderer was looking for – or rather, something that is in it.'

'I see.'

'The manager of the bank is quite willing to hand over the box, but he wants a bit of paper from us to satisfy his bosses.'

'A bit of paper?' Sir William frowned. 'I fail to follow you, Bragg.'

'He says he cannot give it to us without due legal process, sir.'

'And very proper, too.'

'Yes, sir. The trouble is that the Mansion House court is tied up with the Gibson indictment, so we cannot get a summons out of them. We thought you would give us one.'

'I? Give you a summons? You are raving, man!'

'No, sir. Constable Morton remembered that Parliament saw fit to give the Commissioner the status of a Justice of the Peace. It's in Section six of the Police Act, sir. . . If we could have the summons now, we could get the box before lunch.'

The Commissioner held up his hand. 'I know, of course, that the power exists, Bragg. I also know that it has never been used – not by me nor, so far as I am aware, by any of my predecessors.'

'Perhaps they did not remember it was there, sir.'

Sir William snorted. 'Since the act has been in force since eighteen thirty-nine – over fifty years – I think such an explanation is highly unlikely.'

'Well, there is always a first time.'

'No, Bragg. I am sure that, like me, they felt that particular section to be something of an embarrassment. It puts the police in the position of being judge and jury in its own case, if you understand me.'

'I cannot say that I do, sir.'

'Dammit, don't be obtuse! It is too Continental for the British public; too Frenchified. They would never stand for it.'

'But –'

The Commissioner held up his hand. 'Enough! I commend your enthusiasm, Bragg. But I totally fail to understand the urgency you plead. You have apparently located the box. As I understand it, no one is likely to anticipate you in examining its contents. Certainly its owner is unlikely to!'

'We are convinced that whatever the murderer was looking for is in that box. The slightest delay in examining its contents might give the killer the time to escape.'

Sir William sniffed. 'This sounds more like a story from the *Boys' Own Paper* than serious police work,' he said dismissively. 'No, Bragg. There is nothing in this case which persuades me that I ought to disregard the usage of half a century, and grant your application. You will have to go through the police court in the ordinary way.'

After the Commissioner's rebuff, Bragg felt too irritated to settle to anything as mundane as looking at pieces of paper. Accordingly they tramped off to Petticoat Square again. Bragg knocked on the door of the Johnsons' house. After a few moments it was opened by Mrs. Johnson.

'Ah! I wondered when I would see you next,' she said sharply. 'Mrs Plumb said your young man told her to go and clean up next door. But nobody has a key but you.'

'I am extremely sorry, ma'am,' Morton said hastily. 'There has been a misunderstanding. It is entirely my fault. Please apologise to her for me.'

'Yes, well . . .' the woman said, scarcely mollified.

'I'll tell you what,' Bragg said genially. 'Why don't we leave her old key with you? I expect all sorts of odd people will be popping in.'

'Like what?'

'Well, his executors will have to take possession of his furniture, for one thing. And I expect the landlord will be anxious to re-let the house.'

She shivered as she took the key. 'I can't see anybody wanting to live there,' she said. 'It's bad enough being next door. Our Lily hasn't slept a wink since.'

'She will, when she is tired enough,' Bragg said. 'Life goes on. . . By the way, do you know which doctor Mr Chisnall used to go to?'

She frowned. 'I don't know as how he's ever been ill,' she said. 'People round here go to Dr Allison, in Hutchison Street – opposite the market. Mind you, Mr Chisnall might have been too uppity to go to him.'

'We will give him a try. Thank you, ma'am.' Bragg raised his bowler hat to her and turned away.

Hutchison market lay on the eastern fringe of the City. Beyond it was the warren of narrow streets and decaying buildings where Jack the Ripper had struck terror a mere six years before. The market itself did not seem to be thriving, Bragg thought, though a Thursday was probably a poor day for trade. Most of the area was deserted. There was a greengrocer's stall, with bunches of sage and lavender dangling down. There were some nice-looking broad beans on it; but to Bragg the rhubarb looked old and tough, and the potatoes were scabby. In Dorset, where he came from, they would have been fed to the pigs. Apart from that, the market was limited to a second-hand clothes stall, and one selling zinc buckets and brushes. A few people were picking over the clothes and peering at the vegetables; no one seemed to be buying.

'I think that the doctor's surgery must be in the middle of that terrace,' Morton remarked. 'There is a brass plate on the wall. If I am right, I suspect that we may be in luck. I imagine that is the doctor's horse and trap which is tied to the street-lamp outside.'

They crossed the street. Accepting Morton's hypothesis, Bragg thought, doctoring could not be very profitable in this neighbourhood. The trap was sound enough, but badly in need of a coat of varnish; and the pony was old and dejected. He stroked its nose to cheer it up. Then the door of the surgery opened, and a man in a dingy frock coat and top hat bustled out. He put his Gladstone bag in the trap and began to untie the reins from the lamp-post.

'Are you by any chance Dr Allison, sir?' Bragg asked.

'Not by any sort of chance, sir, but by damned hard work!' the man replied aggressively. 'Out of my way!' He threw the reins into the trap and prepared to step into it.

'We would like a few words with you, sir. We are police officers. Here is my warrant card.'

The doctor brushed it aside. 'I have a confinement to see to, half a mile away. Stand aside!'

Bragg took hold of the pony's bridle. 'It is interesting, isn't it, sir?' he said mildly. 'You are concerned with birth, we with death – or murder, to be more precise.'

'I cannot help that! I am needed elsewhere.'

'One of your patients was murdered on Monday night. A Mr Alan Chisnall.'

The doctor frowned and bit his lip. 'I have no recollection of the name,' he said. 'Let go of my horse!' He reached for his whip.

Bragg put his hand on the rein and with a jerk tore it out of the doctor's hand. 'If you are not careful,' he said harshly, 'you will spend a day or two in the nick, for obstructing the police! Get down, before I bloody fetch you down!'

The man looked at him, irresolute, then dropped his whip and stepped down from the trap. In resentful silence he walked back into his surgery. Morton secured the pony, then followed. When he entered the room the doctor was thumbing through a large index-book. He checked and smoothed down a page.

'Yes,' he announced in a subdued voice. 'It is true that one of my patients is named Alan Chisnall. He gave his address as seven Petticoat Square.'

'That's the man,' Bragg said cheerfully. 'Now I will tell you why I want to talk to you. When Professor Burney was doing the post-mortem, he discovered that Chisnall's heart was in poor shape. He talked about fatty degeneration of the tissue, and said he would not have lived much longer anyway.'

A flicker of interest crossed the doctor's face.

'What I want to know,' Bragg went on, 'is whether Chisnall came to see you about an illness recently.'

'Yes, he did,' Allison said reluctantly. 'On the 7th of May. He was complaining of intermittent pains in his chest. I see that I diagnosed weakness of the heart, and advised that he should adopt a more sedentary course of life. I prescribed a medicine containing a minute amount of digitalis, which has the effect of regulating the heartbeat. I could do no more.'

'Hmn. . . Well, I am sure you will be pleased to know that he did not die from a heart attack,' Bragg said grimly. 'He was battered to death so that his own mother would not recognise him.'

There was no sign of interest or concern on the doctor's face. 'Have you satisfied your curiosity now, officer?' he asked coldly. 'May I be about my legitimate concerns?'

'Why, yes,' Bragg said equably. 'And thank you for your help.'

Bragg and Morton found a cool bar in a cellar off Aldgate, and ate their lunch. Then they went back to Old Jewry. Bragg pulled out his tobacco pouch and began to cut thin slices from a rope of twist, with his juice-stained knife.

'Interesting, that,' he remarked, rubbing the tobacco between his palms, and feeding it into his pipe.

'What is that, sir?' Morton asked.

'Why, that Chisnall knew he was not long for this world.'

'But there is no evidence he was aware that his heart condition was so serious,' Morton protested.

'Don't be stupid, lad.' Bragg struck a match and laid it across the bowl of his pipe. Soon his head was wreathed in a cloud of blue smoke. He gave a sigh of contentment. 'No. If a doctor tells you that you have a bad heart, says you must take life easy, you would have to be a numbskull not to realise you were going to kick the bucket before long. . . The question is, would that have made any difference to Chisnall – to the way he thought, to what seemed important to him?'

'Inevitably, I suppose.' Morton turned and surveyed the boxes that had been brought from Chisnall's house. 'Ah well, I must try to bring a little more order to this mess. I can leave the newspapers for the moment; but there are six boxes crammed with miscellaneous papers to be sorted.

A smile formed under Bragg's ragged moustache. 'It's a pity I cannot help you,' he said smugly. 'But it's best for one person to know about it all, and where everything can be found. It is not a job you can safely split. . . But let me know if you find anything interesting. I can be thinking about it!'

Morton grimaced, then tipped the contents of a box on to his table. He began to sort them into piles; bills on one, financial circulars on another, articles about racing on another. . .

'One thing I find mildly surprising,' he remarked after some minutes. 'I have not seen any correspondence; no letters from family and friends, no business correspondence even.'

'They might be in the other boxes,' Bragg suggested.

'Perhaps. But I have already handled their contents, and I cannot recollect seeing any letters.'

Bragg knocked out his pipe in the big glass ashtray on his desk. 'Maybe that was what his killer was burning in the grate.'

Morton laughed. 'That involves a considerable assumption on our part,' he said. 'But I suppose it is possible.'

'Have you thought any more about your bit of paper – the one you rescued from the chimney?' Bragg asked.

'I have thought, yes; but arrived at no conclusions. The letters "op" are commonly used as a contraction for *opus* which is the Latin word meaning a work. But since the "it" was written in cursive script, one would have expected that the "op" would have been written similarly. Again, "op" is frequently used with another Latin contraction, *cit.*, to refer to a literary work previously mentioned. You will see *op. cit.* throughout any work of scholarship; but I have never seen *cit. op.* Indeed, on my fragment there is no point after the "it", which suggests that it was not a contraction at all.'

'Unless it was done by some ignorant person like me, trying to ape his betters,' Bragg said sourly. He got up and walked over to the window. Then he turned. 'Let me give you a hand. Are these boxes still to do?' he asked.

'Yes, the wine boxes. The whisky cartons have at least been looked at.'

Bragg bent down. 'Let us start with the Château Margaux, shall we?' He lifted the box and upended it on his desk. Some of the papers slithered on to the floor. He bent to rescue them.

'Hullo,' he said, picking out a small bound book. 'This looks like a diary . . . for this year too!'

Morton came across and looked over his shoulder.

'Not much in it,' Bragg muttered. 'Mostly just a single initial and time. . . Appointments I suppose. . . Never says where they are.'

'Since he was working alone, he would presumably have no doubt about whom he was meeting,' Morton said.

'I don't know, lad. There are plenty of "J"s in here. How many names beginning with that letter are there? John, Jacob, Jeremiah . . . perhaps something as outlandish as James.'

Morton grinned. 'Or even Joseph! But I confess I had assumed that a single initial represented a surname. . . See, here are two letters, "M H". That must represent Christian name and surname.'

'So where does that get us?' Bragg said grumpily. 'We still cannot tell who the letters stand for.' He turned page after page then stopped abruptly.

'Look at this, lad! For once we have a name – Adelaide. Not long ago either. Monday the twenty-fifth of June.'

'A mere ten days ago. . . Why do you think he put that name in full, sir? I cannot recollect seeing a letter "A" in the earlier entries.'

'Nor I,' Bragg muttered. 'Perhaps he treated his women clients with more decorum – assuming all these are clients.'

'Adelaide is exceptional in another way also,' Morton said lightly. 'If I am not mistaken, she is the only person whom he has seen in an afternoon, since the start of the flat-racing season! She must be fascinating indeed!'

'All you can think of is women, lad. Use your brains! There are not many women who have control of their financial affairs – and they will have bank managers by the score sucking up to them. But there is a state in Australia that has Adelaide as its capital.'

'Absolutely right, sir! I scored a hundred and thirty-four in the 'ninety-two test match there. We won by an innings and two hundred and thirty runs! I am astonished that I should ever forget it!'

'I am not,' Bragg said sourly. 'You lost the series, for all that. . .'

There was a knock on the door and Catherine Marsden came in. She was wearing the blue tailor-made and white jabot that constituted her working clothes; a little feathered hat nestled on her upswept hair.

'I hope that I am not disturbing you,' she said brightly.

The men stood up, and Bragg waved her to a chair that Morton set by his desk. Catherine settled herself elegantly.

'You asked me to enquire into the antecedents of Alan Chisnall,' she said with a bright smile. 'I am sorry that it has taken a little time.'

'Don't you worry, miss,' Bragg said. 'We are glad of any help we can get. I don't mind telling you that we are clutching at straws.'

'I cannot think that my discoveries will add much to your store of knowledge,' Catherine said. 'I fear that it comes very much in the category of ancient history.'

'You can never tell. . . What have you found out?'

'First of all, my sources are the financial editor of the *Star* and, more importantly, a young reporter on the *Financial News* who has been most helpful.' She glanced across at Morton, but he was staring out of the window. 'Charles Anstruther could only relay to me what he had discovered from others; but David Rose of the *Star* actually worked with Chisnall long ago.'

'Well then?' Bragg prompted her.

'It appears that Alan Chisnall was employed for a time by a firm of stockbrokers called Pim Vaughan & Co., in Drapers' Gardens. This was in the late eighteen fifties, so it could be that this was his first permanent post after leaving school. I presume that he remained in stockbroking for some years. According to David Rose, Chisnall was still a raw journalist, when he joined the *Financial News* himself; and that was in 'sixty-six.'

'I am sure that I have seen an assurance policy somewhere,' Morton said. 'That ought to give his date of birth.' He got up and went over to the pile of boxes.

'Go on, miss,' Bragg said.

'David joined the paper straight from school. So, despite the difference in age, they were both starting with no journalistic experience.'

'And was Chisnall no good?' Bragg asked.

Catherine smiled. 'On the contrary, he was very highly regarded. His experience in stockbroking gave him an insight into the workings of the City that his colleagues did not possess; and he had a wide circle of contacts in the various institutions. Because of this he got some scoops for the paper, and the proprietors formed a very high opinion of his abilities. There was even talk that he would eventually become editor.'

'Which, I suppose is a job of power and influence,' Bragg remarked.

'Indeed!'

'I have it!' Morton exclaimed triumphantly. He brought over the document to Bragg's desk. 'A Prudential assurance policy. According to the schedule on the back page, his date of birth was the second of June eighteen forty.'

'Hmm. . . So he had just turned fifty-four,' Bragg mused. 'Right. Go on, miss.'

'There is not a great deal more to tell,' Catherine said, piqued at having been interrupted. 'He worked at the *Financial News* for almost ten years, becoming an experienced reporter no doubt. Then suddenly he left.'

'Why?' Bragg asked. 'You would think he was set up for life.'

Catherine nodded. ' That was precisely my reaction. As you can imagine, I pressed David Rose on the point. I can only describe his reply as evasive. I raised the matter in general conversation with some *Financial News* journalists. They either did not know about the subject or affected not to do so.'

'It is almost twenty years ago, miss,' Bragg said tolerantly.

'Yes.' Catherine glanced at Morton. 'But Charles Anstruther picked up some gossip for me. According to him, Alan Chisnall did not leave of his own volition; his services were summarily dispensed with!'

'Why?'

'The whole affair was kept very quiet, so there is a certain amount of speculation in the report. But according to Charles, Alan Chisnall used confidential information given to him by a company, for his own personal advantage.'

'I see, miss.' Bragg scratched his chin thoughtfully. 'And that kind of thing is not tolerated.'

'Certainly not on the scale reported. . . It seems to have been an act of total recklessness.'

'You cannot give us more detail I suppose, miss?'

'No, sergeant,' Catherine said firmly. 'In fact I have given you all the information I possess. I promised Charles that on no account would I enquire further.'

'Ah! You mean that doesn't bind us!' Bragg exclaimed. 'Well done, miss! I begin to think we should enrol you in the force.'

Catherine looked up angrily. 'If you make any enquiries whatever, you will damage my credibility and ruin my career! Do not dare!'

'I'm sorry, miss,' Bragg said abashed. 'I get carried away at times . . . and we couldn't do without your help, could we? Not on this case anyway.'

Morton intervened. 'I would have thought that our purpose has already been served by Miss Marsden,' he said. 'Something that happened so long ago could hardly have a direct bearing on Chisnall's murder. But your acquaintance's suggestion that the man was disreputable powerfully reinforces our impressions.'

'Really?' Catherine said.

'We had already concluded that whoever killed him was looking for something in his house. And, in view of the extreme brutality, it seemed likely that Chisnall had a hold over the murderer.'

'I have been thinking,' Bragg broke in. 'We know that the visitor tapped Chisnall on the back of the head, then went to look for whatever it was – some document or other. I reckon that if our visitor had found it, he would have left Chisnall as he was. Even if the attacker thought he was only unconscious, there would have been no point in killing him. Once the incriminating evidence had been retrieved, or burnt, Chisnall would have no hold over him.'

'I see,' Morton remarked. 'So the fact that he was battered after the search, and more particularly the savage nature of the attack, suggests that the murderer did not find what he was seeking.'

Catherine shuddered. 'I did not realise . . .' she began.

'Don't you give it a thought, miss,' Bragg said warmly. 'We are very grateful to you for what you have done already. . . Now, I don't suppose you know any Adelaides do you?'

'Adelaides? You mean women named Adelaide?'

'That's right, miss. There is an entry in Chisnall's diary for three o'clock on Monday the twenty-fifth of June. We think it might have something to do with his death.'

'Three o'clock,' Catherine mused. 'One thing is certain; that is not a society time.'

'I don't follow you,' Bragg said.

Catherine laughed. 'I am sorry. Let me explain. In society the time for luncheon would be from one o'clock to, say, half-past two. On the other hand, the time for afternoon At Homes is from four o'clock to seven in the evening.'

'Are you saying that society murders can only take place between half-past two and four?' Bragg said sardonically.

Catherine blushed. 'I . . . I am now totally confused,' she stammered.

'Not at all,' Morton broke in. 'Miss Marsden makes a perfectly valid point, and one that I am sure we would never have identified for ourselves.'

'Oh?' She looked gratefully at him.

'If Adelaide were indeed a society woman, then three o'clock would be an admirable time for her to receive, or be received, for a private tête-à-tête.'

Bragg grunted. 'So this Adelaide entry might be important after all?'

'I think it might well be, sir.' Morton turned to Catherine. 'Can you shed any further light on the matter?' he asked.

'Well, Adelaide is a rather old-fashioned name. I do not suppose that anyone would christen a child Adelaide nowadays. I would think that my mother's generation was the last to embrace it.'

'That's my generation,' Bragg said. 'And Chisnall's too.'

'I suppose so. Indeed,' Catherine added with a chuckle, 'the only Adelaide I am personally aware of is about to become James's sister's mother-in-law!'

'Adelaide Smith?' Morton murmured. 'Do you know, I cannot think of any other Adelaides either.'

It was six o'clock as Catherine ascended the elegant curving staircase of Lanesborough House. By now the afternoon callers should be on the point of drifting away, if they were not already gone. She had no inclination to spend time in empty chit-hat. She paused at the enormous portrait of her godmother, which had been painted when she was the toast of London society as a young woman. It had been her father's first important commission, and had established his position as the foremost portrait painter of his generation. A group of fashionably dressed women came through the doorway from the drawing-room. One of them gave her a haughty stare as she passed; no doubt she was being censured for wearing *démodé* clothes to visit one of London's greatest mansions! Thank goodness she had insisted on making use of her education, and taken a real job, or she would have ended up like them! She turned and went into the drawing-room. It could not have been planned better! Lady Lanesborough was sitting with her crony, Mrs Gerald de Trafford, by a window overlooking the garden. There was no one else in the room. She kissed her godmother on the cheek.

'I hope that this is not an inconvenient time,' she said breezily. 'I am afraid that I had to complete an article for our Saturday edition. It would have been more than my life was worth to have missed the deadline!'

Lady Lanesborough sniffed. 'If you would like my opinion, child,' she said, 'your life would be a deal more promising if you did lose that wretched post. A talented young woman like you should not be wasting her time journalising for a newspaper. There are far better things in life.'

'But it is immensely enjoyable and fulfilling!'

'I only hope that you will not regret it in the end. . . By the way. . .' Lady Lanesborough affected a light insouciant tone. 'Did you know that young Lord Alderley is up for the Season – or what remains of it?'

Catherine laughed. 'I am sure it is most un-god-daughterly to treat so lightly your constant efforts to marry me off!' she said. 'But I would prefer to make my own choice.'

Lady Lanesborough's brows knitted peevishly. 'Had I known that you would develop into such a self-willed young woman,' she said, 'I would not have promised at the font to be responsible for your well-being.'

'But you have been my model in everything! Like you, I am level-headed, self-reliant, sceptical, opinionated. . .'

Lady Lanesborough tapped Catherine's arm with her fan. 'I should chastise you, child,' she said reprovingly. 'I so seldom see you. And when I do, it is only because you seek a favour. . . I suppose you are wanting some tittle-tattle for that wretched policeman of yours.'

'Come, you are unfair! Not only can he not be stigmatised as belonging to me, he has many qualities that you would normally regard as admirable. He has a fine physique, a cultured outlook, an amiable disposition, an amusing manner. . . What more could one reasonably expect of a man?'

'That he should come to the point, child; make up his mind. It is very unfair of him to keep up this friendship with you, year after year, and not make his intentions clear.'

'But Lady Lanesborough –'

'I know perfectly well that he is eligible,' she overrode her. 'I am aware that his line goes back to the Norman Conquest; that he will probably inherit the baronetcy; that he has in his own right a satisfactory fortune from his American grandparents, and will undoubtedly inherit more. But what is the good of all this if you cannot get him to the point of proposing marriage?'

Catherine gave a gasp. 'Good heavens! I do believe that, with you as his advocate, he might prevail in the end.'

'And what do you mean by that, child?'

'I mean, dear godmother, that he has already proposed marriage to me . . . and I have refused him.'

Lady Lanesborough looked at her uncertainly. 'Was that wise?' she asked.

'To refuse him? I think so. The circumstances were inauspicious. . . But I really came to tell you about the arrangements for Emily's wedding!'

'That would be Emily Morton, I suppose. . . It is a great mistake to be a close friend of one's admirer's sister, my dear. Sisters gossip so.'

Catherine laughed. 'You are such an incorrigible matchmaker!' she said. 'Let me tell you about the wedding. . . The service is to take place in the lovely little Saxon church on the estate. Emily has asked me to be a bridesmaid. And you will be intrigued to learn that Reuben Smith has asked James to be his chief groomsman. Think of the possibilities!'

'That seems almost incestuous,' Mrs de Trafford remarked. 'Is it not rather unusual?'

'Reuben has no brother, and I gather that he and James have been acquainted for some years. In fact, James actually introduced Emily to him.'

'So what will you be wearing?' Lady Lanesborough asked eagerly. 'The bride will be in white, of course.'

'I have just this moment come from Worth's! The fit of the bodice is absolute perfection! I shall have to forswear cream cakes until it is all over!'

'What is your dress like?' Mrs de Trafford interrupted impatiently.

'Well, it is in the most exquisite apple-blossom surah silk you could ever imagine. The bodice comes down to a point in front; the sleeves are tight and long to the wrist. . .'

'And the skirt?'

'A gored bell-shape. It should be quite beautiful.'

'Did you say that Worth's are making it?' Lady Lanesborough asked in surprise.

'Yes! The wedding dress, and the dresses of all four bridesmaids.'

'Then they are not stinting.'

Catherine laughed. 'Good heavens, no! She is their only daughter, after all.'

'But what is the bridegroom's background?' Mrs de Trafford asked. 'I am told that she is marrying beneath her.'

'One might say that,' Lady Lanesborough replied. 'The Smiths are as rich as Croesus, but have no pedigree. Not that that need be a hindrance to being accepted; but I believe that the menfolk seem to scorn society.'

'Do they work?' Mrs de Trafford asked suspiciously.

Lady Lanesborough pursed her lips. 'I believe that they do. There is a family bank in the City. That is where the money comes from.'

Catherine smiled. 'Am I not right in thinking that Reuben's father is the only other male in the family?' she asked casually.

'Yes . . . yes, I am sure of that. I have met him once or twice, in connection with charitable work. Theodore is his name. A very dull little man I thought him; well suited to grubbing away in an office all day.'

Catherine laughed. 'I believe you despise men who earn their living by the sweat of their brow,' she said.

'Despise? Not at all! Lanesborough works too, I will have you know! He goes down to the country, even in the Season, to chat with his land agents. No, there is nothing at all wrong with work; but it does so seem to take the sparkle out of people!'

'Who was his wife, before she married?' Mrs de Trafford asked.

'Adelaide? Now, she was a Hollyer. Another wealthy family; made their money in the East Indies. There were brothers, I think, so she may not have had a great deal of money of her own. Surely you have seen her at functions? The Smiths have an enormous mansion, practically next door to Buckingham Palace!'

'Adelaide seems to be a rather old-fashioned name,' Catherine said offhandedly.

Her godmother mused. 'I do believe you are right,' she said. 'I scarcely know any under the age of eighty.'

'I know of one other,' Mrs de Trafford added. 'But she lives in the wilds of Northumberland!'

Catherine got to her feet with a smile. 'Well, I must ask to be excused. I have enjoyed our conversation immensely.'

'Ah! But there is something that I wish to say to you,' Lady Lanesborough exclaimed. 'If you mean to go on with your wretched journalism, I would have thought that you would find this more congenial. I gather that the editor of *The Lady* has resigned, and that they intend to invite applications for his successor. I think that you ought to apply. It would be better than bothering your head about Lord Mayors' shows and Guildhall banquets. And unless you do apply, they will be stupid enough to appoint another man.'

'That would be insupportable, would it not?' Catherine teased her.

'Ah, so you are interested?'

'But of course! How could I fail to be?'

'Good, good.' Lady Lanesborough pursed her lips. 'Well, off you go, child,' she said. 'I also have work to do.'

4

Bragg and Morton left the train at Manor Park station, and walked the few hundred yards to the City of London's cemetery in Little Ilford. It must have been a shock, Bragg thought, when they stopped burials in the City itself. In the old days people could have popped down with a bunch of flowers, on the spur of the moment. Now it had to be an expedition. . . But they had got to using the same graves over again – nearly as bad as Paris. And, once they had removed the gravestones, grassed or paved over the churchyards, they made very pleasant public places. It was more wholesome, more seemly, to have them full of pretty young girls posturing in the sunshine, than rows of mouldering stone slabs leaning drunkenly in all directions.

They made their way to the little stone chapel. There was no one about. To kill time they wandered down the long avenues. Only about one third of the available space was in use as a cemetery. The rest was as well groomed as the grounds of a country mansion; the grass was mown, wooden benches were set in the shade of yews and weeping willows. All in all, Bragg thought, it was a pleasant enough place to lie and while away eternity. He had always intended that he should be buried in Bere Regis. It had seemed proper that he should be returned to the Dorset soil of his childhood. But perhaps that was a bit old-fashioned. If you were going to rise again, what did it matter? And if you weren't. . . They turned a corner and came upon a monstrous headstone of black marble – massive, shiny, assertive, alien. The grave of someone who thought that he would be able to buy his way in heaven, as he had done on earth; who would expect to have a servant to play his harp for him. . . No, let it be cremation for him, rather than have to mix with this lot.

'There is a hearse coming through the gate,' Morton remarked. 'And . . . yes, one other carriage.'

Bragg quickened his pace, so that they arrived at the chapel before the cortège. A man detached himself from the side of the porch, where he had been furtively smoking a cigarette.

He was not dressed in mourning clothes. His only concession to the solemnity of the occasion was a black cravat. He came across to them.

'Have you come to the Chisnall obsequies?' he asked, with a touch of flippancy in his voice.

'Yes,' Bragg said. 'Are you a relative?'

'Good Lord, no! I doubt if I ever set eyes on the man. I represent the *Financial News*'s genuflexion towards convention. I was the unlucky one.'

'Do you happen to be Charles Anstruther, by any chance?' Morton asked curtly.

'Would that I were! Charles's family owns a fair chunk of the paper.'

'So the *Financial News* people still regard Chisnall as one of their own, despite everything?' Bragg remarked.

The young man looked at them uncertainly. 'You seem to know a great deal more about him than I do,' he said. 'What newspaper are you from?'

'We are police officers,' Bragg said flatly. 'We are interested in anybody who comes to the service.'

'Ah! The theory that the murderer is drawn to his victim's funeral. . . But surely that is a fiction?'

'I'm damn certain I would keep away, if I'd done it,' Bragg said. 'But then, I am sane.'

The young man grimaced. 'I thought that this would be no more than a bit of a jaunt,' he said lightly. 'And here I am, under suspicion of murder! I expect you will be demanding my name and address next!'

Bragg looked at him contemptuously. 'No. I think we are looking for somebody with a bit more bottom than you. . . But if I am wrong, we know where to find you.'

He turned as the coffin was borne towards the chapel on the shoulders of the undertaker's men. It was followed by a pitifully small straggle of mourners. Ernie and Alice Johnson were there, with a handful of other people that Bragg had seen at Petticoat Square. Mrs Plumb had evidently decided that respects were no longer in order.

Bragg and Morton followed the mourners into the chapel. The officiating priest hurried through the funeral service in an irreverent gabble. In no time at all the coffin was being carried to the hearse again, for Chisnall's final journey to a hole dug in the yellow clay.

Bragg restrained Morton from following. 'I think we can opt out of the interment,' he said. 'Did you see anything of interest?'

'No one struck me as sinister, or under great emotional stress, or struck by grief or guilt,' Morton said. 'I do not know what we expected to find.'

'No. . . Anyway, we have found out a bit about Miss Marsden's informant. With that sort of background, Anstruther should know what he is talking about.' He cocked an eye at Morton. 'Yes. . . I should think we could trust him, wouldn't you?'

Immediately on getting back to the City, Bragg and Morton hurried to the Mansion House police court.

'You got my note, I hope,' Bragg said to the clerk. 'Only I had to go to a funeral. . . The magistrate hasn't gone, has he?'

'No, sergeant, he is still here, but he is not best pleased at being kept waiting. You will find him in the justices' room. It is Mr Ponsonby; he can get a bit sharp at times, so watch out.'

They found Ponsonby peering irritably at an etching hung in the gloom of a corner. He swung round as they entered.

'Are you the officer who wants the summons?' he asked in a clipped, hard voice.

'Yes, sir,' Bragg said meekly. 'I apologise for having to keep you here.'

'Never mind that! Have you got the paperwork?'

'I, er. . . Did the clerk, not give it you, sir?'

'No. Had you kept the nine o'clock appointment which was given you, no doubt the machinery of justice would have functioned smoothly. But since you deferred presenting yourself here, you can hardly expect the clerk to divine your wishes.'

'It is a witness summons,' Bragg said. 'I will pop to the clerk's room and get the form.'

'Very well; but hurry. I am already late for an appointment!' His face was flushed red with suppressed anger.

Bragg returned in a matter of moments and laid the form on the desk. Ponsonby took his seat, visibly trying to regain a judicial remoteness.

'What is the name of the person to whom the summons is directed?' he asked curtly.

'Mr Ashworth Caldwell, the manager of the Bank of Montreal branch in Abchurch Lane.'

Ponsonby entered the particulars on a form in a careful copperplate script. Then he leaned back. 'And in what connection do you wish Mr Caldwell to give evidence, sergeant?'

'The Chisnall murder, sir. The journalist who was bludgeoned to death in his house at Petticoat Square.'

The magistrate's face showed a flicker of interest. 'And how is this Mr Caldwell able to help us?' he asked.

'Chisnall deposited a strong-box with the bank, as long ago as eighteen seventy-two. We have a key that fits it, we reckon. The manager will not let us have access to it without a warrant; he won't even let us try the key in the lock!'

'And you are expecting to find something specific? Or is this merely a fishing expedition?'

'Not at all, sir,' Bragg said earnestly. 'We have already been given access to a bank account in his name with another bank; but that one does not give a complete picture. We need to be able to examine the contents of the box to see if they will round off our information. . . Of course, it might be that we would find nothing to help us. Chisnall might just have deposited something twenty years ago, and forgotten all about it. Nevertheless,' Bragg added piously, 'we would be failing in our duty if we ignored its existence.'

Ponsonby frowned judicially. 'Yes . . . yes, I suppose that is entirely reasonable. So you want a summons to produce it.'

'That's it, sir.' Bragg gave an encouraging smile.

'Very well.'

The magistrate entered the rest of the particulars on the form and signed it with a flourish. 'Here you are,' he said, holding out the warrant. 'And be sure that you never keep me waiting again!'

Bragg and Morton had their lunch in a pub on Cheapside. Bragg even lingered over a second pint of beer, to make sure that they would not be kicking their heels in Abchurch Lane. At half-past two they left the pub and made their way to the bank. But when they arrived, Caldwell was still not back from lunch.

'It was late when he left,' the young clerk explained apologetically.

'Never mind, sir,' Bragg said expansively. 'We have come with a warrant to examine the strong-box of Alan Chisnall. Perhaps you could be getting it out. It will save time.'

'Yes, sergeant... of course. Would you like to wait in Mr Caldwell's office? I am afraid there is nowhere to sit here.'

'That is very courteous of you.'

The clerk showed them into the manager's office, and shortly afterwards came back with a metal deed-box. It was about sixteen inches by ten, and no more than eight inches deep. He placed it on the desk in front of Caldwell's chair.

'Thank you,' Bragg said warmly. 'Now, don't let us keep you from your work. We will be quite happy to wait here for Mr Caldwell.'

The clerk had no sooner closed the door behind him than Bragg was on his feet, Chisnall's bunch of keys in his hand.

'Listen out, lad,' he said. 'I want to know if we are going to fall in the shit.'

As Morton went over to the door, Bragg put the elaborate key in the lock. There was a click as he turned it. He raised the lid an inch, then dropped it and relocked the box.

'Can you be quite well, sir?' Morton said solicitously. 'I expected you to have the contents spread out over the desk by now!'

'What, and be in breach of the summons?' Bragg said craftily. 'It's for him to produce them to us. We can wait.'

There came a murmur of conversation in the corridor; Bragg recognised the manager's voice, raised in anger. Then the door was flung open. Caldwell looked uncertainly at the box inviolate on his desk and the two policemen sitting beside it.

Bragg rose. 'Good afternoon, sir,' he said. 'We have brought the summons you asked for.'

Caldwell subsided into his chair. 'I have not yet received guidance from my head office,' he said primly. 'I sent a telegraph to them yesterday morning, but I have not yet received a reply.'

'It must be difficult, operating half a world away,' Bragg said sympathetically. 'Anyway, here is the warrant you insisted on. You are covered now.'

'It is not a matter of being covered, as you express it! I wish to operate within the code of practice laid down by the bank. I do not have any personal discretion in this field.'

Bragg wrinkled his brow. 'I think I would agree with you there,' he said. 'Whatever your head office may think, both you and the bank are subject to the laws of this country, even if it is a foreign company. . . I accept that the bank might shrug its shoulders, but that is hardly the point. After all, it is your name that is on the summons.'

Caldwell took the document and glanced at it reluctantly. 'And what would be my position if I refused to comply?' he asked.

'Why, that would be a serious contempt of the legal process,' Bragg said blandly. 'They would lock you up until you had purged your contempt.'

Caldwell swallowed hard. 'And how long would that be for?' he asked.

'Oh, they would just leave you to rot until you had complied with the summons. So you see, you cannot defy the law in this country. Now just give us the box and stay out of trouble.'

'Can it not wait until I have heard from Montreal?' he asked plaintively.

'No, sir. We are after a very violent and dangerous man. Every hour that passes increases the danger that some other innocent man, woman or child might be butchered.'

'I suppose so.' Caldwell unhappily let his eyes drift down the printed page. Then he stiffened. 'It says here that I am summoned to appear at the police court hearing, and to bring the strong-box with me,' he exclaimed.

'That is just a form of words, sir. We will take it with us now. We need to see what is in it this very afternoon.'

'It is not a mere form of words to me,' Caldwell exclaimed angrily. 'You say that the law requires me to surrender this box. Very well, I shall do so, but only within the terms of this document.'

'You realise that this amounts to deliberately obstructing our enquiries into this murder,' Bragg said coldly.

'That is of no matter to me. I have other obligations.'

Bragg sprang to his feet. 'Well it bloody matters to me!' he shouted. He seized the box and made for the door. Caldwell tried to intercept him and was sent sprawling. The clerks in the main office looked up startled, as Bragg marched out triumphantly with the box in his hands. He turned to Morton as they reached the street.

'Well, lad,' he said. 'I think we can say that summons was well and truly served!'

By the time they got back to Old Jewry, Bragg's euphoria had begun to fade.

'I reckon we had better look at this lot before all hell breaks loose,' he said gloomily.

He set the strong-box on his desk and unlocked it. He peered inside and grunted. 'Well, I hope it was all worth it,' he said, and piled the meagre contents on his desk.

Morton picked up a large bundle of envelopes tied with red ribbon. He undid the bow and selected one. The writing on the envelope was strong and rounded, there was a faint trace of perfume. He pulled out the letter. The first paragraph was couched in warm personal terms.

'Old love-letters,' Morton remarked, replacing it in the bundle. 'So our friend Chisnall was a romantic!'

'Let them keep, ' Bragg said. 'Have a look at these loose papers first. . . Hullo! What's this? His last will and testament by the look of it – and only made in May this year.'

'What date?' Morton asked.

'The twenty-third.'

'Then that ties up with his having learned from Dr Allison, on the seventh, that his health was precarious.'

'Made in the knowledge of imminent death, eh?' Bragg browsed through the document, then began to laugh. 'I don't know if he had any relatives or not,' he said. 'If he has, they will be disappointed. He has left all his worldly goods for the benefit of a charity to help injured jockeys!'

'A fair indication of his priorities in life! But did he have much to leave them? I half expected to find a bundle of share certificates and bonds here, but so far there is nothing of the sort... Ah! What have we here? An envelope containing two hundred pounds in twenties! Do you think that this was his piggy-bank, his secret reserve against adversity?'

'Well, a farm labourer has to bring up a family on less than half of that a year. But it would not last Chisnall long. He used to lose more than that on a day's racing, and not think twice about it... No, I think he dealt in cash most of the time. There are no bank-books in the box, are there?'

'No.'

'Hmn... We have no indication of any account except the one with Derenburg's; and we know that one nothing like reflected his income and expenditure.'

'As you say, he was able to place substantial cash bets all through the flat-racing season.'

'So where did it come from? He must have been getting hold of it in some way.'

'You did suggest blackmail earlier,' Morton said. 'There are reputedly people in society who make it a way of life.'

Bragg snorted. 'From the way that snotty little sod carried on at the funeral, I don't reckon Chisnall moved in those circles.'

'But he was getting large amounts of money – of cash – from somewhere, and apparently spending it as if there was no end to it.'

'I wish we had a clearer idea of the kind of work he did,' Bragg said thoughtfully. 'He was employed by the *Financial News*, then left. So far as Miss Marsden's informants go, he does not appear to have worked for any other newspaper.'

'It might be that the answer lies in the boxes of papers over there... Ah, there are some financial articles here, in the papers from the strong-box.' Morton slowly turned them over. 'They do not appear to be articles from newspapers; rather they are financial circulars, dealing with the prospects of one or two companies only.'

'Is that unusual?' Bragg asked.

'No... not in itself. They are the kind of thing that a stockbroker might send to substantial clients.' He picked one at random and glanced rapidly through it. 'This, for instance, is examining the prospects of a cotton weaving concern; analysing the market trends for the product, and the cost of variables such as labour and raw materials.'

'Is it a professional job? You must have seen thousands in your time.'

Morton laughed. 'It is superficially impressive, certainly. Since I know nothing about the cotton trade, I cannot pronounce upon the value of it.'

'Maybe that was how he made his living – doing that kind of circular for stockbrokers.'

'It is possible. Though I have yet to see a stockbroker's name on any of them. And they do not appear to be merely drafts. The paper is of very good quality.'

Bragg picked one out of the pile. 'There is a name written in red, at the top corner of this one,' he said. 'Can you make it out? Your eyes are younger than mine.'

Morton took it from him. 'It is "Porthos",' he said. 'Strange. . . The name can have no connection with the subject of the circular, nor can I think of a firm of brokers it could refer to. Indeed, the only occasion on which I have met the name is in the romance by Alexandre Dumas, *The Three Musketeers*.'

Sir William Sumner sat at his desk and gazed out of the window at the tower of St Olave's church. He could just see the tops of the trees which surrounded it. The breeze was ruffling their leaves, pigeons fluttered in their branches. It was peaceful. . . That was what he liked about Saturday morning. No one wanted to get argumentative, or make trouble. For the bankers and financial people, Saturday morning was a social occasion rather than a time for serious work. They would pop into their office, open the post, chat to underlings, then off to a coffee shop or a hotel bar. Not that they would turn up their noses at a deal; but it was all more relaxed. And certainly they were not concerned to complain about tangled traffic in the streets, or the shortage of beat constables. Consequently Saturday morning was the only part of the week that he genuinely enjoyed.

He got up and went to the window. The sun was lost in a hazy golden halo, but the heat beat down relentlessly. It had been like this in India – and not just for the odd fortnight, either! Close his eyes and he could be back in the club, a whisky in his hand, the soft flop of the native servants' slippers, the monotonous thud of tennis racquets. He had been happy then. A peacetime regiment was like a piece of clockwork. All the parts had their function, interlocked with each other. A gentle pressure from above – the mere presence of the commanding officer – kept it all going smoothly. . . Yes, he had been satisfied with life then, even proud of his achievements. Hilda and the children were safely at a distance, in England; he had been his own man. He sighed. Had he been left to his own devices, he would have retired perfectly happily to Tunbridge Wells. He had never been fiercely ambitious. His promotions had come more by effluxion of time than his own strivings. He had been competent and agreeable; others had fallen by the wayside. So he had ended up a Lieutenant-Colonel in command of an infantry regiment. That had more than satisfied his expectations. . . But Hilda was ambitious; relentlessly ambitious. Not for herself – though she patently enjoyed being addressed as Lady Sumner – but for him. She thought that his backwardness was mere modesty; his disinclination to involve himself a gentlemanly courtesy. So when it had been suggested, at a social occasion, that he might be interested in becoming the Commissioner of the City of London police, she had jumped at it. Overriding his reluctance she had lobbied the wives of City figures, insisted on his attending functions. . . Her campaign had been triumphant, and now he was wearing laurels he did not really want.

Police work was not like the army; that was the trouble. There was nothing predictable about it. Every day there seemed to be a problem that had never been faced before. There was no rule-book, no Army Act to rely on. And, worst of all, he was personally accountable. Not only for the actions of his officers, but for the overall cost of their operations. The police committee was not a government department, remote and inert. Its members were in and out of the Guildhall or the Mansion House all the time. One whiff of inefficiency or financial excess, and they were round in person to investigate. He had never had to fight his corner before; he found the whole experience distasteful and demeaning. Perhaps if he talked to Hilda. . .

There was a knock on his door, and the desk sergeant came in. 'There are two gentlemen downstairs, sir, who insist on seeing you,' he said apologetically. 'I cannot get rid of them.

Do you want me to say that you are out?'

Sir William turned reluctantly from the window. 'Why do they wish to see me?' he asked.

'I dunno, sir. Looks like trouble to me. Only the Commissioner will do, they say.'

'Oh well, I suppose that I must agree.'

'Do I send tea up, sir?'

'By no means! I have no intention of being pushed on to the defensive.'

The sergeant disappeared. Sir William took an old report out of his desk drawer, picked up a pencil and began to leaf through it. There was a soft tap at the door, a squeak of the hinge as it opened. He became aware of two frock coats beyond the edge of his desk, the irritated clearing of a throat. He placed a precise tick in the margin of the report, then looked up.

'You must be the gentlemen who wish to see me,' he said coolly. 'Please sit down.'

'This is not an occasion for social niceties,' one of them exclaimed aggressively. 'It is a matter of the most serious public concern! Here is my card.'

He was short and paunchy, with pallid skin and thinning red hair. A gold Albert was draped across a waistcoat that was threadbare at the edges; his coat was crumpled. Something of an enigma, the Commissioner thought. He was glad that he had not risen to greet them.

'Nevertheless, Mr . . . er.' He glanced down at the square of pasteboard. 'Mr Framblington-Smith . . . we will observe the normal courtesies to the fullest extent possible. Please be seated.'

So Ernest Framblington-Smith practised as a solictor in Stoke Newington . . . eight or nine miles north of the City's border. Had he been of any eminence in his profession, he could easily have travelled in to a City office from there. . . Things were not quite as bad as he had feared.

'Do I understand, Mr Framblington-Smith, that you have some information which you wish to convey to me personally?' he asked in a neutral tone.

'Information?' The red-haired man was bursting with indignation. 'No, sir. It is not information that I wish to lay before you, but a most serious complaint. The conduct of one of your officers has been high-handed to the point of criminality! He has threatened my client with assault, committed actual assault upon his person, and taken away by force a strong-box committed to his charge!'

A sense of foreboding enveloped the Commissioner. 'What is the name of this officer?' he asked.

'A certain Sergeant Bragg. There was another officer, but he took no part in the assault.'

'I see. Did he force his way into your client's presence, or was he there by invitation?'

'He tricked his way into my client's office!'

Sir William turned to the second man. 'May I have your name, sir?'

The man glanced towards his solicitor, but he was occupied in glaring at the Commissioner. 'I am Ashworth Caldwell,' he said firmly.

'And you reside at. . . ?

'Seven Clissold Park Road, Stoke Newington.'

Sir William wrote the details on his pad. 'And was it at those premises that the alleged assault occurred?'

'No, sir. It was in my business premises in Abchurch Lane.'

'I see. So you are alleging a crime within my jurisdiction, also.'

'Yes indeed, sir!' the solicitor broke in. 'It was the most flagrant misuse of police power since . . . since the French revolution!'

Sir William raised his eyebrows. 'Very well,' he said. 'Now, can you give me more factual information. . . What is the nature of your business, Mr Caldwell?'

'I am not in business on my own account, I am the manager of a branch of the Bank of Montreal, in Abchurch Lane.'

'Ah. And are you here on your own behalf, or in your capacity as the Bank of Montreal's manager?'

'It is a distinction without a difference,' Framblington-Smith snapped.

'But you are specifically representing Mr Caldwell?'

'Yes.'

'And not the Bank of Montreal?'

'That is correct.'

'I see. . . And is it on your advice that Mr Caldwell has come to see me this morning?'

'Yes, indeed!'

The Commissioner made a brief note on his pad, then turned to Caldwell. 'Will you give me the essential facts relating to this matter?' he asked.

Caldwell took a handkerchief from his pocket and dabbed at his bald head. 'It was on the afternoon of Wednesday, this week,' he began hesitantly. 'I recall that it was just before we were due to close the public counter. . . I suppose it was a quarter to three, or thereabouts. . .' He seemed to be losing himself in endless verbiage.

'A little before three o'clock,' Sir William said, and made a note.

'One of my clerks came to my room and said that a Sergeant Bragg wished to see me. I consented to an interview. . . In answer to his questions, I told him that the bank held in safe-keeping a box deposited by a Mr Alan Chisnall.'

'Just one moment.' The Commissioner pressed a bell, then sat drumming with his fingers on the arms of his chair until a clerk appeared.

'Will you ask Sergeant Bragg to come up for a moment?' he said. 'If he is not in, bring me the file relating to Alan Chisnall from his cupboard.'

'Very good, sir.' The clerk withdrew deferentially.

Sir William turned to Caldwell. 'Were you aware at the time, that your client had been murdered?' he asked.

'No. But the sergeant acquainted me of the fact. He then proceeded to demand access to the strong-box deposited by Mr Chisnall. I refused.'

The Commissioner stroked his beard in thought. 'When you refused,' he said, 'were you acting as an individual, or on behalf of your employers?'

'I . . . as both!' he said defiantly.

'Had you specifically received instructions from your employers on that matter?'

'No. But their handbook for managers covered the situation.'

'That you should not co-operate with the police in the case of a client that is murdered?' the Commissioner asked mildly.

'No. That information relating to clients should not be given to a third party without specific authority.'

'I see. . . But you presumably realised that you were not going to receive authorisation from your client?'

'Yes. . . I accepted that he was dead. But I needed head office approval for any action I might take.'

'Even though that might hinder the efforts of the police in their attempts to apprehend his killer?'

Caldwell was looking flustered. 'I needed a formal order from a competent authority,' he said. 'Those are my instructions.'

There was a knock on the door. The clerk returned and laid a folder on the desk. 'Sergeant Bragg is out, at the moment, sir,' he said and went out.

The Commissioner gazed gravely out of the window for some moments. 'So the position on the afternoon of Wednesday,' he remarked, 'was that my sergeant had requested access to the strong-box, and you had declined.'

'That is correct.'

'Had you any reason to suppose that the Bank of Montreal would have refused to co-operate with the police in this matter?'

'My client cannot specifically answer on behalf of his employers,' Framblington-Smith interrupted aggressively. 'I see no point in this line of questioning.'

'In a sense you make my point for me, Sir William said mildly. 'It must at least be possible that the Bank of Montreal would wish to co-operate with the police. A lawyer of your undoubted experience must surely realise that there is a possible conflict of interest here. You say that you act for Mr Caldwell; I would have thought it in the highest degree improper that you should seek to act for his employers also.'

'They have made their attitude abundantly clear in their handbook,' Framblington-Smith said pedantically.

'In the general, perhaps, but not in the particular.' The Commissioner turned to Caldwell. 'And what steps did you take to obtain your employer's specific acquiescence to my sergeant's request for access?'

Caldwell frowned. 'I did send a cable, to which I have not yet received a reply. But I had already told Bragg that I needed a proper legal document, requiring me to act. My head office is presumably waiting to hear that I have received it.'

The Commissioner leaned back in his chair and gazed at him coldly. 'Do you seriously believe,' he said, 'That a bank registered in one of the great cities of the empire, doing business in the City of London, licensed to do so by the government of England, would actively seek to frustrate the efforts of the police to apprehend a murderer?'

'I . . . er. . .'

'And were you so convinced of the validity of your actions that you neglected to take any steps in anticipation of their response?'

Caldwell was silent.

'So what happened then?' the Commissioner said with contempt in his voice.

'The sergeant accepted my refusal and left the building. . . I saw no more of him that day. Then yesterday afternoon he came back with a younger officer. I had not yet returned from lunch, and he tricked one of my clerks into bringing the strong-box to my office. When I arrived he served on me a summons, which he said required me to deliver the box up to him. I had, however, the presence of mind to read the document. I saw that it only required me to attend at the police court and bring the box with me. I drew your officers' attention to the terms of the summons, whereupon your sergeant forcibly seized the box and took it away from the premises of the bank.'

The Commissioner paused for a moment then: 'It seems to me that you were deliberately obstructing my officers in the execution of their duty,' he said harshly. 'I am sure your solicitor will tell you that, despite the form of the summons, it is not the magistrates or their officers who carry out criminal investigations, but the police. Fortunately we are no longer in the era of the Bow Street runners!'

'That is correct,' Framblington-Smith murmured.

'In the circumstances,' Sir William said coldly, 'we might legitimately wonder why a responsible officer of a reputable institution should show such studied inertia, in a case involving a violent murder. I find it difficult', he went on portentously, 'to believe that the Bank of Montreal would for one moment have wished to thwart the efforts of the police to discover the perpetrator of this sickening crime. . . One can only suspect the motives of any individual who would seek to do so.'

He opened the folder and drew out a bundle of photographs. He dealt them out like playing-cards before the men.

'Look!' he said angrily. 'These are the post-mortem photographs of the victim. Can you recognise him, Mr. Caldwell? Can you even see that it is a human head? Or have you seen it before?'

Caldwell glanced at them and went white. He fumbled in his pocket for a handkerchief, jerked to his feet and stumbled to the door.

Framblington-Smith got up shakily. 'I am sure that my client would follow my advice, and withdraw all allegations, Mr Commissioner,' he said, then hurried out.

Sir William swivelled round to face the window. He felt quite light-headed. Elation was flooding through him; he wanted to laugh out loud. He had met these experts on their own ground and routed them! He was not a totally useless figurehead, after all. . . But it would not do for Hilda to hear of it. He would have to keep it from her.

When Catherine arrived at London Bridge station, she realised that she was ridiculously early. The platform was deserted, the train had not even arrived. She mentally kicked herself. She ought to know better than appear too eager. Men became bored with girls who were too easily available – or so her mother said. When men settled down, they liked to feel it was with someone who had been worth subduing to their will. . . Of course, her mother thought that she tended too much to the other extreme – that she was cold, aloof; that she put men off by her independent manner. Well, there was some truth in that. It was very useful when she was being pestered by some vain nincompoop who only wanted her as a trophy. But she was sure that she could glow as decorously as any woman, in the right company. . . Not that there had been many occasions on which she had been determined to scintillate. In truth, there was only one man for whom she would consciously wish to appear alluring. But she and James were apt to meet in the course of their work. She could hardly go around London dressed like a mannequin, merely because she might bump into him.

She glanced at her portmanteau, which the porter had placed at the end of the platform with other luggage. It was a pity, she thought, that she had not brought one of her best gowns. Dinner at The Priory would certainly be a grand affair that night. She had been stupid! Her friendship with Emily Morton, and her somewhat equivocal relationship with James, had made her feel too much like one of the family. Lady Morton had been the daughter of John Harman, the American ambassador to the Court of St James, when she met her future husband. He was then a major in the cavalry, and had distinguished himself in the Crimean war. As the daughter of a foreign diplomat, Charlotte had been duly presented at Court. That had been in eighteen fifty-seven, when Albert the Prince Consort was still alive. Lady Morton still loved to describe the glittering social whirl into which she had plunged. It had sounded far grander than the raffish hedonism indulged in by the coterie now surrounding the Prince of Wales. Charlotte Harman had enjoyed her Season in full measure. But when her handsome cavalry major had proposed marriage, she had happily surrendered a life in high society, to become the chatelaine of his ancestral domain. That was her American level-headedness, she would say. However enjoyable it might be, life was to be taken seriously.

There was a lesson for herself, Catherine thought moodily. She had fallen into the arrogant notion that she could postpone indefinitely a decision on what she wanted from life. So long as James hovered around her dutifully, she felt she could indulge her notions about a modern woman's place in society. She could enjoy the distinction of holding down a proper job; having achieved in her field a reputation which few male journalists could rival. But in her self-critical moments, she would admit that the job had initially been created for her, as a result of her father's influence with the proprietor of the *City Press*. And her fame had arisen largely out of her association with Sergeant Bragg and James. From that had come the scoops which had made her name. But it in no way diminished her achievements, she would tell herself. Women were so constrained and restricted by rules made by men – made to keep them in domestic subservience – that it was legitimate to use any artifice to break free. In her modest way she had blazed a trail. She was the most respected woman journalist in London; not only in women's organisations, but by her colleagues also. . . Yet, in her weaker moments, she would confess to herself that she was no rampant feminist; that ultimately she wanted to marry, have children, embrace domesticity.

She looked round and saw that the train was backing into the platform. There was now a fair sprinkling of intending travellers, but still no James. It was always possible that he had been detained – or had even forgotten. . . No, he would not forget, she thought ruefully. His cousin Violet would have arrived at The Priory by now. They had intended to sail from New York on the new Cunarder, and there had been no bad weather. Joshua Harman had brought his wife and daughter over for last year's Season. Catherine had uncharitably hoped that they would be otherwise engaged this summer, that they would have to miss Emily's wedding. But no . . . nothing was to be allowed to stand in the way of their attending it. She had been stupid not to bring her new gown! She knew that James had been sweet on Violet a couple of years ago. Moreover Joshua had made no secret of his hope that James would go to live in America, and take over from him when he retired. Previous generations of Harmans had built up a large coal and iron undertaking centred on Philadelphia. Latterly they had extended the scope of their businesses throughout the entire United States. This had led to a division of day-to-day control between the two brothers. Thomas, the elder, had stayed in Philadelphia and looked after the coal and steel plants. The other interests had been so geographically scattered that Joshua had decided he could equally well administer all of them from Boston. The previous summer she had heard Violet airily talking about her life there. It seemed a pleasant, cultured city. . . Of course, James had been in earshot. It could all have been part of a grand design to lure James over there; to found a Morton dynasty spanning the Atlantic Ocean.

'You can get up now, miss.' The porter's voice broke in on her reverie. How stupid! She had been standing gazing at the train for minutes. Everyone else had boarded it.

'First class, I take it?' He opened a door to an empty compartment.

'Thank you. I was day-dreaming!'

She stepped into the carriage, and the porter closed the door after her. She sat by the window, facing towards the rear of the train. From there she was able to see the barrier. People were trickling through it on to the platform. Still no James. But there were ten minutes to go. . . Now a group of well-dressed travellers was walking up the platform, peering into the compartments. They were clearly hoping to find an empty one. What should she do if they came into this one? Should she attempt to reserve a seat for James? Yes . . . that would be a perfectly acceptable action, in a woman travelling alone. So which seat should she keep? The one next to her, so that they could converse; or the one opposite, so that he would gaze at her? . . . As the leading man of the group laid his hand on the door handle, she dropped her bag on the seat beside her. She immediately felt guilty. They were considerably more elderly than they had seemed in the distance. With gasps and grunts they lodged coats and handbags on the racks. Catherine counted them quickly as they began to subside gratefully into their seats, then quietly put her handbag on to her lap again.

There were a mere two minutes before departure time, when James appeared on the platform. He sprinted along the train, valise in hand, until he saw her. Her heart jumped as his face lit up with pleasure. He bustled into the compartment.

'I am sorry to be so late,' he said, finding a space for his bag on the rack. 'It is entirely my own fault that I shall have to stand. I was so enthralled by a certain mound of incomprehensible papers, which I had taken home with me, that I lost all track of time!'

'But you caught the train,' she said lightly, 'so you cannot be late!'

A whistle shrilled and with great gasping heaves the train pulled out of the station. James leaned back against the door, and as the train picked up steam she was aware of the pressure of his leg against her knee. She decided that it was not incumbent upon her to avoid the contact.

5

When Morton arrived at Old Jewry on the following Monday, he found Bragg already at his desk. He had dismantled his pipe, and was scraping the accumulated carbon from its bowl.

'Have a good weekend?' he asked gruffly.

'Excellent, thank you, sir! After the rehearsal, you may be assured that the performance in two weeks' time will be flawless.'

'Let's hope the marriage is, as well. . . Did you get anything from Miss Marsden?'

'About the Chisnall case? I did not even enquire. There were far more wholesome things to occupy us.'

Bragg looked at him speculatively, then thought better of pursuing the matter. He had said time and again that they would make a perfect couple; that if Morton wasn't careful he would lose her to some society numskull. But it hadn't made him see sense. He was too much of an idiot gentleman. So they danced around one another, each waiting for the other to make the first move. Bragg cleared his throat.

'I went over to Petticoat Square again, on Saturday morning. You will be glad to know that Mrs Plumb has cleared up your mess.'

Morton grinned. 'And were you struck by any lightning flash of inspiration?' he asked.

'No. It's going to be a hard slog. . . I think we were born a year or two early. There is a new book in the library downstairs, by a man called Galton. I took it home this weekend. He is on about fingerprints, how no two people have the same pattern on the skin of their finger ends. Talks about arches, loops and whorls.'

'I seem to recall some such theory from a Scotch physician working in Japan. But I do not think that he suggested the patterns were totally individual.'

Bragg picked up the stem of his pipe and pushed a pipe-cleaner through it. 'This Galton chap is certain of it. From what he says, you could reduce police investigations to just paper-work. What we should have done last Tuesday, was to get our camera people to take a photograph of the fingerprints on the handle of the poker. Then we could have sat here, with a book full of everybody's prints, and said, "Ah! It was Tommy Davenport, from Hackney Wick. Let's go and pick him up!" Bloody silly!' He moodily began to reassemble his pipe.

Morton crossed over to the boxes of papers and emptied one on to his table. 'I suspect that the humdrum will not be eliminated yet awhile,' he said. 'I suppose I might as well continue with this.'

He picked up paper after paper, scrutinising each briefly then dropping it on one of the piles at the other end of the table. Either by accident or design, the murderer had so jumbled the documents that it was a major task to sort them out again.

'This is an odd one,' he remarked, taking it over to Bragg's desk. 'It consists of columns of initials, each entry with a small pencil tick beside it. But look what is at the head of the first column!'

'It says, "Musketeers"!' Bragg exclaimed. 'You mentioned something about them last week.'

'Exactly!' Morton crossed to his press and brought out a folder. 'Here is the financial circular we put aside. The one with "Porthos" on it. There must be a significance. It cannot be mere flippancy on Chisnall's part.'

'All right. But what? I skipped through *The Three Musketeers* when I was young, but it was a bit slow for my liking. It started off all right, with the duels and suchlike; but then it turned into a woman's book, all romance and history.'

Morton laughed. 'So much for fame!' he said. 'But there is one point we ought to give our minds to.'

'What is that?'

'If there is a Porthos connected to our case, there must logically be also an Aramis and an Athos.'

There came a soft tap at the door and Catherine came in. Her face was pink and she was breathing quickly.

'I hope that I am not intruding on some vital conference,' she gasped. 'I am sorry, I have just run from Cheapside. The entrance to Old Jewry was blocked by a van, and my cab could not get by.'

'Sit down, miss,' Bragg said solicitously, 'and get your breath back. There will be time enough.'

'As you can see,' Morton said with a smile, 'I am still occupied in bringing some sort of order – almost any sort of order – to these confounded boxes of papers. I took three home with me. But Mrs Chambers was so taken aback to see them strewn all over the floor, that I fear I shall have to bring them back again.

I declare that my evenings will henceforth be an empty void!'

'Why then, James, I shall have no need to play the temptress!' Catherine took a deep breath. 'Goodness! I ought to run more often, or not at all!'

'Not at all, if it serves only to inform me the more speedily that I have not anticipated your slightest whim!'

'Don't mind him, miss,' Brass interposed. 'He has a bad attack of moonshine, or sunstroke. What is it you want to tell us?'

Catherine smiled. 'I have determined to set aside my maidenly modesty and ask you, James, to accompany me to the theatre!'

'Then I shall honour your virtue, and rescue my own tattered reputation by accepting without question!'

Bragg frowned. 'There is more to it than that, isn't there, miss?'

'Yes. When I arrived at the office, this morning, the editor called me in. It seems that he had been sent two complimentary tickets to the first night of a new play. He asked if I would like to use them.'

Morton frowned. 'A new play? In the middle of the Season? I have not heard of one. When is it opening? What is it called?'

Catherine laughed. 'One could hardly say that it is at a West End theatre. In fact it is opening on Friday the thirteenth of July, at Gatti's Music Hall! And for one week only.'

'That is the little theatre under Charing Cross railway station,' Morton exclaimed. 'How bizarre!'

'The thirteenth is this Friday,' Bragg said. 'I would have thought you would have more important things to think about, lad, unless we have already cracked this one.'

The smile faded from Catherine's face. 'Nevertheless I feel that James will wish to accept my invitation. You see, the name of the playwright is . . . Alan Chisnall.'

'Alan Chisnall?' Bragg exclaimed. 'When did your boss get the tickets?'

'On Saturday the thirtieth of June. It seems that he had intended to go. But when the news of Chisnall's death became public, his wife thought it would no longer be proper.'

'And is it still going to be on?'

'Apparently so. Mr Tranter received an assurance from the theatre to that effect.'

'Good God! . . . Sorry, miss!'

She smiled and turned to Morton. 'Do you still wish to accompany me, James?' she asked.

'Indeed I do! Not the more because of the circumstances; but because any moment spent with you is a delight.'

'Then you will call for me? Eight o'clock will suffice.'

'Excellent! And a light supper afterwards at Romano's?'

'When you two have finished sorting out your private lives,' Bragg said acidly, 'perhaps we can get on with some work!'

'Then I will go.' Catherine got to her feet, settled her hat on her head and went serenely out.

'What do you think about that, lad?' Bragg asked. 'Is it too much of a coincidence that he was murdered just before his play was coming on?'

'One might legitimately have wondered that, had the performance of the play been prevented by his death. As it is. . .' Morton shrugged his shoulders.

'I tell you what, lad,' Bragg said grumpily. 'It would have been a bloody sight better if she had given both of us a ticket, instead of going with you herself. Now I shall have to scrabble round for one.'

Morton laughed. 'It should not be too difficult. Gatti's does not have much of a reputation for drama, amongst the sophisticated populace; and their normal patrons would run a mile from anything more demanding than Marie Lloyd!'

Bragg's moustache lifted in distaste. 'Sometimes, lad, you sound no better than any of the others in your under-worked, over-indulged class. . . Now, where does this get us?'

Morton perched on the corner of his table. 'Why should Chisnall – I assume it must have been he – why should Chisnall have sent complimentary tickets to the editor of the *City Press*?' he mused. 'It must have been *qua* editor; but why? And why to him?. . . Unless he was only one of many. . .' He turned and picked up the paper covered with columns of initials. 'Yes! Here we are, "C P" . . . and there is an "F N", which must be the *Financial News* . . . and an "Ec" for the *Economist*!'

'You mean to say, he was sending free tickets to all the newspapers?' Bragg asked incredulously.

'And not to newspapers only, is my guess. There are initials here that could easily be City institutions and firms. Look!' He took the paper over to Bragg's desk. ' "B o E" can only mean the Bank of England. . . "N P B" the National Provincial Bank, "S M" Samuel Montague's bank, "S E" the Stock Exchange!'

'But if every one of those initials means two free tickets, he was never going to make any money!' Bragg exclaimed.

'But suppose that making money was not the object of the exercise?' Morton asked. 'Ah! "Q B". That can only be Quilter Balfour & Co.! I know a junior partner in the firm. May I go and make judicious enquiries?'

'If you must,' Bragg said grudgingly.

Morton half walked, half ran to King's Arms Yard, off Moorgate. He arrived at the premises of Quilter Balfour & Co., and went through the imposing lobby.

'Is Mr Pargiter in, please?' he asked the clerk in the enquiry-room.

'Why, yes,' he said with a smile. 'It's Mr Morton, isn't it? Mr Pargiter has just come back from the Exchange. He will be in his room, I expect. You know the way, don't you, sir?'

Morton charged up the stairs, and arrived panting at a small attic room looking over the house-tops. Gerald Pargiter was sitting at his desk in his shirt-sleeves, checking items in a ledger. He looked up.

'Ah, James! Good to see you!' He rose and held out his hand. 'I have just got back from the floor. Things had gone a bit quiet. If you are thinking of buying, now could be a good time.'

Morton grinned. 'You will never be poor, if you can turn an honest penny by disingenuous charm,' he said. 'It is not your expertise as a broker that I seek, Gerald, but information – pure and unadulterated if possible.'

Pargiter sniffed. 'I shall send you a bill!' he warned.

'Very well. Mark it for the personal attention of the Commissioner of the City of London police!'

'Hmn. . . That's different! You have all the resources of Quilter Balfour at your disposal – on the strict understanding that all my peccadilloes, past and future, will be overlooked!'

'I do not need you to be resourceful,' Morton said. 'I just need a little innocuous information. I gather that complimentary tickets for a play at Gatti's Music Hall have been sent to various City firms. Have you received any?'

'Rather! The senior partner received two last week. I gather that the author has been murdered. Is that what you are involved in?'

'Yes. I understand that the play is going to be performed, despite his death.'

'So I believe. You cannot get a ticket for love nor money now. I volunteered to go on behalf of the firm, but the senior partner said he would not miss it for all the tea in China!'

'But why?'

'Hints of scandal, James. The noise of dirty washing being aired will resound through the City – if that is not too much of a mixed metaphor!'

'You are exaggerating, surely?'

Pargiter's face became serious. 'Not by much,' he said. 'I was not ragging you when I said that trading was thin. The market has been dropping like a stone, all last week. There are some very nervous people in the City at the moment.'

'But the stock market has always been irrationally volatile.'

'Yes, but it has never been like this before. Not in my time, nor in my father's time. And it is not merely the market. The government is jumpy also.'

'The government?'

'It is the close of the parliamentary session. Right?'

'Yes.'

'It is customary at this time for the Lord Mayor to give a banquet in Guildhall, to honour Her Majesty's ministers.'

'That is so.'

'Well, I gather that the Prime Minister, having accepted on behalf of his ministers months ago, is now declining to attend. The whole government is boycotting the banquet! It has never happened before. There must be something serious behind it.'

'I find that astonishing!' Morton exclaimed. 'And will the banquet go ahead?'

'It is not yet certain. The Court of Common Council is busy lobbying, no doubt; trying to save face. But can you have *Carmen* without the cigarette girl?'

When Morton left Old Jewry, Bragg found himself at a loss as to what to do next. Morton was involved in looking at the financial circulars, and he had best be left to get on with it. To interfere, to try to do part of them himself, could mean that he might discard something as meaningless, which might seem of vital significance to Morton. He went over to the strong-box, took out the bundle of letters, and undid the red tape. There were about forty of them. He looked at the postmarks. They had been sent over a period of some three years; from the twentieth of January eighteen sixty-three to the twenty-seventh of June eighteen sixty-six. Chisnall had slit each envelope open carefully, as if to preserve it as nearly intact as possible. Bragg read the first letter, intent on getting the feel of the relationship. Often in a letter between a man and a woman, what was not said, or was referred to cryptically, could be revealing. And the more so when the writer was the woman. This was a straightforward thank-you note. Chisnall had escorted her home from a party, and she was grateful. But the words were . . . well, not exactly coquettish; not pert either – she was much too well brought up for that. Lively might be the best description. When she said that she hoped she would see him again soon, it didn't come across as an empty remark. She was trying to make herself interesting and amusing in his eyes.

He began to read through them steadily, in order. He wondered how Chisnall had replied to them – indeed, if he had replied to them. Here was one describing her eighteenth birthday party. . . So he had not been invited. Why not? Was he not in their social circle. . ? Probably there was no significance in it. When the letters started she had been only seventeen – but a self-possessed, forward seventeen-year-old. By the end of eighteen sixty-four, the warmth of feeling expressed had become intense. If Chisnall had replied in similar terms, and her parents had seen the letter, they would have written her off as a wanton, and banished her to relations in Australia! But perhaps it was just playfulness. . . It was difficult to judge a correspondence when you only read one side. But the girl had plenty of freedom, that was for sure. She was constantly referring to their encounters in the most provocative terms, deliberately titillating his emotions. Whatever had happened to chaperons? It sounded as if, at a ball in these big mansions, it was the easiest thing imaginable to slip away upstairs for half an hour. And he had always thought that these society girls were pallid insipid creatures, who wouldn't part with their honour till a marriage contract was in the safe!

But perhaps it depended on how powerful or wealthy her family was. . .

The series of letters continued in this playful, teasing, sensual vein until the summer of eighteen sixty-six. For about a year there had been some two letters a month. There was only one letter in April. In May there were none. One letter remained, dated the twenty-seventh of June. Bragg picked it up, feeling the same foreboding that Chisnall must have experienced. It was a short, courteous note, verging on the impersonal. It said how much she had valued their friendship; how sad she was to end it; but that since she was to be married, ended it must be. Bragg put down the letter and leaned back in his chair. Chisnall would have been badly hurt by it. He must have believed that she was serious about what she had written earlier – and it had not stopped at writing letters, that was for sure. The excitement and affection she felt had cried out from the page. . . Then this cool, almost perfunctory note ending it all. Chisnall must have felt angry, betrayed, diminished. Why had he kept the letters all these years? Why had he not torn them into shreds and thrown them on the fire? Perhaps he had really loved her, and that was stronger than the feeling of betrayal. Bragg felt at a loss. He could not fathom the picture of Chisnall that was emerging. The man seemed to have tamely accepted his fate. . . But it seemed certain that the girl was from a much higher social level than the son of a timber merchant. Whatever she had said in the letters, her expectations would have been much higher than Chisnall could have supported. Once she decided not to break from the herd, he would never have been able to compete. She probably ended up shackled to some randy old lord, who looked on her as a plaything, along with his horses and his gun-dogs.

There came a tap at the door and the Commissioner came briskly in. 'Ah, Bragg,' he said. 'There you are.'

'Yes, sir.'

'What is that you are reading?'

'Love-letters, sir.'

'Really?' He picked one up and glanced through it. A flush of embarrassment came over his face. 'I . . . er. . . Was this written by a woman?' he asked incredulously.

'That one?' Bragg looked at the postmark of the next in

sequence. 'She was all of nineteen years old, when she wrote that one, sir.'

'Good heavens! Was she a professional woman . . . a strumpet?'

'I wouldn't say so, sir. She seems to have been from a very good-class family. She was Chisnall's friend for a time.'

'A good deal more than a friend, if this is anything to go on. . . It is merely signed with an "A". Do you know who she is?'

'No, sir. I cannot say that she is at all relevant to our investigation. The last letter is dated as far back as June eighteen sixty-six. But Chisnall did keep them all these years, in his strong-box.'

'I see. . . Talking of strong-boxes, Bragg, I had a little skirmish with the manager of the Bank of Montreal and his solicitor, on Saturday morning. Where were you, by the way?'

'I was at the scene of the crime, sir.' Bragg said stolidly. 'Just making sure we had overlooked nothing.'

Sir William looked suspiciously at him. 'Well, it was probably a good thing that you were not here, or there might have been blood spilt. That Caldwell man seemed exceedingly self-righteous; and a more pompous, dogmatic lawyer I have never met! A formal complaint against you, they said; for threatening assault, committing actual assault against the person – they had a whole rigmarole. But I saw them off, Bragg. I saw them off! These inflated, self-important City people expect us always to dance to their tune. But there are occasions when a few corns have to be stepped on. . . Not that I necessarily condone your taking the strong-box from the bank by force. I have no doubt that, in strict law, you overstepped the mark. But all the same, I will not have my officers wilfully obstructed in their duty. I saved your neck on this occasion, Bragg. "High-handed to the point of criminality," they said; and I can well believe it. See that it does not happen again.'

'Indeed I will, sir,' Bragg said contritely.

'Yes. . . But they withdrew their complaint when I had finished with them!' A smug smile settled on the Commissioner's features. He drifted over to the window. 'Just like India out there, Bragg. Never knew such weather!' Then he turned and marched briskly out.

Bragg smiled to himself, then turned back to the letters. He began to jot down the important facts that emerged from them.

Chisnall and the girl had been young; she had been prepared to flout convention, as no doubt hundreds of modern upper-class girls were; in the end she had faced up to reality and backed away. So what was special about that? Take away the tupping and it was the stuff of a penny romance. Except that Chisnall had been battered to death. Nothing romantic there. . . Why had he kept her letters? Was he still besotted with her, after all these years? Or did he think some day they might be useful?

The door burst open and Morton marched in. He was grinning widely. 'I think, sir, that we may be involved, yet again, in a matter of earth-shattering complexity and importance!' he said. 'I have been told tales of widespread corruption, of multiple ritual suicides, of politicians scrambling from sinking ships! I tell you, chaos threatens!'

'Oh, yes?' Bragg said drily. 'Have Consols dropped half a point or something? . . . Come to think of it, it might do us all a bit of good to have a real clear-out at the top. Now then, let me have it straight. What have you found out?'

Morton leaned back in his chair. 'Well, there is certainly something very odd going on. The stock market is said to have dropped like a stone, last week. So now is the time to get all those sovereigns from under your mattress and buy securities!'

'Like hell I will! And what do they think is behind it?'

'Gerald Pargiter is convinced that it has something to do with Chisnall's play. It is rumoured that it will pull the dust-sheets off some pretty rickety deals. The whole City is agog with expectation; tickets are changing hands for a king's ransom!'

'So much for my chances of getting one.'

'Oh, I would think that you could legitimately attend in your official capacity, sir.' Morton's voice became serious. 'I gather that Lord Rosebery and the whole of his government have withdrawn from the Lord Mayor's end-of-session banquet in honour of the Queen's ministers. I know that there has been some political friction, but nothing to justify such a grand gesture.'

'Hmn. . .' Bragg tugged the corner of his moustache in thought. 'So you think the politicians are backing off, do you?' he asked. 'Well, they should be able to smell corruption if anybody can. But surely somebody like Chisnall could never get anywhere near being involved in something shady on that scale?'

'One might certainly consider that to be so. But the City

trades on its reputation for absolute integrity – and with justification. So even the smallest hint of dishonesty among the financial community can have a disastrous effect. Without doubt there have been cases of fraud; we have ourselves convicted several men operating on the fringe. But can you tell me when there has been an allegation of malpractice against one of the major firms?'

Bragg pondered. 'No. Not for years. . . There has been the odd case where a partner has retired a bit early, or a firm has been merged with another. But I cannot recall any complaint being made to us about the big boys.'

'No. Because the Bank of England steps in, dispenses its own brand of justice, and the wider world is never allowed to know. But I am convinced that a financial journalist would hear rumours, acquire confidential information. He could build up a fairly accurate picture.'

'So you are saying that Chisnall had two options – blackmail them, or write a play.'

Morton grinned. 'Well, his executors will become possessed of the box-office receipts! Of course, he could already have tried blackmail and failed.'

'Then, what would he gain from putting on the play, except a piddling amount of ticket-money?'

'Why not revenge?' Morton suggested. 'They say it can be sweet. . . As I see it, Chisnall included references to real situations, murky events in his play, but disguised his characters enough to avoid the libel laws. On that same basis, the play would pass the Lord Chamberlain's scrutiny.'

'Hmn. . . I still think blackmail was at the back of it. After all, he could easily cancel the performance, if his victims paid up.'

Morton pulled a face. 'Blackmail is so sordid,' he said. 'But revenge can be inspiring!'

'Somebody got their revenge all right. But Chisnall did not seem to be inspirited by it. . . I have been reading the bundle of letters Chisnall kept. I cannot decide why he kept them. He might have done so out of sentiment, or because he thought they could come in handy sometime.'

'More blackmail? May I see them?'

'No, lad. You are a bit immature for that. They might warp

your young mind.'

'I would gladly take that risk for the greater good!'

'No. I am serious. . . Here, you can read the first and the last.'

Morton took the proffered letters. 'January eighteen sixty-three?' he remarked. 'That is ancient history. . . Merely signed "A" . . . It seems fairly innocuous. From some lady, presumably.'

'It is the only one with an address.'

'I see. . . Twenty Bruton Place. That is off Berkeley Square; a good address.'

'Full of society people, is it?'

'Indeed. I wonder what the young lady's name was. You clearly suspect that she was Adelaide.'

He went over to the press and took out a tattered street directory for the West End. 'This is somewhat later than the date of the letter,' he said. 'But I would not think that the inhabitants of Bruton Place were given to changing houses lightly. Here we are. . . Bruton Lane. . . Bruton Place. . . In eighteen seventy-five the inhabitants of number twenty were graced with the name of Hollyer. . . Oh, Lord!'

'What is it, lad?'

'I am just recalling a conversation with Miss Marsden, over the weekend. . . Have you got that old *Who's Who*?'

'In my cupboard.'

Morton crossed over, a worried look on his face. He took the volume back to his desk and began to flip through the pages. 'I thought as much,' he said sombrely. 'Listen to this. "Smith, Theodore. Principal of Smith Payne & Smith's, bankers. Born the eleventh of November, eighteen forty-seven . . . educated at Eton . . . married on the twenty-eighth of June, eighteen sixty-six to Adelaide Hollyer, daughter to Jeremiah Hollyer of Bruton Place, SW. Private address, fifteen Buckingham Gate, SW" . . . I very much fear that Chisnall's Adelaide is about to become my sister's mother-in-law.'

'It gets even murkier, lad. If you look at the second letter I gave you, she was writing to break off her relationship with Chisnall on the very day before her wedding.'

'So your refusal to show me the ones in between shows an unaccustomed delicacy on your part?'

'It's best that way. . . There is a peculiar thing, though. One letter – same paper, same handwriting, same sort of subject – is signed "Your constant Constance". I cannot make that out.'

'Constance? Why, she is another character from *The Three Musketeers*. How extraordinary!'

'They seem to have been playing some sort of game,' Bragg said darkly. 'Only I think one of them had a different set of rules.'

'We have the reference to a Porthos, and now a Constance,' Morton exclaimed. 'But who are Athos and Aramis?'

After a late lunch, Bragg decided that they should go to Buckingham Gate and talk to Adelaide Smith. He uncompromisingly overrode Morton's protests about conflicts of interest. They took an underground train from Mansion House station to St James's Park, then walked through the tree-lined streets to the Smiths' house. It was a fine Regency mansion, austere but elegantly proportioned. It had an air of restrained confidence and good breeding, of a gracious age long gone. It stood in its lawns like an elaborate doll's house on a billiard table. There were no other houses like it. On the area around, terraces of grand town houses had been built, dwarfing it. That it existed at all proclaimed the unassailable wealth of its owner. Bragg pulled the bell at the main entrance. After a few moments a servant appeared. His manner was grave and aloof.

'Can I help you, gentlemen?' he enquired.

'Police,' Bragg said shortly. 'We have come to see Mrs Adelaide Smith.'

'I see. Is she expecting you?'

'Not specially.'

The man raised his eyebrows, then stood back. 'If you will come this way, I will see if madam can be found.'

They followed him down a central corridor hung with stiff, gloomy portraits, to a small room at the back of the house. It overlooked the gardens, and was flooded with sunlight. An elegant writing-desk stood near the french windows, chintz-covered chairs were grouped around the flower-filled fireplace.

'What a beautiful room,' Morton said in admiration. 'The Smiths may not be laden with titles, but they have the most exquisite taste.'

'You cannot see a murderer living here, eh?' Bragg said gruffly. 'I tell you, nobody gets up the greasy pole as far as this, without a bit of skulduggery somewhere.'

'Come, come, sir! What of your strictures about keeping an open mind?'

'James!' A shapely woman in her early fifties was in the doorway. There were strands of grey in her dark brown hair, her face was round, her complexion clear. There were crinkles in the corners of her eyes, as if she laughed often; her lips were full and sensual.

'Good afternoon, Mrs Smith,' Morton said in some embarrassment. 'I little thought, when I said adieu yesterday, that I would see you again so soon. However, as you will have gathered, I am here as a constable of the City police. This is my superior, Sergeant Bragg.'

She smiled warmly and held out her hand. 'It is good to meet you, sergeant,' she said. 'I am sorry that I cannot offer you tea, but the staff are still at leisure.'

'That is no matter,' Bragg said curtly. 'We are come here in the course of our duty.'

Her smile faded somewhat. 'In that case, let us sit down.' She sank decorously into one of the chairs by the fireplace, and the men followed suit.

'We wanted to have a chat with you about a certain Alan Chisnall, ma'am,' Bragg said. 'I believe you knew him.'

She was suddenly watchful. 'At one time that would have been true,' she said.

'And when would that have been?'

She laughed, and the warmth of her personality flowed over them. 'Why, many years ago, sergeant. A lifetime! When we were all very young.'

'You know he's been murdered?'

Now the face showed a nice blend of concern and regret. She ought to have been on the stage, Bragg thought. 'My husband told me about it,' she said earnestly. 'What a dreadful end!'

Bragg leaned back in his chair. 'I don't mind admitting we are stumped with this case,' he said stolidly. 'We are left with picking up crumbs of information from anybody who knew him.'

'I see.'

'What kind of man was he?'

'What kind?' She put her head on one side to demonstrate the effort of recollection. 'I always found him charming and attentive . . . humorous and, well, polite.'

'He sounds like a paragon, ma'am.'

She raised an eyebrow. 'Well, a pleasant companion, certainly.'

'Yes. . . I suppose I find it difficult, looking at you as you now are, to think of you as ever moving in the same circles as him. He was never in the same class, surely?'

Her glance approved his discrimination. 'True. But a hostess cannot afford to be too nice in these matters. In my youth, as now, there were always far more young ladies than young men. Sometimes of the order of six to one. Those are long odds by any standard! So if the girls were to dance, one had to search the highways and byways for young men!'

'And compel them to come in, eh? But not only for dancing in the ballroom.'

If she was aware of his *double entendre* she did not show it. Her face was utterly composed.

'Could you tell me where you first met Alan Chisnall?' Bragg asked.

'Goodness! That is so long ago. All I can say is that I was introduced to him by my husband. They shared lodgings together in Monkwell Street.'

'I am sorry, ma'am, Bragg said earnestly. 'You have lost me. Do you mean that you were introduced to Chisnall by the man who later became your husband?'

'Yes, that is correct.'

'Theodore Smith?'

'Yes, sergeant.'

'Can you remember if anyone else shared those rooms?'

Her brow wrinkled slightly in an effort of remembering. 'There was a third young man. John . . . John Teverson. They used to go the rounds of all the parties together.'

'So you saw a fair bit of all of them?'

'I suppose one might say so.'

'And did Chisnall ever marry?'

She shrugged. 'If he did, I never became aware of it.'

'Right. Thank you. I think I have got that straight.' Bragg

looked across at Morton and paused until he had completed his notes. Then he put his hand into his pocket and drew out two envelopes. 'I now hand you two letters, ma'am, which we have reason to believe were written by you. Will you please examine them?'

She glanced at them, her face wooden.

'Will you confirm that that is your handwriting?'

She took the earlier one from its envelope and scrutinised it. 'Yes, sergeant. He had been courteous enough to accompany me to my home. It was elementary good manners to write and thank him.'

'Of course, ma'am. And the other?'

She glanced at the postmark on the other envelope, and her mouth tightened. 'I have no need to read it, sergeant. I know well enough its contents.'

'Yes... We found a bundle of about forty in a strong-box at Chisnall's bank. And let me say that, apart from those two, nobody else has read the letters but me.'

She looked at him uncertainly. 'Thank you for that assurance,' she said. 'Perhaps I was somewhat closer to Alan than my earlier remarks would suggest. There was a little foolish flirtation, but marriage between us would have been impossible.'

'In a way that marriage to Theodore Smith wasn't?' Bragg asked sardonically.

She sighed tolerantly. 'It was not a mere matter of money, if that is what you are thinking,' she said.

'Money is never "mere" to the likes of me, ma'am. But perhaps you will explain what you mean.'

'I mean that a young girl is easily attracted by superficial qualities. But more is looked for in a husband. Alan was entertaining, he was a wonderful companion. But he lacked application; he would never have made a success of his life.'

'From what I have seen, you are right there! Did you ever meet him after your marriage?'

'Occasionally. One grows away from one's youthful attachments, when children come along.'

'I see. And when did you see him last?'

She looked into the distance, a frown on her brow. 'It was ages ago. He had dropped out of our circle. He was no longer sociable; he had become moody.'

'Hmn. . .' Bragg pulled his watch from his pocket and gazed at it intently. 'And what did you think of him two weeks ago at this time?' he asked.

She flinched. 'I do not understand,' she said in a hard tone.

'There is an entry in his diary for three o'clock on Monday the twenty-fifth of June. Did you meet here?'

'No!' She pouted prettily, like a child caught out in a fib. 'No, we met in Regent's Park.'

'And what did he have to say for himself?'

'I have other things to think about than superficial social conversations, sergeant,' she said with some spirit.

Bragg regarded her amiably. 'You know, ma'am, you have more to gain from being open with us than from fighting us,' he said.

She dropped her head. 'He wanted money,' she said at length.

'Hmn. . . A lot or a little?'

'I prefer not to answer that, sergeant.'

'So he was trying to sell you back your letters? . . Or was he threatening to send them to the *Reynolds News* unless you paid him?'

She looked up, the incarnation of a helpless female. 'He was going to send them to Theo,' she said. 'It would have been a disaster. But I have no money at my immediate disposal, and Theo would have insisted on knowing what I needed it for. . . In the end I promised to sell some jewels to pay him.'

'I see. And how much did you get?'

'I have not yet disposed of them.'

'Did you think he was bluffing?'

'Oh, no!' she cried wide-eyed. 'I knew he was capable of any vile course; he seemed desperate. But I was in great difficulty myself. I could not suddenly cease to wear my emeralds, in the middle of the Season.'

'I suppose not. . . Then suddenly he is dead, and you are off the hook. You must have been relieved.'

She looked at him steadily, but said nothing.

Bragg let the pause grow. He turned to look out of the window, where a gardener was cutting hollyhocks and lupins. 'There was one letter that you signed "Constance",' he remarked.

She managed a little laugh. 'Oh, that was a foolish charade. There were three of them lodging with Mrs Tickle; Theo, Alan and John Teverson. They used to go round all the parties together. They became known amongst the hostesses as The Three Musketeers. When they became aware of it, they began to consciously act the part. "All for one, and one for all." Even I was drawn into it, if what you say is true.'

'I see. And who was who?'

She paused, considering. 'I really cannot remember. It was of no consequence. . . I think that Theo was Athos, because of his somewhat restrained manner. I really cannot help you further.'

'I see. . . By the way, ma'am, where were you around six o'clock a week ago?'

'A week ago today, you mean?'

'Yes, Monday the second.'

She frowned, then gave a radiant smile. 'Of course,' she said. 'I went to have tea in town, with Anne Murray, an old friend of mine. We had a lovely long chat.'

'But you would have been back here before six?'

'No, sergeant. I think that it would have been after seven o'clock. Anne was going back to America, she is married to someone in oil.'

'Hmn. . . But no doubt the head waiter or whatever will remember seeing you there.'

A hint almost of mockery crossed her face. 'I doubt it. You see, we took tea in the refreshment room at Waterloo station. Anne was catching the seven o'clock boat train.'

Bragg took the letters from her and got to his feet impassively. 'I should tell you, ma'am,' he said, 'that we are now going to see your husband. It is not, at the moment, my intention to tell him about the existence of the letters, or their contents. What you decide to do about it is your own affair.'

Bragg and Morton took the underground train back to Mansion House station. By the time they reached Lombard Street, the public counter of Smith's bank had closed. They went to a discreet doorway further down the street, and rang an electric bell. After some time they heard the sound of a lock turning and bars being drawn. The heavy oak door was pulled open a crack, and an irritated face peered out.

' 'Ere! Wot you after? The bank's closed!'

'I know that!' Bragg shouted. 'Why the bloody hell do you think we rang the bell?'

The door swung open to reveal a uniformed messenger. 'Wot you want?' he asked in a surly voice.

'Police. We want to see Theodore Smith.'

'But he's the big boss! You can't see him without an appointment.'

'If I like, I can put him in the next bloody cell to yours! Get out of my way!'

The man stepped aside, and Bragg pushed into a narrow ill-lit corridor. Once through the door at the end, they found themselves in a large room lit by a central glass dome. Around them were solid oak desks, with a slender gas standard rising out of each. At them clerks were sitting, their heads bowed over ledgers. Beyond them brass railings could be seen, which presumably marked the public counter.

The messenger elbowed his way past them and went to a man with pince-nez, and a flower in his lapel. He looked up frowning, then marched over to them.

'I trust that you can justify this unwarranted intrusion,' he said icily.

'Not to you, I won't,' Bragg retorted. 'Tell Mr Theodore Smith that I would like to see him.'

The man gave Bragg a long stare, then walked away. After a few minutes he returned and ushered them into an office off the main banking-hall. It was richly furnished in heavy old pieces that betokened a century of tradition and integrity. A short man with receding hair stood up as they entered. As he saw Morton his frown disappeared.

'James, my boy!' he said in a dry, rather bleak voice. 'Why did you not say it was you?'

'We are here on police business, sir,' Morton said quietly. 'This is Sergeant Bragg, who is my superior in the detective division.'

'I see.' Theo held out his hand to Bragg. 'Good-day to you, sergeant. Please be seated.' He settled back in his swivel chair and looked at them coolly. 'And how can I be of assistance to you, gentlemen?' he asked.

'We are investigating the murder of Alan Chisnall, sir,' Bragg said. 'I am talking to everybody who knew him.'

A smile briefly touched Theo's lips. 'And are you of the opinion that I belong in that category?'

'We are aware that you knew one another when you were younger.'

'That is true.' He swivelled round to gaze out of the window. 'Yes. . . We were young together; starting in the City at the same time. . . It all seems so long ago.'

There was a pause, then: 'How did you come to meet him?' Bragg asked.

Theo swung to face them. 'We were three youngsters lodging in Mrs Tickle's house,' he said reflectively. 'Alan Chisnall was there first. His parents had moved to the country somewhere, so he had to take diggings. He seemed to be having such a splendid time, that I managed to persuade my parents to allow me to join him. . . It was no easy matter, I can tell you. My mother thought it faintly absurd that, living in Buckingham Gate, as we did, I should wish to take lodgings a mere three miles away! But Alan was such a personable chap that, once she had met him, her doubts were put to rest.' He smiled briefly. 'The fact that the house was in Monkwell Street, and that there was a Congregational chapel a few doors away, seemed to dispel her fears!'

'I expect she saw you settled in, though.'

'No,' Theo said impassively. 'My mother seldom set foot out of the West End. The City was a man's world – and still is, I suppose.'

'Yes. . . You said that there were three of you in your group.'

Theo pursed his lips. 'Four strictly, I suppose. John Teverson joined us at Mrs Tickle's shortly after I went there. And there was Robin Yeulett. He lived with his parents, in Finsbury Circus. We used to call him the day-boy!'

'Does that mean you others had all been to boarding-school?' Bragg asked.

A brief smile crossed Theo's lips. 'By no means, sergeant. It is true that I went to such an establishment. However, the others had all been to day-schools. Chisnall and Teverson were at the City of London School, and Yeulett at St Paul's. . . No, we called him the day-boy because he could not always join us in the evenings. His parents kept him on something of a tight rein.'

'Was that unusual?' Bragg asked.

'We thought it unfortunate – for him. My own father was of the opinion that young men ought to sow their wild oats; and before they were given responsibility, not after it.'

'And, of course, you had plenty of money.'

'Enough. Whoever was in funds paid the bills. But you would be surprised how little one needed. There was always something going on – a party or a dance. During the Season, that is from April to the end of August, there was a plethora of dinners, drums, picnics, balls. . . And almost any young man was welcome, provided that he was reasonably presentable.'

'It is surprising that you were awake enough to do anything during the day,' Bragg said mildly.

'Ah, one had limitless energy in those days. And one had a certain responsibility to prepare for the future.'

Bragg scrutinised Theo. He seemed so composed and undemonstrative, it was hard to imagine him at wild parties. Would he have been any more boisterous when he was young? 'And what form did this preparation take?' he asked.

Theo looked surprised. 'I take it that you regard this as relevant,' he said.

'Well, you never know,' Bragg replied. 'To be honest, although I have been a policeman in the City for near a quarter of a century, I have precious little idea how it works.'

Theo gave a wintry smile. 'I could hardly hope to enlighten you in. . .' He took out his watch. 'In a mere half-hour.'

'No. But was it like it is now?'

'Much the same. In what I suppose one might call the initial phase, we endeavoured to acquire an all-round knowledge of the City's workings, before settling into our chosen niche. I remember that I began in Teversons' stockbroking office. Then I went to the bond-brokers owned by Yeulett's father, for another six months. One moved round, gaining experience all the time. It has been invaluable. When, say, a metal broker asks for a loan, and begins to talk about market movements and terms of trade, not only do I understand him, but he knows he cannot bamboozle me!'

'I see. . .' Bragg pondered. 'So there were three of you, living in the same diggings, rattling around the City together,' Bragg said amiably. 'I bet you got known as The Three Musketeers.'

Theo shrugged. 'Inevitably, I suppose. The story must have been at the height of its popularity then.'

'And which were you? Athos?'

'That would be to flatter me! As I recall it, Athos was of distinguished appearance, full of wit and wisdom, a man of unfailing good humour!'

'Is that so. . . ? And your wife. Was she Constance?'

Theo looked up irritably. 'Adelaide had no connection whatever with Monkwell Street,' he said. 'Her world was that of West End society.'

'I see. So she never met Porthos and Aramis.'

'If you mean Chisnall and Teverson by that remark,' he said icily, 'then the probability is that she did know them. London society is composed of comparatively few people. She would have been bound to encounter them.'

'Very good. . . And had you kept in touch with Chisnall over the years?'

'One is bound to bump into people in the City; but I have not actively maintained the relationship.'

'Really? But you were close friends, with the same sort of interests.'

'No. On my marriage, in eighteen sixty-six, I was made investment manager of the bank by my father. It was a responsible and demanding post. I had little time for roistering.'

'So you put away childish things. . . But did you never have a professional relationship with Chisnall in later years?' Bragg asked.

'A good bank has no need of publicity, sergeant, as you ought to know. In fact we actively eschew it.'

'Ah. I keep my spare money in an old teapot; you will have to forgive me. . . Did Chisnall ever bank with you?'

'Fortunately not!'

'Why fortunately?'

'In banking, to lose a customer is unfortunate, to have one murdered is a disaster!' He smiled in triumph.

'I see you have a touch of the Oscar Wilde's, sir,' Bragg said stolidly. 'I would avoid it, if I were you. It looks bad on the written report – a bit flippant, if you understand me. . . Can you tell me where you were at six o'clock last Monday?'

Theo looked somewhat crestfallen. He opened a drawer in his desk and took out a diary. 'I see that I had no appointments in the late afternoon. . . Ah yes! On the following morning I had a potentially difficult conference with several of our important clients, concerning a development. It is difficult to give impartial advice and support in a situation where a particular course of action is to the clear advantage of one client, but potentially to the detriment of another. I remember feeling that I must get away from here, and think the whole thing through in more tranquil surroundings.'

'I see. Did you go home, then?'

'No. The house is hardly tranquil when my wife is at home! I went to the park.'

'And which park would that be, sir?'

'St James's Park. I normally travel by underground railway, as did my father. I merely lingered in the park after leaving the station, instead of walking straight home.'

'What time did you leave the bank, sir?'

'At five o'clock.'

'Did you see anyone you knew on the underground train, or in the park?'

'I have no recollection of anyone.'

'And what time did you eventually arrive home?'

'Perhaps a little after seven. The butler would know.'

Bragg paused till Morton's note-taking had caught up, then: 'Would this problem of your clients' have any connection with the receipt of certain tickets, for a dramatic production?' he asked.

'Tickets? Why, I was certainly sent some! I gave them to Reuben in case he wished to go. But I imagine he has other things on his mind!' Theo smiled in Morton's direction, but he was preoccupied in recording the answer.

'You will be aware that the stock market has been falling for a week,' Bragg said.

'That is true.'

'Then, you will have heard the rumour that Chisnall's play is going to put the cat among the City pigeons.'

Theo gave a dry cackle of laughter. 'I do not subscribe to the theory that anything so evanescent as a play could bring about a stock market upset!' he said.

'Then what has?'

'I take it that you are not interested in my unsubstantiated speculations, sergeant, therefore I will refrain.'

Bragg cleared his throat, then looked hard at Theo. 'Has Chisnall ever demanded money from you, sir?' he asked.

'Demanded money? Why should he?'

'By way of blackmail.'

Theo snorted. 'There is nothing in my life which could form the basis of blackmail, sergeant. I have scrupulously observed a banker's probity in all my dealings, both business and private.'

'In that case, sir, I take it you will have no objection to our examining your private bank accounts. There are deposits in Chisnall's account we would like to match.'

'My dear sergeant, if I were intent on paying off a blackmailer, I would do it in cash, not by way of a cheque drawn on Smith's bank!'

'Nevertheless, it can only be in your interests to convince us that we can eliminate you from the investigation. I could not in conscience do that, unless we had seen your bank account.'

Theo frowned. 'You must accept', he said, 'that I have no desire at all to frustrate your efforts. And have no fears as to the outcome. But before I consent, I shall have to consult others. Firstly I must take advice from my solicitor; and secondly I shall have to obtain the consent of my partner-to-be.'

'And who might that be?'

Theo smiled. 'On his marriage to the sister of this young constable, I intend to take Reuben into the firm.'

Morton put down his pencil and closed his notebook on it. 'My position has become totally untenable,' he said irritably. 'Who will believe that I can act impartially, when my sister could be affected by the outcome of the investigation?'

Bragg swung round and looked at him angrily. 'What the bloody hell are you on about, lad?' he demanded. 'What do you think a village bobby does, when one of his cronies might have thieved a stray pig? Send his resignation to the Chief Constable? There are no half-measures. You will do your job, like it or not!'

There was an angry silence, then Theo intervened. 'For my part,' he said coolly, 'I would have no objection to Constable

Morton's being involved in my examination of the books of the bank. Indeed, I can only see advantages in any such investigation's being performed by a gentleman.'

6

When Bragg arrived at Old Jewry next morning, he found Morton already there. He was sitting at his table, moodily turning over and sorting the loose papers.

'You taken to sleep-walking?' he asked. 'Or did you not bother to go to bed at all?'

Morton looked up. 'I must confess that I am extremely concerned about the conflict of loyalties I am caught up in,' he said.

'Concerned? What have you to be concerned about?' Bragg asked roughly. 'Theo Smith told you himself that it was what he wanted. And one gentleman could not possibly let down another gentleman, could he?'

'Nevertheless, I can see great problems ahead.'

'That's the trouble with too much education, lad. You can see so far ahead, you end up doing sod all!'

'Even were that so, sir, it hardly solves the difficulty I am in.'

Bragg glared at him angrily. 'Let me tell you, lad, you are only of use to me because you are out of the top drawer; so you know what these buggers can get up to! In a minute you will be telling me that I ought to come off the case too; because I know your sister, and because her intended may be a murderer. You don't put things right that way!'

Morton looked up startled. 'Reuben Smith a murderer?' he exclaimed.

'Well, why not? Do you not get family loyalty among the nobs? The way I see it, Adelaide Smith had a first-class motive for killing Chisnall. Even you will go that far with me. . . But are you going to tell me that Theo Smith had no idea what Chisnall and Adelaide Hollyer were up to, when they tiptoed upstairs at a ball? Of course he did! I bet you they were all at it!'

'I would have thought that such conduct would render a girl virtually unmarriageable, particularly twenty-five years ago.'

'Well, that just shows how stupid you are, doesn't it? In your class people might hop in and out of bed for love; but they marry for advantage. Adelaide Hollyer was from a moneyed family. As long as she hadn't got a string of bastards, she would always have been marriageable.'

Morton's lip curled in distaste. 'Even if one accepted your theory in principle,' he said, 'there would still be difficulties. According to Adelaide, Chisnall threatened to send the letters to Theo. On that basis Theo did not know of the liaison.'

'You are a damned sight too simple-minded, lad. It would all be kept unacknowledged – like a lot of things in your class. Discretion they call it, don't they? Theo could hardly go to her father and say, "I know she's anybody's screw, but make her dowry big enough and I'll take her off your hands." But that was the way of it, I reckon.'

'I would have thought that the Smiths had already enough money to put them above that kind of expedient,' Morton said coldly. 'Apart from that, your theory destroys the very basis of Chisnall's blackmail threat to Adelaide. If Theo was aware of her affair with Chisnall, she could hardly be blackmailed by a threat to inform him of it.'

Bragg gazed at him blankly, then: 'Ah, I keep forgetting that you have not read the letters that matter.'

'Then perhaps I ought to read them.'

'No, lad. You might yet end up related to her.'

Morton snorted angrily. 'Well, if I am to be placed in the position of speculating without knowing the full facts, I cannot be expected to understand how Theo is supposed to be a suspect.'

'That's an easy one. Chisnall goes to Theo and says, "Unless you come across with ten thousand quid, I take the letters to a gutter newspaper like the *Reynolds News*." That would be a killing matter for Theo. He could never risk those letters becoming public.'

'And Reuben?'

'You know how boys think their mothers are saints. If Chisnall tried to put the screws on Reuben – and just as his own wedding was coming up – he would swat him dead like a fly!'

'All of which reinforces my conviction that I should take no further part in the investigation.'

'Oh! You think you would be doing everybody a favour, do you?' Bragg said sarcastically. 'Let me tell you this. If it is left to some cloth-head like me, who cannot see the wood for the trees, the suspicion never will be lifted from them.'

Morton sighed. 'Well, I did spend some time, last evening glancing through *The Three Musketeers*. In fact, I realised that the descriptions of the characters confer attributes on them which are seldom, if ever, demonstrated by the plot. You will recall that Theo described Athos as of distinguished appearance, full of wit and wisdom, a man of unfailing good humour.'

'That was what he said.'

'Yet in the book he is also described as being proud, aloof, reserved, almost a recluse. Not, you would think, the natural qualities of a bon viveur.'

'But it's only a story, lad.'

'True. However, we have heard from both Adelaide and Theo that, to some extent, the *habitués* of the Monkwell Street house acted out the characters of the book.'

'All right – so they could pick whichever quality suited them. . . Constant Constance could have been either faithful, or constantly at it!'

'I would gladly believe that – at least since her marriage – Adelaide has been the first, if one has to choose between them!'

'Me too,' Bragg said quietly. 'And I hope she comes out of it as white as snow. I am not muck-raking to get at the rich, if you think I am. . . And what about Porthos? We have a bit of paper with that name on it.'

'In the book he is a vain, womanising braggart. I think that, of the trio in Mrs Tickle's house, Porthos must have been Teverson.'

'Why is that?'

'Well, if Chisnall had been Porthos, he would hardly have needed to put that sobriquet on the circular.'

'That makes sense. So what about Chisnall himself?'

'It follows that he must have been Aramis – a lover of women, but unconvivial; ingenuous but mysterious.'

'In a way that fits part of what we know of him pretty well,' Bragg mused.

'One could even stretch the theory to extreme lengths, with

regard to Constance,' Morton went on with a smile. 'In the novel Constance is poisoned by Lady de Winter, who turns out to be Athos's wife. So figuratively one might say that Adelaide, the intimate of Chisnall, was eliminated when she became Adelaide the wife of Theo.'

'Now we are just playing bloody games,' Bragg said crossly.

Morton laughed. 'At least I noted one precept that Chisnall appears to have followed. "To know about a man's private life always gives one a moral advantage over him." '

'Particularly if you are not very moral yourself. So where has all this got us?' Bragg moved over to his desk. As he did so, his newspaper slipped to the floor.

Morton bent to rescue it. 'Good heavens!' he exclaimed. 'Have you seen the Stop Press item in your *Standard*?'

'No. Why?'

'There was a fire at Gatti's Music Hall last night!'

'Gatti's? That's where Chisnall's play is going on! In my book, that's no accident! Come on, lad, let us have a nose round.'

They took a hansom cab along the Strand, then walked down the steep hill by Charing Cross station, towards the river bank. Already the air was tainted with the smell of burnt wood. At the bottom of Villiers Street the slope levelled out. There was an open, paved area with an elaborate gas-lamp standard. To the right was the monumental bulk of the abutment of the Hungerford railway bridge. Here the piers of its arches had been bricked in to form the theatre. An elaborate semicircular doorway had been constructed, mirroring the curve of the arch above it. The door was of heavy mahogany. One of its panes of etched glass had been shattered, the woodwork damaged as the door had been jemmied open. A man in a crumpled frock coat was talking to a uniformed constable. Bragg crossed over to him.

'I thought there was a fire here,' Bragg said. 'I expected the whole place to have been gutted.'

The man looked at him suspiciously. 'You did, did you, sir?' he said. 'And why would you think that, eh? How would you know what to expect?'

'I can read.'

His eyes narrowed. 'Now that's interesting. You see, none of the papers had a report of a fire. It happened too late.'

'What time was it?'

'About four o'clock, as I suspect you very well know. I must ask you, sir, to come along to the police station with me.'

Bragg laughed and put his hand in his coat pocket. The uniformed constable leapt forward and seized his arm. 'Now, just you come along quietly,' he growled.

Morton savoured the tableau for a long moment, then produced his own warrant-card. 'I am sure that you do not wish to waste time arresting Sergeant Bragg, of the City police,' he said with a grin.

'Who? . . . What the devil are you doing on my patch?' the man spluttered.

'On duty,' Bragg said, wrenching his arm out of the constable's grasp.

'Well, keep out of my bloody way!'

'And who might you be?'

'Inspector Bingham, based at Bow Street.'

'I see. Well, sir, the most you can get for arson is penal servitude for life. We are investigating a capital offence, so we should get preference.'

'Like hell, you will!'

Bragg stared at him coldly. 'I have been appointed coroner's officer in a very violent murder,' he said. 'The victim was the man who wrote the play that is due to be performed here on Friday. Now the theatre has been set on fire, by all accounts. If you want to be hauled up before Sir Rufus Stone, to explain why you prevented us from examining the site of the blaze, then that's your affair. I expect you would get a few weeks inside, for contempt of court, and be reduced to constable. But it's your choice.'

Bingham's gaze dropped. 'It is not much of a fire,' he muttered. 'You will find the chief of the fire brigade in there, with the manager. . . And if you get anything on the arsonist, I want to know,' he added aggressively.

'Of course, sir.' Bragg beckoned Morton, and they strolled into the foyer of the theatre. Morton whistled in surprise. Although it was small, it was decorated with Grecian pilasters; gilded friezes topped the walls, elaborate gasoliers hung from plaster bosses in the ceiling. 'This is astonishing,' he said.

'Can you find the fire brigade chap?' Bragg asked. 'He should be able to get to the bottom of this, if anybody can.'

Morton pushed through a door, and they went down a narrow flight of steps into the theatre. 'There is no visible damage here,' he remarked, 'though there is a strong smell of smoke.'

The auditorium was about two hundred feet long, but rather narrow. Half-way down, the pillars of the great viaduct obtruded. The rake of the seating was gentle, because of the restricted headroom; otherwise it was much like any other theatre. The interior echoed the decorative style of the foyer, the soft light from the gasoliers adding to the sumptuous effect. As they walked down the central aisle, a man emerged from a low doorway to the right of the stage. He was wearing a silk-faced frock coat, and carrying a silk top-hat.

'Excuse me, sir,' Bragg called. 'We are looking for the chief of the fire brigade.'

The man looked across. 'I am he,' he said.

'We are police officers.'

His gaze became hostile. 'What, more police officers?' he exclaimed irritably.

Bragg went over to him. 'The man who wrote the play that was supposed to be opening here, in four days' time, has been murdered. Naturally, when we heard that there had been a fire here, we thought there might be a connection.'

The antagonism faded from the fire chief's face. 'In that case, I will do all I can to assist,' he said. 'My name is Halliwell by the way. . . It is at least certain that the fire was not accidental, if that is of interest to you.'

'Arson, was it, sir?'

'I would have thought that attempted arson might have been a better description, since there was comparatively little damage.'

'Where was the fire?' Bragg asked.

'Backstage. . . Just look at this place,' Halliwell exclaimed in disgust. 'It is nothing less than a fire-trap. It must hold six hundred people, not to mention cast and stage crew. And the only means of egress is that wretchedly inadequate doorway you came in by. The gangways are far too narrow to allow for speedy evacuation in an emergency. In the case of a fire there would be panic; women would trip over their dresses on the stairs; other people would fall over them, clogging the only means of escape. There would be carnage! I really do not know how the Middlesex justices can bring themselves to grant a licence for public performances here!'

'Could you show us where the fire was, sir?' Bragg asked.

'What? Oh, yes. Follow me.'

He led them back through the door by the stage, into a whitewashed corridor. Through an opening on the left, Morton saw steps leading up into the wings. In the gloom he could see that the stage was furnished to represent a drawing-room. A man was sitting on a settee, his head in his hands. Halliwell took them into a room at the rear. Its walls were begrimed with smoke. A charred wooden press stood in the corner; the floor was covered with ash and half-burnt papers. A man was sitting at a desk on the other side of the room; he was dolefully sorting through bundles of singed papers. Morton felt a pang of sympathy for him.

'You see how it was done?' Halliwell said, pointing to the pipe of a gas-light hanging drunkenly from the wall. 'The intruder pulled that down from the wall, twisted it so that the jet would play on the cupboard, lit it and made his escape. . . The whole place would have gone up, but for a most fortunate circumstance. The door of this room was left open; smoke escaped down the corridor and out of an open window in the backstage urinal. A passing railway worker raised the alarm.'

'At four o'clock in the morning?' Bragg asked in surprise.

'A cleaner, apparently; going to his work at the station. . . Well, I must be off. If there is anything that I can do to assist you, please do not hesitate to ask.' He turned and marched out of the room.

Bragg went over to the desk. 'Who are you?' he asked.

The man looked up dazedly. 'My name is Wallis,' he said. 'I am the manager of the theatre.'

'Where is Mr Gatti?'

'Dead. Rosa is the one who matters now. I don't know what I am going to say to her!'

'Try the truth,' Bragg said shortly. 'Is this the only damage?'

'Yes.'

'Then, it is not too bad. . . It looks as if all they wanted to do was to destroy the cupboard. But why?'

'How do I know?' Wallis said peevishly. 'To me it seems that the arsonists were disturbed before they could complete their preparations.'

Bragg looked round the room. 'I doubt that,' he said. 'It would take some time for the smoke to get out of the building; and it was a long shot for anybody to see it, at four in the morning.'

'There are several spent matches on the floor, sir,' Morton said. 'More than would be necessary to light a gas jet. It seems likely that the intruder first made a heap of papers in the middle of the floor, and set light to them there.'

'Hmn. . . That would have made it pretty thick with smoke in here.' He turned to Wallis. 'What did you have in that press?' he asked.

'Scripts, in the main; we do an annual pantomime. They were hardly of great value, but we might have repeated one or two of them.'

'Scripts, eh? What about the script of the play you are putting on this Friday?'

'Oh, that is safe and sound. The producer's copy is the only complete one. Fortunately he had taken it home with him.'

'What about incomplete ones?'

Wallis frowned. 'I really cannot be certain. The actors were given scripts containing only their own lines, plus cues. They presumably still have them in their possession.'

Morton gave an exclamation and, squatting down, picked up a half-burnt page. 'At least we have the answer to one of our problems,' he said. He took the paper over to Bragg. 'At one point in this particular pantomime, one of the characters has to leave the stage. So there is a stage direction "Exit OP". I suspect that the fragment from Chisnall's grate is part of just such a stage direction.'

Bragg swung round to Wallis. 'What does it mean?' he asked.

' "OP" is short for "Opposite Prompt", which is stage right,' he said.

'So Chisnall's copy of the play was burnt by his murderer,' Bragg murmured. 'Then he came here to destroy the rest.'

'Or she,' Morton suggested.

Bragg frowned. 'I suppose so. The lock on the entrance door was not up to much. It could have been opened up with quite a small lever.' He turned to Wallis. 'Where can we find this producer man?' he asked.

'A short time ago he was sitting on the stage. He may still be there.'

'Right. What is his name?'

'John Todd.'

Bragg marched out of the room and up the steps to the stage. The man was still sitting in the gloom.

'Police,' he said. 'I understand that you are the producer of this play that is being performed on Friday.'

The man roused himself. 'That is true,' he said in a mincing voice. 'Though whether it will happen is anybody's guess.'

'But you have the full script.'

'Why, yes. Here it is, if you are interested.' He gave a feminine wave of the hand. 'But don't be surprised if it never goes on. From the way that chief of the fire brigade was talking, they may take away Gatti's licence!'

Bragg sat down opposite Todd. 'Tell me about the play, will you, sir?' he said. 'I gather that it was out of the ordinary for this theatre.'

'Oh, it is, officer! This is a music hall really. They hardly ever do a straight play. . . Not that this was going on for the money.'

'You mean that you were doing it for love?'

Todd smirked. 'No, officer. I mean that Mr Chisnall was having to pay to have it performed. Some playwrights are dreadfully vain!'

'I see. Did he engage you to produce it for him?'

'That's right! He let me engage the cast, and arrange for the scenery and stage furnishings. It all fell on me, really.'

'I see. You know Chisnall is dead, I suppose.'

'Yes. But there is no reason why that should stop the performances. He has paid all the expenses. Mr Wallis says that we are under a duty to continue with the production – unless they close the theatre, that is.'

Bragg pondered. 'So our joker might have been trying to set fire to the theatre, after all. . . Tell me, sir. Who else was aware that Chisnall had paid in advance?'

'Why, Rosa Gatti must have received rental for the rehearsals, and the actual performances. And Mr Wallis was paid for the scenery, costumes and properties weeks ago. . . Then there is the cast, and the backstage people. Oh, a score of people must have known.'

'And anyone they talked to, eh?'

'That's right!'

Bragg considered for a moment, then: 'Was it a good play?' he asked.

Todd snorted in derision. 'It was the most boring play I have ever been involved with! It was so bad that you could hardly call it drama. The only good thing about it was that it was short. Its plot consisted of seven awful men conversing, in various combinations, about events in the City of London and what not. I understand Mr Wallis was assured by the author that it was all fiction. But that hardly made it any more entertaining! I said as much to Mr Chisnall. He said he was going to stand in the wings. If he thought the audience had not taken his point, he was going to come on stage to explain it all! The very thought made me shudder! But I decided that he had paid well, so he was entitled to call the tune.'

'Did he give you any specific instructions?'

'Instructions?' Todd bridled at the word. 'No, not as such. But he did want the actors to emphasise some phrases. He underlined them in red ink on my script. I must admit I was a bit piqued, being told what to do. After all, I am one of the leading West End producers. I, if anyone, should be able to judge where the stress of a line should fall. But. . .' He shrugged.

'But you had been well paid, eh? May I take this script with me?'

Todd hesitated. 'If you must, I suppose. If we are not ready now, we never shall be. But I might ask for it back. . .'

Bragg and Morton made their way out of the theatre, and strolled back up Villiers Street.

'We seem to be getting in deeper and deeper, lad,' Bragg remarked.

'It seems to me, sir, that Chisnall brought down Nemesis upon himself,' Morton said. 'Having arranged for his play to be staged at his own expense – which is an exceptional event in itself – he then sent out scores, possibly hundreds, of tickets to City luminaries. Indeed, since he seems to have been an extraordinarily rash fellow, I would not be surprised to learn that he had himself started the rumours which have had such a startling effect on the City, and the ministers of Her Majesty's government. But why he should take such a course eludes me.'

'Revenge,' Bragg said emphatically. 'You have to remember that his doctor had only given him a short time to live. We decided he might have been prepared to blackmail people to keep the bookies in the style to which they have become accustomed. But this is a horse of a different colour altogether. You had it right earlier. It must have been revenge!'

7

'I am sorry if I am a little late, this morning,' Morton said. 'For some reason Chambers overslept; and Mrs Chambers seemed all fingers and thumbs, when she was getting my breakfast. I suspect that they had an over-convivial evening at one of the local hostelries!'

'You poor helpless sod,' Bragg said sarcastically. 'It must be hard, not being able to get through life without someone to wipe your arse!'

Morton grinned. 'I must confess that, in the absence of my trusty retainers, life would be considerably grimmer.'

'That's the trouble with you nobs,' Bragg grunted. 'Your money lets you opt out of the humdrum things of life. So you spend your time on candy-floss doings. You don't realise it's the humdrum, the drudgery that makes life worth while.'

'Ah! Here beginneth the first lesson; I ought to abandon my worthless life of self-indulgence, persuade – against all the probabilities – Miss Marsden to marry me, and raise an endless brood of little Mortons.'

'And what is wrong with that?'

'Nothing. Except that the lady does not share your idyllic vision of domestic bliss.'

'Huh! I don't know what has got into city folk nowadays. When I was young, the country lasses knew what life was about, all right. They didn't fight it. Most of them were three months gone when they walked to the altar, and none the worse for that. It was part of the natural way of things. . . You lot think you can go against nature. When you find out you are wrong, it will be too late.'

'Then, the Fabians will only need to wait one generation and the despised upper classes will wither away! However, I feel justified in pleading for your indulgence on this occasion. I spent several hours after dinner, last evening, in reading an unutterably boring and undramatic play. I assure you that Todd, the producer, was restrained in his criticism yesterday.'

'Did you find anything?' Bragg asked.

'I am sure that someone *au fait* with City matters would have been able to appreciate references which went over my head. To an outsider like me, it was largely incomprehensible. What I would suggest is that we consult my friend Gerald Pargiter. I am sure that he would be able to bring enlightenment.'

Bragg considered. 'The trouble is, the play might not go on now. And if Pargiter read it, all the City would know in twenty-four hours. We might have put ourselves in the position of publishing a libel. I cannot see Sir William backing us on that one; and quite right too.'

Morton sighed. 'I suppose that must be so.' Then he brightened. 'You will recall that Todd was instructed by Chisnall to have certain phrases emphasised by the actors.'

'Yes.'

'I fear that he was exaggerating the extent of the interference. I found only three instances where a phrase had been underlined in red ink.'

'And what were they?'

Morton took out his notebook. 'The first appears to contain the name of a City institution. The whole phrase was: "for Brown Glass & Brown's, integrity appears optional".'

'What do you make of that, lad?'

'At the moment, nothing.'

'And the other two instances?'

'They were phrases occurring in different scenes of this shapeless conversation that Chisnall called a play. The first was: "profitable enlightenment", the second: "misled ever so daintily".'

Bragg frowned. 'It hardly sounds like a killing matter, does it? Who are Brown Glass & Brown's, I wonder?'

'Am I allowed to consult Pargiter to that extent?'

'You are forgetting! Even these stuffy City firms are connected to the telephone system nowadays. Just look in the classified directory.'

Morton took the volume from the press and leafed slowly through its pages. Then he looked up, troubled. 'I am afraid', he said, 'that Brown Glass & Brown's do not appear; and so, on your hypothesis, do not exist. The name can only be an oblique reference to Smith Payne & Smith's.'

'Theo's bank, you mean?'

'Yes. As to what he wished to convey by the phrase: "integrity appears to be optional", I cannot imagine.'

'But a City audience would know?'

'Presumably so.'

'I see. . . How far is Theo's house, at Buckingham Gate, from Gatti's theatre?'

'I suppose, rather less than a mile.'

'I see. So Theo could have got up at three o'clock, walked to the theatre, broken in and set fire to the scripts, and been back in bed by half-past four.'

'It would have been possible, certainly.'

'Yes. . .' Bragg gave a fierce smile. 'Nobody would have been wandering about, at that time in the morning. I bet even Adelaide never knew, since nobs sleep in separate bedrooms.'

There was a knock at the door, and the desk sergeant poked his head in. 'The Chisnall case hasn't been closed down, has it, Joe?' he asked.

'No, it bloody hasn't!'

'Only there is a young lad by the name of Johnson downstairs. Lives next door. He says Chisnall's house has been broken into.'

'Right, I'll see to it.'

Bragg sprang from his chair, grabbed his bowler from the hat-stand and rushed downstairs. Morton caught up with him in Old Jewry, and waved down a passing hansom. Bragg glared at him resentfully, as if he needed some violent exercise to relieve the frustration building up in him. He sat wordless and fuming as the cab trotted easily along the streets, from blinding sun to shadow to sun again. When they arrived at Petticoat Square he flung back the flap and leapt out, leaving Morton to pay the fare.

The door of Chisnall's house had been forced open; the wood round the lock was splintered.

'A jemmy?' Morton enquired jauntily.

'It looks of a piece with the theatre, doesn't it?'

The front door of the adjacent house opened and Mrs Johnson appeared. She was wearing an apron, and a cotton cap enclosed her hair. She held a duster in her hand. 'I sent our Alan,' she said. 'I hope I done right.'

'Indeed you did, Mrs Johnson,' Bragg said warmly. 'It may have nothing to do with the other affair, but you never can tell. When did you discover it had been broken into?'

'Not half an hour ago! Our Alan had finished his breakfast, after his paper round. He was on his way to the shop – he works at the ironmonger's in Cutler Street – when he noticed the door was open a little bit. We knew it had been closed last night, because we came past on the way from the pub. So I sent him to tell you.'

'Thank you. Did you go into the house?'

She hesitated. 'I went in as far as the door to the front room. It were in such a state, I daren't go any further . . . in case it was like last time.'

Bragg laughed. 'I hardly think that would be likely,' he said. 'Did you hear any noises next door?'

'What, in the night? No. Like I said, the two landings are between us. Now, on the other side of us, you can make out everything that goes on. They would be surprised if they knew some of the things we've heard!'

'No doubt. Now, can you arrange for this door to be secured, once we have had a look round?'

'Well, the rent collector is due round today. I could tell him.'

'Well done!'

Bragg pushed open the door and went into the hallway. The door to the front room stood open. All the books had been taken from the shelves again and put on the floor. But this time it had not been done in a frenzy. The empty drawers had been removed from the desk and piled by the fireplace, as if someone had been searching the spaces behind the drawers for something.

'Perhaps this represents a last desperate attempt to find the documents we found in the strong-box,' Morton said.

'Maybe.' Bragg led the way upstairs. The bedroom at the back had been ransacked. The clothes had been taken from the drawers and the wardrobe, and placed neatly on the bed.

'Our housebreaker was at least methodical,' Morton remarked.

'Yes. . . To me, it wasn't the same person. This looks . . . well, more like a woman's way of going about things.'

Morton started to laugh. 'This is worthy of a West End play in itself,' he said. 'Theo Smith and Adelaide Smith creeping about in their vast house in the early hours; almost bumping into each other; tiptoeing into the darkness – he to burn theatres, she to break into houses – then flitting through the dawn to their separate beds! You have missed your vocation, sir!'

'Huh! You would be laughing on the other side of your face if it were true, wouldn't you?'

The grin vanished from Morton's face. 'Indeed I would,' he said soberly. 'You are right, sir . . . I most certainly would.'

Since it was barely past eleven o'clock when they had finished at Chisnall's house, they walked back to the centre of the City. At the Bank crossing they turned into Lombard Street. They went into Smith's bank and approached the counter.

'We would like to see Mr Theodore Smith,' Bragg said. 'Is he in?'

The clerk looked at them with a mixture of curiosity and uncertainty. 'Yes, he is in. I will see if he is unengaged. You are the policemen who called on Monday, are you not?'

'That's right.'

'Just one moment.' He locked his cash drawer and went away.

Bragg stepped back and studied the mosaic decoration around the central dome. St Paul's had a lot to answer for, he thought; heathen rubbish!

'Will you come this way, gentlemen?'

This time Theo contented himself with standing up as they entered. He did not offer to shake hands. His eyes were red-rimmed, and he looked tired. His voice, though firm, held a note of irritation.

'I thought I had seen the last of you,' he said coldly.

Bragg sat on one of the chairs and made a business of straightening the frock of his rumpled coat. 'Criminal investigations are funny things, sir,' he said amiably. 'You think you have got one part of it straight, then something comes up which shows that you were wrong.'

Theo waved Morton to a chair, then sat himself. 'And what has occasioned this visit?' he asked.

Bragg looked up reproachfully. 'You were going to arrange for us to see the books,' he said.

Theo frowned. 'I did consult my solicitor,' he replied. 'His opinion was not exactly helpful. On the one hand he urged on me the duty of confidentiality towards our clients. On the other he pointed out the advantages of voluntary co-operation, since otherwise compulsion was a probability.' Theo swivelled round and gazed out of the window for a space, then he swung back. 'I discussed the situation with my son, Reuben,' he said, 'and I confess that I was impressed by the maturity of his judgement.' A brief warmth touched his face. 'He observed that it would be a flagrant breach of trust, were we voluntarily to give access to the records of our clients' affairs. On the other hand, the bank itself has nothing to hide, and nor has its principal. He suggested, therefore, that we would make available to you the records of any transactions which do not directly involve our customers.'

'Right. And what about your own private affairs?'

Theo shrugged his shoulders. 'You are welcome to investigate to your hearts' content. You will find nothing.'

'Is that because there is nothing, or because it is too well hidden?'

Theo looked at Bragg contemptuously and did not reply.

'Where were you between three o'clock and six o'clock, yesterday morning?' Bragg demanded gruffly.

'What? In the early hours? I was in my bed, of course.'

'I don't see there is any "of course" about it, sir... Can anyone vouch for that?'

Theo's brows knitted. 'I suppose not,' he said finally.

'Your wife?'

'I take it that she was asleep in her own room.'

'You take it... Is there any particular significance in that choice of words, sir?'

Theo was watchful. 'No, sergeant. So far as I know, my wife was asleep. I certainly was.'

Bragg allowed a pause to grow, his eyes fixed on Theo's face, then: 'Have you ever heard of a firm in England called Brown Glass & Brown's, sir?' he asked.

Theo smiled. 'Brown Glass & Brown's? No. Never! It almost sounds like a parody of...'

'Go on, sir.'

Theo gave a half-laugh. 'Well, of Smith Payne & Smith's, of course.'

'Yes,' Bragg said portentously. 'That is what we thought. You see, we have got hold of a copy of Chisnall's play.' He watched Theo for any changes of countenance, but his face only displayed a mild interest.

'Everybody knows it was to be a muck-raking job,' Bragg went on. 'And when we read it, we found this reference to Brown Glass & Brown's.'

'In what context?'

'Read it exactly, will you, constable?'

Morton turned back the pages of his notebook. 'The remark was put into the mouth of a purported Bank of England official, but we do not see any particular significance in that,' he said. 'The exact phrase was: "for Brown Glass and Brown's, integrity appears to be optional".'

Theo frowned. 'I have not the remotest idea as to what that is intended to convey,' he said irritably. 'Integrity is never optional with a bank – or with any successful financial institution.'

Bragg leaned back in his chair. 'You can see our problem, sir,' he said earnestly. 'Chisnall told the producer of the play to emphasise certain phrases – to make sure the audience got the point, you might say. This was one of them. So naturally we have to think there was something in it, some good reason for it.'

Theo looked up angrily. 'Then you will discover that you are wrong, sergeant!'

'I see.' Bragg pondered, gazing into space. 'I expect you will have remembered by now that you did see Chisnall shortly before he died,' he said mildly.

A look of apprehension was immediately overlaid by an apologetic smile. 'You are perfectly right, sergeant. As it was purely a social meeting, it had quite slipped my mind!'

'Yes, I'm sure,' Bragg said drily. 'When exactly was it?'

'Exactly?' Theo picked up his diary and leafed back through the pages. 'On Tuesday the twenty-sixth of June . . . I see that we lunched together.'

'A week before he was murdered?'

'Ah . . . why, yes. I suppose that must be the case.'

'Where did you lunch?'

'Here in the bank. We have a small partners' dining-room.'

'I see. A social occasion you say?'

'Yes, which was why it slipped my memory.'

'And who else was there?'

Theo gave him a level stare. 'There was no one else present,' he said.

'I see. So it was a . . . what do they call it? . . . a tête-à-tête?'

Theo did not reply.

'And what did you talk about?'

'Just old times. I found it somewhat boring, in fact.'

'Yes, well you would . . . you being so high, and him fallen so low. But surely you were interested in his play?'

'He made no mention of it, sergeant.'

'Goodness me!' Bragg said expansively. 'What a strange man he was! By then he had your name on the list for tickets; I expect he already had yours in the envelope, yet he never mentioned it!'

Theo glared at him and said nothing.

'You said, when we saw you on Monday,' Bragg went on, 'that Chisnall had never attempted to blackmail you. Do you still stand by that, sir?'

'I do, sergeant. There would have been no substance for such an action.'

'Then, why do you think Chisnall should go to the lengths of putting a name in his play that everybody would recognise as your bank?'

Theo shrugged. 'I would not attempt to explain the workings of a deranged mind,' he said shortly.

'Deranged?' Bragg ruminated. 'Do you know, of all the people we have talked to, no one else has suggested that he was off his rocker.'

'Well, then, it was done out of pure malice,' Theo exclaimed harshly. 'Does it matter?'

'Something mattered to Chisnall, didn't it? . . . Of course, he never forgave you for pinching his girl.'

'Pinching his. . . What on earth are you talking about?' Theo exclaimed angrily.

'Why, Adelaide – your wife.'

'Now you are being ridiculous! There was never any question of Adelaide's marrying Chisnall. They were merely part of the same social set at one time.'

'I see. And he showed no resentment when you married her?'

'None whatever. You amaze me, sergeant. Why, the man was a groomsman at our wedding!'

'Hmn. . . Then it does sound like pure malice. It's about the first pure thing we have discovered about Chisnall, I can tell you, sir!'

Theo pulled his gold half-hunter from his waistcoat pocket and glanced at it. 'I have a luncheon appointment in the City now,' he said tersely. 'If you have any more questions they will have to wait.'

Bragg got to his feet. 'Very well, sir. We would not wish to detain you at the moment.'

A look of alarm flitted across Theo's face.

'There is one thing though,' Bragg went on urbanely. 'If you could get one of your staff to show us the books that you are prepared to let us examine, we would get an idea of what is involved.'

Theo hesitated. 'Very well,' he said. 'If you will stay here a moment, I will send someone to you.' He took his top-hat from the stand, nodded briefly at them and went out.

Bragg and Morton kicked their heels for almost ten minutes, before there was a knock at the door. Then the clerk in the pince-nez came in.

'Mr Smith has given me certain instructions,' he said frostily. 'If you will come this way, I will show you the record books that will be made available to you.'

They followed him across the banking-hall into a room on the other side of the building. It was little more than a cubby-hole, the small barred window admitting a dim light. A plain deal table under it was piled with books and ledgers. The clerk stood in the doorway as Bragg and Morton turned over the volumes. Suddenly Bragg jerked alert. At the bottom of one pile was a quarto book, on which the word 'Options' was embossed in gold letters.

He nudged Morton and gestured to the ledger. 'Integrity appears optional,' he whispered. 'Distract his attention, lad.'

Morton turned to the clerk. 'Is there a water-closet here that I could use?' he asked.

The clerk turned to the door, pointing. As he did so, Bragg grabbed the options book, and held it inside his jacket with his arm. 'I wouldn't bother, constable,' he said. 'We've finished here. Just tie a knot in it till we get back.'

He marched out of the bank with Morton on his heels. Once in the street, Bragg broke into a run. He dodged down St Swithin's Lane, pounded along Cannon Street and disappeared down the steps of the Mansion House underground railway station. When Morton caught up with him, he was leaning against the wall of the booking-hall grinning like an urchin.

'That'll show the buggers!' he gasped. 'By the time they wake up, we will have everything we need!'

'If you are caught with that book in your possession, sir, we will both have more time than we need – to repent in! I cannot believe that you would be so reckless!'

'Repent! We will leave all that to Chisnall's murderer.' Bragg tapped the book under his coat. 'Chisnall wasn't a fool, whatever else he was. I reckon we have all the evidence we need, here in this ledger!'

Morton shook his head in disbelief. 'But we cannot commit a crime in order possibly to solve another,' he said. 'We are supposed to be guardians of the law, not brigands ourselves!'

Bragg scowled. 'Oh, the Commissioner will back us up. He sorted out that sod Ashworth Caldwell for us.'

'The Bank of Montreal is very small beer compared to Smith Payne & Smith's.'

'Are you telling me there should be one law for the little banks, and another for the big?' Bragg demanded self-righteously.

'I am saying that your action is utterly indefensible, and Sir William is enough of a soldier not even to attempt to defend it. If you recollect, we gave Theo the full text of the play's reference to Smith's. When he realises that the options book is missing, he will know full well who has taken it.'

A worried frown settled on Bragg's face. 'You think that, do you?'

'Indeed I do!'

'Then we had better get rid of the swag. Quick, lad, go and buy some brown paper and string. I will get tickets for St James's Park.'

'St James's Park?'

'Adelaide... Hurry up!'

Morton went up the steps again and hurried along Cannon Street. There was no evidence of unusual police activity. Perhaps luck had been with them, and the clerk had preferred to go to lunch rather than return the ledgers whence they came. He bought a sheet of brown paper and a ball of string in a stationer's shop, then strolled back to the station. He eventually found Bragg lurking in the gentlemen's toilets.

'Right... Well done! Give it here!' Bragg seized the paper and string and disappeared into a cubicle.

Morton strolled back to the platform. A train was coasting into the westbound platform, the engine spewing out steam and smoke. The train stopped, and a handful of passengers alighted. Morton opened the door of a compartment, lest the train should go without them. The guard scowled at him and shouted an oath. But Bragg was emerging from the toilet, a neatly tied parcel in his hand. He climbed into the compartment as the train began to move.

'Have you got a nice blunt pencil?' he asked.

Morton fished a stump from his pocket. 'Will this suffice?' he asked.

'Just the thing! Now we write in big capitals: "Miss Catherine Marsden". Then underneath: "To be called for". Like that...'

'Why Miss Marsden's name?' Morton asked.

'It is as good as any other. Women are always forgetting things. Now it looks like a parcel that she arranged to pick up from a shop, then left on a train.'

Bragg sat in the corner smiling smugly to himself, until the train stopped at St James's Park station. Then he jumped out and bustled importantly up to the guard.

'This parcel has been inadvertently left on the train by some departing passenger,' he said pompously. 'Could you please take care of it?'

The guard touched his cap. 'Thank you, sir. I will.'

Bragg turned with a self-satisfied smirk. 'There you are, lad. We have got no options book! But when the coast is clear, it will be waiting for us in the lost property office at Mansion House station!'

They bought pork pies from a stall by the entrance to the park, and sat on a bench in the shade to eat them. Bragg felt his spirits rising again. It was nearly as good as being in the country, he thought. Better in some ways. You didn't get this parade of young women, with their bouncy breasts, in Bere Regis. It did a man good. They were so confident, so exhilarated by their beauty. And yet, in ten or fifteen years they would be faded and worn out from scrubbing floors and rearing children. A man wouldn't look twice at them then.

'You intimated that we are going to see Adelaide,' Morton said, interrupting his reverie.

'Yes. What a pity that we cannot consult Miss Marsden on whether this is a society time or not!'

Morton laughed. 'Who would have thought that would prove to be such a barbed remark,' he said. 'If you are so irked by inaction, we could go to Adelaide's house now, and wait there if she is not in.'

'So long as Theo hasn't slipped back for something, eh? All right. I cannot bear to sit here wasting my life.'

By the time they had reached Buckingham Gate it was almost two o'clock. The butler informed them that his mistress was in the garden, and showed them to the same room that they had been in on their previous visit. It was not long before Adelaide appeared at the french window.

'I did not expect you to haunt me like this!' she said with some spirit.

'Haunt?' Bragg savoured the word. 'I would not call it that, ma'am,' he said. 'We just wanted a bit of a chat.'

'And if I refuse?'

Bragg sat on the settee with great deliberation. 'Somehow, I think you are much too sensible for that,' he said. 'You are in a spot of trouble and frankly we are the only ones who can get you out of it.'

She sank into a chair despondently. 'I can accept that, officer. But I cannot envisage that you will exert yourself on my behalf.'

'Well, look at it like this. You are too intelligent not to have realised that we suspect you could have killed Chisnall. We need not talk about murder, at the moment. He had a thin skull, you might not have meant it. A little tap could have been enough.'

She looked up. 'I had nothing to do with his death!' she said vehemently. 'I had left him hours before he died, and I can prove it!'

'Oh yes. Winifred the waitress from Waterloo station,' he said sardonically. 'Then, if what you say is true, would it not be better to help us find who did kill him?'

'I am not at all convinced of it.'

'All right,' Bragg said formally. 'Where were you between three o'clock and six o'clock yesterday morning?'

'But that was in the middle of the night!'

'That is so.'

She gave him a harassed glance. 'I was in my bedroom. I got up at two o'clock to take a sleeping draught. I must have fallen asleep before three. And I did not wake until eight.'

'Have you anyone who can vouch for that?'

'My maid came to my room at half-past eight, with my breakfast. But that is well outside the times you mentioned.'

'And what about during last night?'

'I was in my bedroom from eleven o'clock until my maid woke me.'

'At half-past eight this morning?'

'Yes.'

'I see.' Bragg paused. 'The trouble is, we know that you have not told us the full story,' he said earnestly. 'So how can we start to believe you? Now, why don't you unburden yourself, so that we can begin to put your pieces of the jigsaw into place.'

'If only I could trust you, sergeant.'

'Well, let us see how far we can get, shall we? How long has Chisnall been blackmailing you over those letters?'

'Oh, for years. At first it was infrequent, and for small amounts. But for the last few years it has been more frequent. I must have paid him fifteen hundred pounds during last year alone. I was becoming desperate.'

'That doesn't sound all that much, for somebody in your position,' Bragg said.

'Then you deceive yourself. I did bring a considerable dowry into our marriage, certainly. But Theo has invested that on my behalf. I could not realise any of the capital without telling Theo why I needed the money. And the income is not so large as to furnish my personal needs and blackmail demands in addition.' She looked down at her clenched hands.

'So you were running out of money, and then Chisnall came back for more,' Bragg prompted her.

'As I told you last time, it was four weeks ago. I received a letter from him, asking me to meet him.'

'And did you?'

'Yes. On Monday the fourth of June.'

'Where?'

'In Regent's Park, as usual.'

'What did he say?'

'He had heard that Reuben was to be married. He demanded a thousand pounds. He threatened, on that occasion, to send my letters to the gutter press, to ensure that the wedding was ruined.'

'What did you do?'

'I went to Reuben, and asked him to get me a thousand pounds of my money without his father's being aware of it. I hope that he thinks I was planning an extravagant present for Theo. However that may be, he said he could not do precisely as I asked; but he lent me a thousand pounds from his own resources.'

'In cash?'

'Yes.'

'And what did you do with it?'

She gave him a level stare. 'I took a cab to Petticoat Square,' she said,' and pushed it through the letter-box in his door.'

'So you knew where he lived?'

'Oh yes, sergeant. I knew where he lived.'

Catherine Marsden paid off her cab in Covent Garden, and walked past the Opera House towards Tavistock Street. She wanted to steady her nerves for the ordeal which faced her. If she were honest with herself, she would admit to having mixed feelings about the possibility of becoming editor of *The Lady*. Strictly in terms of her career, it would be something of a coup. The editor of the *City Press* had been taken aback when she told him of her intention to apply. Nevertheless, he had declared that she was amply qualified for the post, and that her age should be no handicap. But he had been a little too emphatic for her liking, in his assertion that he would do everything in his power to facilitate her advancement. The truth of it was that Mr Tranter had never been wholly comfortable with her. He had been brought up in the old attitudes, where a woman was either a servant or a plaything; never the equal of a man. She admired the restraint and fortitude he had shown, when she had been foisted on him by the owner of the newspaper. He had been tolerant and genuinely helpful. But she was an anomaly. He would be glad to see her go.

But what of *The Lady*? From what Lady Lanesborough had said, the current editor was a man. She had no idea how old he was. He had apparently resigned, rather than retired. Did that mean elevation to some more prestigious post, or acknowledgement of failure? None of her colleagues seemed to know. But *The Lady* was said to be financially in low water. Perhaps the two were connected. . . In that case, would the proprietors be looking for new blood, or wanting to play safe? Well, she could but do her best.

In many ways, she thought, obtaining the editorship of *The Lady* might compel her to face up to her future more generally. She would demonstrably be a successful woman; and there was no reason why that could not be combined with a normal personal life. She had often fantasised about a future as James's wife; living in his rooms in Alderman's Walk; being looked after by Mr and Mrs Chambers. Going to work as he did; attending glittering balls and first-night theatres with him. She had never actively considered the question of children. Nowadays it was possible to regulate their arrival. Yet she acknowledged that she would quite like some. James would certainly want a son.

His elder brother Edwin, while serving as a subaltern, had been greviously wounded in a minor colonial skirmish. He had been brought back to The Priory paralysed from the waist down; a chronic invalid. His parents had tried to convince him that he could still lead a useful life. When his health had recovered a little, they announced that henceforward he should have the running of the estate that surrounded the ancestral home. Lieutenant-General Sir Henry Morton had by then retired from active soldiering, and had been appointed to the largely honorary post of Lord Lieutenant of Kent. He had declared that he was far too busy to be involved in managing farms; here was a worthwhile job for Edwin, paralysed or not. So he had fallen in with the charade. He would lie propped up in his rooms, with charts of the fields and notes of the crops. The bailiff would come every day to receive orders from him, then go and do what he thought was best.

Catherine had often seen the anger in James's face, when he had returned from a weekend at The Priory. On her occasional visits there, her untutored eye had recognised the malaise that lay on the estate. Sir Henry Morton resolutely refused to accept that it was deteriorating. Or, if he recognised the fact, he regarded it as a worthwhile price to pay in order to give his elder son the feeling that his life had not been wasted. Catherine was sure that it was this impasse that had driven James to turn to the police service. His work was ludicrously undemanding for someone with his background and education. And the fact that he enjoyed it in no way invalidated her opinion. With his fluent command of French and German, he could have had a satisfying career as a diplomat. He could have become a Member of Parliament, in time a minister of the crown. The Prime Minister had once hinted as much. But in truth, he was merely filling in the time, until he could take the inheritance that must pass to him and his sons. . . Yes, James would want children.

Well, she had no long-term objections. Indeed she had often faced up to her mother's strictures that, should he so wish, James was perfectly well placed to marry now; that if she waited too long, she might find he had become attached to someone younger than she. Of course, her mother was far too inclined to listen to Lady Lanesborough; to want her to marry a doddery earl or vacuous viscount, just because a title sounded important. . . She reminded herself that James had already proposed marriage to her. But in circumstances so grotesquely inappropriate that she had rebuffed him. Since then he had kept a warm but respectful distance between them. She had allowed – almost contrived – situations to develop in which he could have renewed his proposal, but he had refrained. Perhaps he was now content with a relaxed, comfortable friendship; perhaps he no longer wished to marry her. She shook off the idea as preposterous . . . but the securing of the editorship of *The Lady* could well be more important than she wished to acknowledge.

She turned into Tavistock Street with a quickening pulse. In a few short weeks this could be part of her daily routine. She walked along the soot-blackened brick terrace. Number twelve struck her immediately as appealing. The mid-blue paint of the door was fresh and shining, the brasswork gleamed, the pavement outside had been washed that morning. It was just as it ought to be, restrained, confident, mildly superior. There was an office at the front, off the hallway. She knocked on the door and went in. 'I have come for an interview,' she said.

A young woman looked up from her desk. 'Ah, yes,' she said. 'Please sit down.' She took a piece of paper from a drawer and set it in front of her. 'What is your full name?' she asked.

'Catherine Ann Marsden.'

'Your age?'

'Twenty-three.'

'Good. . . I see that you are not married.'

'No.'

'Are you going to be?'

Catherine smiled. 'I have no plans to do so.'

'I am sure that will count in your favour. . . Is your shorthand good?'

'Tolerably so.'

The woman looked at her with raised eyebrows. 'I see. . . And your typewriting?'

'I cannot typewrite at all.'

'You cannot. . .' Suddenly her face flushed scarlet. 'Oh! Miss Marsden! You have not come for the secretarial job! You are. . .'

Catherine forced a wintry smile. 'I am to be interviewed in connection with the post as editor.'

The woman got to her feet. 'Please forgive me,' she said effusively. 'It had quite slipped my mind. . . Will you kindly follow me?'

She scuttled into the hallway and up the stairs. Catherine followed her up three storeys and was shown into a small waiting room, where she was left. She must put this silly misunderstanding behind her, she told herself, or it might affect her mood for the coming ordeal. She forced herself to examine her surroundings. The room was comfortably furnished, with armchairs and a table by the window. On the walls were pleasant sporting prints; in one corner an aspidistra lurked glumly. The air was heavy with the taint of old cigar smoke. She made a mental note that the windows would have to be opened more frequently. There was no one else in the room. On the table were recent copies of *The Lady*. She picked one up. In the critical mood engendered by the manner of her reception, it seemed to her old-fashioned, even dull. It was small wonder that the publishers were losing money. In comparison, the *Ladies' Realm* was altogether more appealing. There was certainly room for improvement.

She heard the squeak of the door hinge, and turned. A smart-looking young man came in, his hair plastered down with macassar oil.

'Miss Marsden?' he asked in a soft voice.

'Yes.'

He held out his hand. 'I am so pleased to meet you,' he said. 'Have you come far?'

'Only from Park Lane.'

'Park Lane. . .? Oh! I . . . er, I did not realise that you lived in such a prestigious area,' he said in embarrassment.

Catherine smiled sweetly, but did not reply.

'Yes, well. . . I want to tell you a little about the interview. The chairman of the board will do most of the questioning, I expect. He is Mr. Harbery, and he has interests in publishing outside *The Lady*. His wife will be there too. I confess that I know very little about her. It is said that her fortune keeps the magazine afloat, but that may be mere gossip.'

'So the Harberys own it?'

'Effectively yes. . . Mr Stone, the retiring editor, will be on the interview panel also.'

'Ah,' Catherine said thoughtfully. 'That is something of a surprise. So are they looking for continuity, rather than change?'

The young man wrinkled his brow. 'As to that I cannot say. If the rumours are true, we need either new capital or a timely outbreak of profitability!'

Catherine laughed. 'I expect *The Lady* is not alone in that! Will there be anyone else on the panel?'

'Mrs Empson. I suppose one might describe her as a token member of the readership.'

'Mrs Empson,' Catherine said thoughtfully. 'I cannot say that I have met her.'

'I believe that her sister married into some offshoot of the Hertford family. . . Well, if you will wait a moment, I will find out if they are ready to receive you.'

Catherine walked casually to the window, trying to repress her growing nervousness. She wished that she had asked the young man about the other applicants for the post. There were bound to be some – and probably better qualified than she. Most assistant editors in Fleet Street would have cast an eye over the advertisement; thinking it might be a way to the top, or wondering if it could prove a secure backwater for the rest of their working lives. Well, it was too late now. All she could do was to relax, be herself, say what she genuinely thought. On that basis she would maintain her self-respect at the very least.

The young man appeared in the doorway. 'They are ready now,' he said. 'Good luck!'

He ushered her into a room dominated by a long table. In the centre of one side, four people were sitting. The two men rose as she entered. One of them leaned across the table as she came opposite them, and held out his hand. He was in his mid-forties with grizzled black hair. A pearl tie-pin nestled in his cravat.

'Good morning, Miss Marsden,' he said in a friendly voice. 'Thank you for applying for the post of editor.' He squeezed her hand. 'Please sit down.'

She decided not to drag her chair nearer the table, in case it gave the impression that she needed its support. She put her handbag on the floor and composed her arms in a relaxed posture on her lap.

'My name is Harbery,' the man said. 'I am the chairman of the company which owns *The Lady*. Beside me is my wife, and the lady beyond her is Mrs Empson. This gentleman on my left is Mr Stone, the present editor.'

Catherine smiled and nodded briefly to each. Stone was in his late fifties, with cropped grey hair and a florid face. From the resentful look on his face, he was not departing willingly.

'Well now, Miss Marsden,' Harbery said cordially, 'I propose that the interview should proceed as follows. We will first discuss your background and experience, so that we can get into focus your suitability for the post. Then we will have a more forward-looking discussion. If there is any matter that you do not understand, I will clarify it before you comment. Does that seem reasonable?'

Catherine winced inwardly at the implied condescension towards a member of the weaker sex. 'Perfectly,' she said calmly.

Harbery glanced down at the folder in front of him, and Catherine recognised her own writing on the document it contained. 'It appears that you are twenty-three years of age,' he said. 'Do you not think that this is a somewhat early age to take editorial charge of a publication of national importance?'

She smiled. 'I would regard my age as of no significance, providing always that I have the personality and experience to carry out the work.'

He looked at her approvingly. 'Yes. . . Well, let us go through your curriculum vitae. You are, I believe, unmarried and live with your parents.'

'That is so.'

'Would you say that you were from the aristocracy, the landed gentry, the merchant class. . .?

'My mother's family are minor Hampshire gentry; my father is an artist – but a moderately civilised one!'

Harbery glanced down. 'Ah, yes, William Marsden RA.'

'He painted Lottie Bonham's portrait, last year,' Mrs Harbery interrupted. 'It was a beautiful likeness, but I sometimes think it did not quite capture her true character.'

Catherine contented herself with a smile.

'And, of course, you live in Park Lane, which is at the centre of society's little village,' Harbery said genially.

'That is so.'

'As to your education, in your early years you went to a private day-school in Mount Street, then to Cheltenham Ladies' College. Would you regard that as desirable, in the context of your present application?'

Catherine consciously relaxed her posture. 'Indeed I would. My childhood years were spent in a small cultured family, where I was encouraged to acquire a wide range of interests. On the other hand, Cheltenham taught me to sharpen my analytical skills, and apply a more rigorous discipline in forming my judgements.'

Harbery's eyebrows lifted fractionally. 'Yes. . . yes, I see. And you no doubt retain a lively interest in what is going on around you.'

Catherine smiled warmly. 'Yes indeed!'

'You are undoubtedly aware that our publication is largely concerned with the interests and doings of the upper layer of the country's inhabitants that has come to be known as society,' Harbery said pompously. 'And I see that you were presented at Court in eighteen ninety-three.'

'I was very fortunate, in that Queen Victoria herself was present at that drawing-room.'

'So you would regard yourself as not only having the entry to society, but its ear also?'

Catherine laughed. 'I cannot think that it could be expressed more felicitously.'

Mrs Empson leaned forward to attract the chairman's attention. She was in her fifties, well groomed and tending to plumpness. 'I would like to ask Miss Marsden if she regards herself as part of the Marlborough House set,' she said.

Catherine frowned in puzzlement. 'By no means,' she said. 'How could I be and have a career also? As I understand it, the members of the Prince of Wales's circle have to be prepared to drop whatever they are doing, and dash to wherever his whim takes him!'

'But you are acquainted with him?'

'Yes.'

'And you are aware that we have received a communication from Marlborough House, expressing his Royal Highness's support for your candidature?'

Catherine was thunderstruck. 'I neither have knowledge of it, nor need of it,' she said sharply. 'I would not wish my candidature to proceed on any other basis than my suitability as a journalist for the post.'

'But you do know him well?' Mrs Empson persisted.

'I was once instrumental in saving his life, when an assassin tried to shoot him at Liverpool Street station,' Catherine said sharply. 'But our subsequent encounters have not led to his knowing me in any pejorative, Biblical sense.'

Harbery intervened. 'I am sure that we are all content to consider only your record as a journalist, Miss Marsden. And I have to say that it seems at the same time both impressive yet limited. We, of course, know of the considerable scoops which have made your name in the profession. On occasion, I am sure that you have been the envy of every journalist in London. Yet the stark facts are that your experience extends to only three years.'

'I have been a staff reporter for two of them.'

'Yes. . . But that on the *City Press*, which appears only twice in the week. And when one examines your articles, one finds that in large measure they reflect the cultural background you urged on us, rather than bread-and-butter news-gathering.'

'Well, there is nothing bread-and-butter about *The Lady*,' Catherine said with a smile. 'So I do not see it as a handicap. And I would say that the production rhythm of the *City Press* would be much closer to that of your periodical, than would be the cycle of a daily newspaper. However, you will also see that I was offered a staff post as society correspondent for the *Star*.'

'Yes. But you apparently declined it. Does that suggest that you are basically unambitious?'

'By no means! There were several reasons for my refusing to take the post. An important one was the editorial policy of the *Star*. It is, as you know, a radical newspaper. It has tended to look critically on what it regards as upper-class hedonism. To report on society matters for such a journal would be to cut against the grain with a vengeance!'

Harbery nodded. 'But you still remain an occasional correspondent for the *Star*?' he said.

'Yes. On City matters only. Naturally, if I were offered the editorship of *The Lady*, that connection would lapse.'

'Yes, yes. . .' Harbery brooded for a moment, then: 'What would you particularly urge on us as exceptional in your candidature?' he asked.

'Why, I am a woman!' Catherine said brightly. 'Your magazine is aimed exclusively at women. I have an instinctive feeling for the topics which interest women. And not only that. Women themselves will respond to a magazine whose editorial policy is handled by a woman. . . Moreover, I think that I could more surely guide the profitable evolution of *The Lady*.'

Stone, the editor, was glaring at Catherine as if he would like to strangle her.

Harbery gave her a quizzical look. 'In what direction do you feel we might . . . evolve?' he asked.

Catherine smiled confidently. 'Certainly not to a lower level,' she said. '*The Lady* is a good quality periodical, and it should remain so. Inevitably that means it will be costly to produce. Indeed, such changes as I have tentatively considered might increase the production costs somewhat.'

'And what changes might these be?' Harbery asked in surprise.

'My editorial philosophy would be to create a magazine which the reader would not put down, until she had read it from cover to cover. I would like to see more illustrations. I am told by a friend that, in the foreseeable future, we will be able to reproduce photographs in newspapers, instead of using blocks from etchings. I would want to work towards that day.'

'We are not the *London Illustrated News*,' Stone said acidly.

Catherine ignored him. 'I think that one could incorporate a feature where a portrait of some society lady – say the Duchess of Devonshire, Lady Londonderry and so on – is reproduced in each edition, together with an article about her and her household.'

'But everyone who is anyone in society would know that already,' Mrs Empson interrupted.

'Indeed. But I spoke of evolution. At the moment, *The Lady* does not aim to reach a readership beyond the confines of what we know as society. In many ways it is little more than an *aide-mémoire* to the top five hundred families. It is my belief that one could treble or quadruple its circulation, without sacrificing its essential qualities.'

'And how would you set about achieving that?' Stone asked with a sneer.

'By a conscious effort to widen its readership. Mrs Empson has identified the problem precisely.' Catherine flashed a smile at her and received a look of incomprehension in return. 'The members of society know already what has taken place, who was with whom, who wore what. But there is a great mass of people in the country – merchants, landowners, manufacturers – who long to know these things. For them London is the glittering centre of the nation, which they may never visit, but crave to belong to however vicariously. *The Lady* could be their window on this fascinating world. With the right kind of direction, you could expand your readership immeasurably.'

Catherine sat back in her chair. There was a silence. She heard Stone mutter something about voyeurism. She glanced around. No one seemed to wish to question her further. Finally Harbery got to his feet.

'Well, thank you, Miss Marsden,' he said, holding out his hand. 'You have certainly left us with a great deal to think about. We set out to find a new editor. I think perhaps we ought to find a new chairman!'

8

Bragg hung up his bowler next morning with a sense of impending doom.

'What is that you are doing?' he asked gloomily.

'I have been examining Chisnall's bank-books yet again,' Morton said cheerfully. 'There is no trace of the cash Adelaide Smith is said to have given him.'

'Did you expect there to be?'

'Not really. If we take the words of the bookie at their face value, her contributions would have funded little more than a few days' racing in total.'

'Was she telling the truth, though?'

Morton wrinkled his brow. 'Unless she is a consummate liar, I think that she was. To have invented the incident of borrowing from Reuben, would have given too many hostages to fortune.'

'Huh!' Bragg sat at his desk and took out his tobacco pouch. 'Most of the time, women don't know the difference between truth and lies,' he said grumpily. 'With that lot, life is one long lie. Look at the way they daub themselves with creams and powders, trying to pretend they are twenty years younger. They would not turn a hair at lying to the police.'

'Well, at least we both agree that Chisnall must have had a considerable amount of money from another source or sources, to finance his way of life. Personally,' Morton said airily, 'I incline to a multiplicity of victims, each contributing according to his means and vulnerability.'

'You sound like a bloody parson, lad. . . By God! If you are right, we shall have a damned long row to hoe. You know, getting back to this *Three Musketeers* business, it seems queer that one of the characters should blackmail another.'

'Ah, but Constance was always going to be the sacrificial victim. There would have been nothing romantic in the story otherwise.'

Bragg pulled out his pipe, and began to stuff tobacco into the bowl. 'So you are sure that Chisnall was blackmailing other people too?' he said. 'Do you think the papers that were kept in the strong-box relate to them?'

'That is an interesting idea, sir. And, if you remember, the financial circular annotated "Porthos" was in that box.'

'Hmn. . .' Bragg put his pipe in his mouth and picked up his matches. Then there was a heavy clump of boots in the corridor, and the Commissioner marched in. His little beard bristled with anger.

'This time you have gone too far, Bragg!' he shouted. 'My efforts to support you only serve to encourage ever wilder indiscretions on your part!'

Bragg looked up, his drooping moustache reinforcing the expression of pained innocence on his face. 'Me, sir? I cannot for the life of me think what you are talking about.'

'If I had my way, a firing-party would indeed be the best solution! What on earth do you think you are about? You cannot go riding roughshod over the laws of the country, regardless of the influence of people you antagonise, in pursuit of some fanciful notion of yours! I saved your hide over the Bank of Montreal affair, Bragg, but I will not attempt to protect you this time!'

Bragg put his pipe and his matches down with great deliberation. 'I have to say, sir, that you must be mixing me up with somebody else.'

'I am sure you do have to say that,' the Commissioner interrupted wrathfully. 'But it will not wash this time! I will not be manipulated by you, and put into a position where I am seen to condone your reckless behaviour.'

'Has someone made a complaint about me, sir?' Bragg asked innocently.

'Yes, sir! Someone has, sir! And I am minded to dismiss you from the force without even consenting to hear your version of events!'

'What events were they, sir?'

'You know full well, Bragg! I have just experienced the most painful half-hour of my entire life. I have been pilloried by a lawyer representing Smith's bank. Blackguarded almost. And all because of you!'

'Smith's bank?' Bragg said in surprise. 'Why, we were in there yesterday. We had a pleasant sort of chat with Theodore Smith. He used to be a friend of Alan Chisnall. . . Very co-operative he was, too. He seems quite sure he can prove he had nothing to do with Chisnall's murder. He is even going to let us have a look at the bank's books, to dispel any suspicion we might have.'

'Not any more, I can tell you! He even accuses you of stealing one of the bank's ledgers.'

'Stealing a ledger?' Bragg exclaimed incredulously. 'That's absurd! From what we saw of them, they are damned great books you could hardly lift! What am I supposed to have taken, anyway?'

'The options book. I am told that it is comparatively small.'

'For what purpose am I supposed to have stolen it, sir?'

'Purpose? How do I know for what purpose? Some devious purpose of your own, no doubt. But I will not have it!' Sir William crossed to the window and glared at the church tower.

'We did see a pile of books yesterday,' Bragg said evenly. 'They got them out for us, so that we could assess what was facing us. And a good long time it will take.' He turned to Morton. 'Did you see any options books, constable?' he asked.

Morton frowned. 'I believe there was one at the bottom of a pile. A fairly small ledger, as the Commissioner has said.'

'Hmm. . . Well, sir, you can see for yourself that it is not here. I expect what has happened is that some clerk has put it in the wrong place. . . What I do find interesting is that they should make such a fuss.'

Sir William swung round. 'What the devil do you mean, Bragg?' he demanded.

'Well, sir, there is a reference in Chisnall's play about integrity being optional and, do you know, it could have referred to Smith's. How did it go, constable?'

'"For Brown Glass & Brown's, integrity appears optional".'

'That's it. You know, sir, even Theodore Smith said it must mean his bank. . . And now their options book has disappeared. Well, well!'

The Commissioner frowned irritably. 'What are you getting at, Bragg?' he asked.

'It seems just too convenient for him. But you'll allow it's a stroke of genius to say we have pinched it!'

Sir William looked at him suspiciously. 'Do you give me your categoric assurance, Bragg, that you do not have this options book in your possession?' he asked.

'I do, sir.'

'And that you have not examined it?'

'That is the case.'

The Commissioner took a deep breath, and let it out in a long sigh. 'I have to believe you, of course,' he said.

'Not at all, sir. You can have this room searched, my lodgings in Tan House Lane – I expect Constable Morton's rooms as well. . . I think you ought to, sir; so that there can be no doubt.'

'No. I accept what you say. . . You know, Bragg, sometimes I think that retirement would be an attractive course for me. I get tired of being put under pressure by the various City interests. On occasion I think that I am more of a politician than a policeman.'

'Not for a long time yet, I hope,' Bragg said earnestly. 'We need someone with a clear sense of purpose, and the authority to carry it out. Everybody says that we have had no one to match you, ever before. It would be a great loss to us, if you went.'

The Commissioner cleared his throat. 'Would it, Bragg? Well, at least it is comforting to feel the force is behind me.'

'To a man, sir.'

'Nevertheless, it is I who will have to bear the brunt, if Smith's renew their allegations,' he said plaintively.

'I wouldn't worry too much about that, sir. If push comes to shove, we can cope with Theodore Smith.'

'Oh? How, may I ask?'

'Why, sir, yesterday his wife admitted that she has been paying blackmail money to Chisnall for years. I doubt if Theo would want that made public.'

'Ah, I see.' Sir William stood irresolute. 'At least I have your categoric assurance on the matter,' he said and went slowly out.

Bragg leaned back in his chair and lit his pipe. 'Where were we?' he asked.

'Where we still are – in deep trouble.'

'You sound like a pregnant Sunday school teacher! Don't forget we have got the upper hand at the moment, and it is going to stay that way. . . You were going to look over that circular marked "Porthos".'

'Ah, yes.' Morton went to the strong-box. 'Here it is. It seems fairly innocuous.'

'Hmn. . .' Bragg stood up. 'It will wait. I have a feeling that it would be as well to get out of here for a bit, while things cool off. Who was the last one of the three at Monkwell Street?'

'John Teverson.'

'Good. Where does he hang out?'

Morton took down the classified telephone directory, and turned the pages. 'Here we are,' he said. 'Teverson & Braithwaite – five Tokenhouse Yard.'

'Right, let's be off.'

The day was just as hot, but there was now a haze veiling the sun. It was so humid that they had barely walked a hundred yards before they were sweating profusely.

'There will be thunder before long,' Bragg said. 'And thank God for it! We spend all the winter waiting for a bit of sun, and when it comes it boils you.'

'In little more than a week's time, you will be able to enjoy a weekend in the balmy air of Kent,' Morton said lightly.

'Hmm. . . That is if there is still a bridegroom at liberty. Here we are. . . Teverson & Braithwaite, top floor. I might have known; there is no lift, as usual.'

They laboured up three flights of stairs to a small suite of offices. From the name-plate on the landing it appeared that John Teverson was the only principal of the firm. Bragg pushed into the general office. A shirt-sleeved youth sat at a desk on one side of the window. He seemed to be occupied in adding long columns of figures. Opposite him a typewriter sat at her machine. She looked cool and smart, in her light cotton dress. She smiled demurely.

'Can I help you,' she said.

'I am sure you can, miss,' Bragg said affably. 'We just want a quick word with Mr Teverson. We are police officers – Sergeant Bragg and Constable Morton.'

Her face clouded. 'I will see if he is unengaged,' she said, and hurried out of the room. Bragg felt his depression lifting. So long as you followed your instinct, you would never go far wrong, he thought. It was a pity the Commissioner did not have more backbone – but then, he had a lot more to lose than a lowly detective sergeant.

The typewriter came back, her eyes on Morton's admiring face. 'Mr Teverson is free,' she said brightly. 'If you would like to follow me. . .'

She led them across the landing, and into a large office with a view of the dome of St Paul's Cathedral. As they entered, a man in his mid-fifties rose from behind a big mahogany desk and held out his hand. He was tall and well-built, with an open friendly face, and a full head of wavy grey hair.

'Good morning, gentlemen,' he said in a warm, deep voice. 'This is an unexpected pleasure! How can I be of service to you?' He gestured to them to sit.

'It is just general information we are after, sir,' Bragg said amiably. 'We are investigating the murder of Alan Chisnall, and we are trying to build up a picture of his last days. We understand that you once knew him.'

Teverson looked surprised. 'Indeed I did. But that was long ago! I joined him and Theodore Smith in lodgings in Monkwell

149

Street, when I first came to the City.'

'Mrs Tickle's, yes. We understand from Mr Smith that you were sort of City apprentices, at that stage.'

Teverson smiled, and his face lit up with warmth. 'Yes. I must say that they were the best years of my life. I am not sure that we learned very much, but we had a marvellous time.'

'Theo Smith said that the experience was invaluable to him,' Bragg remarked.

'Ah well, that is Theo. A very serious-minded gentleman, even then. One sometimes felt that he was joining in the revels because it was the right thing to do.'

'Really? A bit stodgy, was he?'

Teverson smiled again. 'Perhaps that is unfair! And, of course, his destiny was to take over a major banking house. I think his prospective responsibilities tended to weigh on him.'

'We got the impression he was tight with his money,' Bragg said.

Teverson paused in thought. 'No, I would not agree with that. In fact, he trod a very judicious path. He had far more money at his disposal than either Chisnall or I. Had he chosen, he could have indulged his whims in a way that neither of us could have matched. Instead he limited his spending to an amount which did not leave us feeling uncomfortable.'

'He sounds a real little gentleman,' Bragg said sardonically.

Teverson looked at him in surprise. 'I would be happy to affirm that he was – and still is, I presume.'

'Good. . . So you do not see much of him nowadays?'

'No. Youthful attachments seldom survive the onset of responsibilities. Once I married, I had sterner matters to attend to.'

'You didn't marry money, then?'

Teverson smiled tolerantly. 'I believe that love and mutual respect are of more importance, sergeant.'

'Not so comfortable though. And did you have children?'

A shadow fell on his face. 'We would have had a son. . . But things went wrong, and I lost them both.'

'Ah. That's bad,' Bragg said quietly. 'And Chisnall never married at all, I gather.'

Teverson's smile was back. 'I think not.'

'Can I ask you about those days at Monkwell Street?' Bragg said. 'We are told that the three of you went around a good deal together.'

'Yes indeed! With such a superfluity of young ladies, we were always welcome at society functions. In retrospect, it seems that never a week went by without some ball or party. In the Season I swear we used to fall asleep at our desks!'

'Do you remember a young lady called Adelaide Hollyer?'

'Why, yes! She was later to become Mrs Theo Smith. Goodness me, yes! She was a most charming girl. In fact, she came to Monkwell Street on more than one occasion.'

'Properly chaperoned, I presume.'

He was momentarily off balance, then: 'But of course!' he said warmly.

Bragg nodded. 'And were you surprised when she married Theo Smith?' he asked.

'Surprised?' Teverson repeated, savouring the word cautiously. 'No, hardly surprised. Knowing their families, it was a perfectly natural alliance.'

'But not a love-match, like yours?'

Teverson shrugged. 'I believe that some couples reserve their demonstrations of affection for the bedroom,' he said. 'But I do not see where this conversation is taking us.'

'It is a bit aimless, isn't it? But you never know when something apparently unconnected with a crime can shed light on it.'

Teverson smiled. 'It would be a very weak ray of light, shining down all those years. But how is this connected with Alan Chisnall's death?'

'Oh, it isn't,' Bragg said simply. 'At least not directly. But we have not been able to find anybody you could say knew him well in recent years. Would you say that you had stayed close to him?'

Teverson looked momentarily embarrassed. 'Well, no, sergeant. I lost touch with him socially at the time of my marriage, and I never took up with him again.'

'Why was that, sir?'

'Well, it is a curious thing . . . when one loses a husband or wife, I believe that one becomes something of a social outcast – as if it were a contagious malady, or you were possessed of some communicable ill-luck! And, of course, in recent years Chisnall rather degenerated.'

'How do you mean, sir?'

'Well, this is largely hearsay, so you should treat what I say with caution. But I do believe that he began to drink heavily, and to gamble. I could not afford to be drawn into that way of life.'

'Afford financially, or socially?'

Teverson considered. 'Morally would perhaps be the right word.'

'I see. So you regard drinking and gambling as degenerate, do you, sir?'

'I would say that to cultivate either to excess would be undesirable, sergeant.'

Bragg shifted in his chair to mark a change of subject. 'I gather that this business belonged to your father,' he said.

'Indeed! Teversons have been stockbrokers in this building for four generations.'

'And the Braithwaites?'

'A mere aberration, fifty years ago. But it sounds well, don't you think?'

'Oh yes. . . And is Theo Smith one of your clients?'

Teverson smiled ruefully. 'Alas no! Neither personally nor as a banker. Would that it were so! But professional relationships in such institutions go back for generations. I could not remotely have expected him to sweep away the web of mutual self-interest and respect, to favour a friend of his youth.'

'And have you banked with Smith's?'

His eyes lit up with mischief. 'No, sergeant! Why should I upset the delicate balance of the City, by moving my accounts from the National Provincial's branch in Moorgate, to Smith's bank?'

'Did you ever have a professional relationship with Chisnall?'

Teverson considered for a moment. 'In the sense of his instructing us to buy or sell shares for him, the answer is no. . . However, when he gave up, or lost, his post at the *Financial News*, my father did have some dealings with him in connection with new issues. My recollection is that he found him unsatisfactory. I have had no dealings whatever with him.'

'I see. . . There is one other matter that I want to bring up. It seems silly at this distance; but there is some evidence that, when you three young men were living at Mrs Tickle's, you were known as The Three Musketeers.'

Teverson gave a guffaw of laughter. 'For a moment I thought it was a hanging matter!' he said.

'Yes, it was a bit pompous, putting it like that. But was it true?'

'I suppose so, in a loose kind of way. The story was popular at the time. We were three young men who, to the hostesses of the day, must have seemed inseparable.'

'And who was who?'

Teverson frowned. 'I do not understand your question,' he said.

'Which of you was matched with which musketeer?'

'Ah, I follow you. . . No, there was no question of any of us acting out the character of, say, Athos or Aramis. We were too preoccupied with enjoying ourselves in our own right.'

'I see. . . That is sorted out, then. . . Tell me, sir, was there any reason why you did not go to Chisnall's funeral?'

'No. Why do you ask?'

'Well we went; and we expected to find a fair crowd of people who had known and respected him. In fact there was a bare handful – and most of them were neighbours from Petticoat Square. In some way it seemed a bit heartless, considering his past career.'

Teverson looked at him warily. 'I am afraid that I was not aware of his death for some days. I was confined to bed with a recurrent illness at the time – a Pauline thorn in my flesh. But I regret the fact. I would sincerely have wished to be there.'

Bragg and Morton ate a sandwich in a pub, so that they could arrive back at Old Jewry in the lunch hour. Bragg caught the eye of the desk sergeant.

'You have not seen me, Bill. Right?'

'Right.'

They crept up the stairs and closed the door quietly behind them. Bragg took off his coat, then loosened his collar and tie. 'Now then,' he said leaning back in his chair, 'what do you think of our friend Teverson?'

'A very self-possessed individual,' Morton said reflectively. 'Not very keen to be thought one of Chisnall's cronies – but perhaps that is understandable. Interestingly enough, his view of the relationship of Adelaide Hollyer with the inhabitants of twenty-one Monkwell Street was far less compromising than you had assumed after reading Chisnall's love-letters.'

'You are right. But don't forget they were Adelaide's letters, not Chisnall's.'

'At any rate, it is clear that a certain slant is being given to their evidence, by both Theo and Teverson. Whether there is anything sinister in that is another matter.'

Bragg cocked his head. 'Of course, you would be glad to find it was no more than two nobs being little gentlemen.'

Morton shrugged and said nothing.

'There is one queer thing, though,' Bragg said musingly. 'Neither of the two wants to admit there was anything in the Three Musketeers business. I cannot swallow that. Miss Hollyer would never have signed herself "Your constant Constance", unless she knew of the charade. She was saying she was part of it – part of it because she was close to Chisnall.'

'And, of course, we have a comparatively modern piece of paper on which Chisnall has written "Porthos" – and, moreover, a list of initials with "Musketeers" at the top.'

'Damn!' Bragg exclaimed. 'I forgot to ask Teverson if he got any tickets for the play.'

'Since everyone in a prominent position in the City seems to have received some,' Morton said, 'I would have thought it a safe conclusion that he had.' He produced the ticket list from his file, and ran his finger down each column in turn. 'This is interesting,' he said finally. 'One would expect to find the initials "T B" here, for Teverson's firm, but they are not.'

'What about "S P S", for Theo?'

'No.'

'Not his own initials, either?'

Morton began again, running his finger slowly down each column. Finally he looked up. 'Neither is included, in any guise,' he said.

'Ah. Are you saying we have a bit of a conundrum?' Bragg said challengingly.

'Hardly. We know that Theo received tickets; he told us so himself.'

'So what is the answer? Come on, lad! You are as slow as a costive camel!'

Morton gazed out of the window, then: 'I suppose that the entry "Musketeers" covers Theo Smith – and Teverson also,' he said.

'My God! That took you long enough! So, where does that get us?'

'Well, according to Adelaide, Theo Smith was identified with Athos. And, since Chisnall wrote the name "Porthos" on the top of the circular, it follows that he himself must have been Aramis. On that basis, Porthos must have been Teverson.'

'Well done, lad! Feel better now?'

Morton grinned and, rummaging through his folder, found the circular. 'Perhaps it will repay closer scrutiny,' he said, 'though we do not know what connection Porthos might have had with it.'

'What is it about?'

Morton skipped through it paragraph by paragraph. 'It appears to be a document intended to be circulated amongst the general public,' he said. 'It discusses the merits of various new issues of shares. Chisnall is fairly lukewarm about the first couple, and positively damning about the next. . . Ah, here is one he deigns to look charitably on. Aurora Electric Lighting Company Limited. That is a splendid title for an enterprise! I can imagine people emptying their piggy-banks, and flocking to subscribe!'

'Aurora? That rings a bell,' Bragg said. 'Where does it hang out?'

'Its registered office is said to be in Chancery Lane, WC. That is in the Met's area.'

'The bottom end is ours. . . Here, lad, pop down to records, while everybody is out. See if we have anything. I'm sure I have heard a mention of this recently.'

As Morton went out, Bragg picked up the circular. It gave minimal information, but foresaw dividends of considerable size being paid year on year to infinity. The crock of gold at the end of the rainbow. . . And the article itself was a masterpiece. Its style was sober and reasonable; the words used were ordinary, factual; there was no attempt to appeal to the emotions or persuade. The conclusion drawn fell just short of a firm recommendation. And yet Bragg would have been tempted to subscribe, if he had had the money.

Morton came back again, a gleeful grin on his face. 'We do indeed have a file,' he announced. 'And can you guess where I found it? Among the closed cases!'

Bragg took it and browsed through its contents. It seemed that the share issue in Aurora had been made a mere six months ago, in January eighteen ninety-four. Towards the end of June a shareholder had complained to the City police, when it became known that the interim dividend would not be paid as promised. Inspector Cotton had made perfunctory enquiries, then closed the investigation... A fortnight later, Chisnall had been found dead.

'This is going to be a tricky one,' Bragg said. 'Have a look at the prospectus, while I think.'

Bragg had been answerable to Inspector Cotton for a good deal of his service. Indeed, he still was in theory. Cotton was a ponderous, forthright man, with a hectoring manner. He was well suited to chasing footpads and burglars, beating a confession out of them and sending them down for a stretch. Anything subtle or complicated bored him. This very fact had produced the *modus vivendi* which existed between him and Bragg. But in this case they seemed to have a common interest – except that Cotton had already closed it down. Normally Bragg would have been able to rely on the Commissioner, to manipulate him and get his support. But at the moment he had been pushed to the limit of his patience. Bragg's position was precarious to say the least; he could end up being suspended, even thrown out of the force.

He sighed. 'Have you made anything of it, lad?' he asked.

'It is in situations like this, that I regret not having taken a science degree,' Morton said ruefully. 'It appears that Aurora was floated to manufacture electric light bulbs. The company was to make use of a new patent filament, which would give vastly longer life than existing light bulbs. The inference is that, with wide patent protection, they would be able to flood the world with their product. On the supposition that there could be no competition for a very considerable period, it is presented as a veritable licence to print money.'

'So what went wrong?'

'I have obviously not mastered the detail of the case. There is a copy of the prospectus here, and the letter from the complainant. There are some jottings which presumably relate to the investigation, but they would be difficult for anyone but Inspector Cotton to decipher.'

'Hmn. . . What was the set-up in the company?'

Morton turned back to the prospectus. 'The company is capitalised at three hundred thousand shares of one pound each. They were to be issued on a half-paid basis.'

Bragg whistled. 'But, even so, we are talking big money! A hundred and fifty thousand quid in the kitty. Were the shares all taken up?'

The file contains no information on that point, sir.'

Bragg pondered for some minutes. 'In the normal course,' he said at length, 'I would not touch this with a barge-pole. But Chisnall was involved in pushing the share issue; and a couple of weeks after the police are alerted, his head is bashed in. . . I reckon Aurora is what the phrase "profitable enlightenment", in the play, refers to. On that basis I cannot see we have any option but to stick our necks out. All the same, we might as well try to prevent Inspector Cotton from chopping our heads off! Come on, lad.'

They clattered down the stairs and into the bustling streets. For once Bragg seemed oblivious of the chattering shop-girls, in their thin blouses. He made no move to find a cab; instead he strode along the pavements head down, a scowl on his face. Morton followed him through St Paul's churchyard, to Fleet Street and on to the Strand. There he turned into the cobbled courtyard of King's College, and went into the porters' lodge.

'I am looking for Professor Porteus,' Bragg said. 'Where will I find him?'

The porter looked up at the great clock. 'He normally gives a lecture at two o'clock,' he said. 'You might find him in his laboratory. He likes to come early.'

'Right. We know where it is. Thank you.'

For some reason, Bragg now seemed almost loath to reach his goal. He strolled across the courtyard, his brows knitted. But when they reached the laboratory his pace quickened, and his anxiety vanished. They pushed through the swing-doors into the long gloomy room. Porteus was sitting by his desk at the far end. He looked up as they approached.

'Ah! Sergeant Bragg, is it not? And may I say that, in your other capacity, Jim Morton, I vastly enjoyed the century you scored last month – even allowing for the fact that it was against Middlesex, my own county!'

'Why, thank you,' Morton said delightedly. 'I have to say, however, that the hard ground made fielding difficult. I ought to have been run out when I was fifteen. . .'

'We have come to see if you can advise us, sir,' Bragg interrupted irritably. 'You have helped us when we were getting out of our depth before; and we are in over our heads this time!'

Porteus smiled. 'You merely indulge a childhood desire of mine to be a detective,' he said. 'What is it this time?'

'Electricity, sir. Or rather a company claiming to have an electric bulb that will beat anything on the market.'

'Is that a criminal offence?' Porteus asked.

'It could be, when the company collapses almost as soon as its capital has been subscribed.'

'Ah. Well, as you know, sergeant, I am a professor of chemistry, not of physics. However, in an area which is, I suppose, technological rather than scientific, I might well be able to assist. If it is beyond me, we can consult one of my colleagues. . . Do sit down.'

Bragg pulled the prospectus from his pocket. 'The concern is called the Aurora Electric Lighting Company Limited, and their claim is that they can produce a new electric light bulb that will be infinitely better than Edison's. Let me read what they say. . . "The bulb designed by Mr Edison yields only three lumens of light per watt of energy. In laymen's terms, this means that little more than one half of one per cent of the electrical energy is converted into light." That sounds a bit wild to me, sir. What do you think?'

Porteus pursed his lips. 'I know that electric lighting is exceedingly inefficient, in scientific terms. The arc lights on London's major streets are massively wasteful. It is certainly an area where scientific advance could be immensely beneficial.'

'Hmn. . . Well, this company claimed it had the answer. Apparently Edison's bulb has a filament made of carbonised cotton thread. Aurora's bulbs were to have a filament made from a special metal named proteum.'

'I have never heard of it,' Porteus said. 'However, it may be a new alloy, that they have christened themselves. . . A metal filament, eh? And what are the advantages claimed for proteum?'

'Apparently it glows more brightly, and lasts much longer, than Edison's carbonised cotton.'

Porteus shrugged. 'Without scientific experimentation I cannot pronounce on the validity of the claim, obviously. But it is in no way preposterous. Work is going on in that field, in every advanced country in the world. Has proteum itself been patented, do you know?'

'The prospectus says patents are pending in a great list of countries.'

Porteus smiled. 'Of itself that means very little, as you no doubt know. And if a patent had been sought in England, I would have expected to hear some high-table gossip on the matter. . . A metal filament . . . I suppose you have no idea where this proteum has been developed?'

'No, sir. But I gather that the Aurora factory was to be managed by a man who used to work for Philips Incandescent Lamp Works, in Eindhoven.'

'Well, sergeant, it sounds entirely plausible. There is some very advanced work going on in Holland. Do you happen to know the name of this man?'

'Binswanger, sir.'

'Hmn. . . I cannot say that I have heard of him. However, as I said, it is not really my field.'

'But does it make sense?'

Porteus laughed. 'Well, may I express it in this way, sergeant. I would be reluctant to proclaim it as scientific flummery without further investigation, lest I was made to look a fool!'

9

Morton tracked Robin Yeulett down to a firm with an office in the Strand. According to his friend Pargiter, Yeulett Norrington & Co. were bond-brokers; so they did not need constant access to the trading floor of the Stock Exchange. From the contemptuous note in Pargiter's voice, the very fact that Yeulett's were outside the City proper made them inferior beings in the financial world.

The next morning, Bragg and Morton were at Yeulett's office when he was still opening the post. He was a tall, wiry man, with receding sandy hair and a pale, freckled skin. He did not offer to shake hands.

'We are here concerning the death of Alan Chisnall,' Bragg said, sitting down with great deliberation. 'We understand that you knew him.'

Yeulett looked at him in surprise. 'But that was in our youth! We could hardly have been said to be even acquaintances, for many years.' He sat down indecisively.

'We realise that, sir,' Bragg said quietly. 'Nevertheless, we were surprised that you did not attend his funeral.'

'I was not aware of his death for almost a week,' Yeulett said. 'I am afraid that my links with City life have become progressively more tenuous over the years.'

'Oh? Why is that, sir?'

Yeulett sighed and looked gloomily out of the window. 'I am not quite sure. Perhaps it is some shortcoming in me. . . Perhaps the days of the specialist are over.'

'Surely not, sir.'

'I think it may very well be the case, sergeant. At all events, I have begun to believe that I ought to have widened the scope of our activities years ago. My father, and his father before him, built up the business by concentrating on municipal finance. In retrospect, it was a mistake to specialise in so narrow a sector.'

'For what reason?'

Yeulett sighed. 'You see, the years of plenty were those when our industrial cities were expanding; when places like Manchester, Birmingham and Leeds needed access to capital funds greater than their ratepayers could be asked to provide. We handled the big loan-stock issues for them. In the seventies and early eighties it seemed as if we could not put a foot wrong. . . But those days are over. When Liverpool issued its first Consolidated Stock, in 'eighty-eight, the corporation appointed local brokers. And that trend has continued. Now we exist on minor loan issues from towns like Wigan and Rochdale. . . The only comforting thought is that I am not myself answerable to future generations.'

'You never married, then?'

Yeulett's lip curled. 'Oh, I married. Indeed I married! But there was no issue – nor will there be.'

'I am sorry to hear that, sir.'

'There is no need to be. . . It is strange,' he mused. 'My wife was a teacher, yet she would not hear of having children. She seemed to dread it. I came to terms with what was a very unrewarding existence. Then one day she announced that she was with child – by someone else.'

'That's rough, sir. Still, I expect you have not had to keep her.'

'No. But it is small consolation, sergeant.'

'It's strange how everybody seems optimistic in their youth,' Bragg said. 'John Teverson was only saying, the other day, what a splendid time you all had when you were first starting in the City.'

Yeulett brightened. 'Yes, they were good days. Our firm had an office in Throgmorton Street then. One felt one really belonged.'

'When did you first meet Alan Chisnall?'

'I suppose around thirty-five years ago. Yeulett Norrington was on the circuit in those days. Aspiring youngsters from the right families would gladly come to see what we were up to. Chisnall was one of them.'

'What about Theo Smith and John Teverson?'

'They also. And I, in turn, spent some time at Teverson's and in Smith's bank.'

'Would you say you were close to them?' Bragg asked.

'As close as I have ever been to anyone.'

'But you never went to live at Monkwell Street with them?'

'No. . . My parents were of a somewhat puritanical outlook. Enjoyment, while not exactly smacking of the devil, was something not to be encouraged. Life was a serious matter, levity a distraction.'

Bragg smiled. 'Well, it would have seemed a bit odd. After all, in Finsbury Circus you were only a few hundred yards from Monkwell Street.'

'Yes. . . Yes indeed.'

'But you did go to parties with the other three?'

'Sometimes. But I could never stay beyond eleven o'clock. I had to be back by midnight, or face a family inquisition. . . Do you know, the others used to call me the "day-boy". Can you imagine that?'

'I expect it was only in fun, sir. . . Did you ever meet a young lady named Adelaide Hollyer?'

A look of pleasure brightened Yeulett's face. 'Indeed I did! She was a most lively and charming girl. Occasionally she would come, with friends, to the Monkwell Street house. . . I have to confess that I very much envied the other three men their freedom.'

'Chisnall was a bright young fellow then, by all accounts.'

'Chisnall?' Yeulett thought for a moment. 'Well, he had an acute mind, there is no doubt about that. But in retrospect I have thought that he lacked application. In his youth he was an attractive and humorous person, and he seemed to sail through life by ingratiating himself with everyone around him. He spent three months working at Yeulett Norrington. After it my father told me, in confidence, that on no account would he offer him a senior post with the firm. I was incredulous at the time, but it would appear that my father was not alone in forming that opinion. When what one might call his probationary period was over, Alan failed to find a post to satisfy his aspirations. So he turned to financial journalism.'

'That must have been a disappointment to him.'

'Yes. Particularly as Theo and John had careers waiting for them in their family firms.'

'And you also.'

'Well, yes. But he did not measure himself by me.'

'Did you lose track of each other at that stage?'

Yeulett thought for a moment. 'Not when he first went to the *Financial News*. Indeed, he made a point of cultivating all his old acquaintances. I suppose that is part of a journalist's method of working. Certainly he used to come into our office in Throgmorton Street grubbing for information.'

'You did not care much for him, by that stage?'

'After you have repeatedly given a so-called friend information in confidence, only to see it broadcast in a newspaper the next day, it is difficult to hold him in continued esteem.'

'And, of course, he did not last all that long at the *Financial News*.'

Yeulett considered. 'I would not quite put it like that, sergeant. After all, within a matter of a couple of years from joining the paper, he had his own column. One might almost say that, ten years ago, he was a minor City figure in his own right.'

'And then?'

'Well, there were almost as many opinions concerning his going, as there were people gossiping about it. Frankly I refused to listen to it all.'

'You had a feeling of loyalty towards him, then?'

'Loyalty?' Yeulett frowned. 'No, not loyalty. But I was sorry for the man.'

'Did you have any business dealings with him, once he had set up on his own account?'

'No. There was nothing he could do in relation to our business. But I heard a deal of uncharitable remarks about him. It seems that he became involved with outside brokers and questionable share issues.'

'Outside brokers?' Bragg exclaimed. 'I have never heard of them.'

'They are brokers operating outside any recognised trading floor. Peripheral agents who are, by the nature of things, excluded from the established market in shares. They are inevitably drawn to questionable, even shady share issues. You probably know them as bucket shop operators; always on the verge of fraudulent trading.'

'Yes,' Bragg said quietly. 'We have sent a few of them down for a stretch in my time; but they are not all that easy to pin down. And how was Chisnall involved with them?'

'He acted as an independent consultant and, frankly, as publicist for them. He was a talented man, make no mistake. His analysis of a company's prospects was never to be disregarded. He could have made so much more of his life.'

'You sound somewhat sour about the publicist bit,' Bragg said.

'Do I? Well . . . it is the usual story about the thin dividing line between sanity and madness, probity and knavery. It is important that the public should have at their disposal accurate information, balanced judgements on possible investments. But at what stage does an objective and honest opinion become a partial and dishonest exercise in persuasion? I formed the view that Chisnall had allowed himself to be used by share-pushers. And, if the stories of his drinking and gambling were true, one can see what impelled him.'

Bragg laughed. 'You have left us way behind, sir,' he said. 'Can you tell us how you think Chisnall was involved with these people?'

'Not with any precision, because I kept well clear of him in those years. But the essentials are simple enough. The instigators form a company with a large authorised capital. They draw up an appealing scheme of trading, with the emphasis on its long-term profitability. Then they find someone like Chisnall, to issue an apparently independent assessment of its business prospects, which recommends it as a sound investment. After that it is merely a matter of sending out enough circulars, and the shares will be subscribed.'

'And Chisnall was involved in that kind of caper?'

'Such is my belief.'

'Hmn. . . I can see why someone in your position would drop him. . . Tell me, sir, did you get any tickets for Chisnall's play? The one due to have opened tonight, at Gatti's.'

'No, I did not! Had he sent any to me, I would have returned them.'

'But you knew about it?'

'No more than snatches of gossip.'

Bragg paused for a moment, then looked up with a smile. 'I wonder, sir,' he said warmly, 'if you can help us. Somebody was talking about options to us, the other day – not connected with this case. I could not make head nor tail of what he was saying.'

Yeulett raised his eyebrows. 'Well, there is no great difficulty. In the normal course one makes bargains to buy and sell securities at the price then ruling on the trading floor. But that is not the only way of dealing. Obviously, if I had shares that you wanted to possess, then I could sell them to you without the intervention of any intermediary. The price would be a matter for us to settle, and it would be a perfectly legal transfer. Now, it would be possible for us to refine the process further. You might not be able fully to make up your mind as to whether you wanted my shares; but you might be concerned that someone else might pressure me to sell them to him. To secure your position you might propose that I grant you a formal option on my shares. By paying me a comparatively small sum of money, you could acquire the right to buy them from me, at some specified time in the future, for a sum agreed now. That is known as a call option. If you subsequently decide not to call on me to deliver the shares at the agreed price, the bargain lapses and the amount you have paid to me is lost.'

'I see. It's a kind of gamble, then.'

Yeulett smiled. 'No City man would countenance that description for a moment! No, it is a device that is generally used to cover open positions. And, of course, it can work the other way. I can enter into what is called a put option with you. Under such an agreement I would acquire the right to compel you, if I should so choose, to buy my shares at a pre-determined price.'

'And you would pay me for the right.'

'Exactly. Not that I would encourage you to contemplate either course! Options are strictly for the professionals. And even they can fall flat on their faces, if there is an unforeseen movement in the market.'

'Why is that?'

'Well, the true value of the shares is determined by their market quotation at the date your option contract is due to mature. If you have guessed wrongly, you can lose a great deal of money.'

'I see. I think I will go on keeping my savings under the mattress! Tell me, sir, do you still live in Finsbury Circus?'

'Yes. . . All on my own, in a three-storey house!'

'I wonder you haven't moved somewhere smaller.'

'So have I, sergeant. I suppose it is partly inertia, and partly that it would scarcely be worth my while. My father obtained a fifty-year lease at what seems now a ridiculously small annual rent. But the unexpired term is so short, that I would get very little for it. The only attraction I can see is that the new occupier would acquire the right to negotiate for a fresh lease. But nowadays City people want to live out in the country, and travel to the City daily. . . No, I will see my time out there.'

'That sounds sensible. By the way, sir, does the phrase "misled ever so daintily" mean anything to you?'

'In what context?'

'Chisnall put it in the mouth of one of the characters in his play. I wondered if you had any ideas about what it meant.'

Yeulett shook his head. 'No, sergeant. I cannot say that I have ever heard it before.'

'So what do you reckon of Yeulett, then?' Bragg was leaning back in his chair, a wisp of blue smoke curling up from his pipe.

Morton smiled. 'He is scarcely an advertisement for the greatest financial centre in the world. He struck me as an indecisive, petulant man.'

'A real old woman, if you ask me! No wonder his wife left him – peevish bugger. Anyway, we now know he was not sent any tickets to Chisnall's play.'

'Yes. He seems to resent no longer being within the mystic circle of the City; but one can only feel that he is himself largely to blame.'

There was a tap on the door and Catherine Marsden sailed into the room. Her hat was at a jaunty angle, there was exhilaration in her every move. 'I have come to make a formal complaint,' she said with a mischievous smile. 'I have reason to believe that I may have been cheated, and by an official personage of great importance.'

'How is that, miss?' Bragg asked.

'I have been prevailed upon to attend a certain function with this eminent individual, but I have reason to believe that there is no such function. I begin to fear for either my safety or his reliability.'

'Oh, Lord!' Morton exclaimed. 'I am so sorry! I totally forgot. No, Chisnall's play will not open tonight.'

Catherine lifted an eyebrow. 'You will never make a courtier, James,' she said teasingly. 'You are my witness, sergeant! He can reduce me to the status of an afterthought, and then mumble, "Oh, Lord, I forgot." What shall we do with him?'

'At least let me make amends,' Morton said.

'I am not sure. I had almost reconciled myself to an evening at home, with my sampler.'

'Sampler? You? Now I know that I am forgiven! Will dinner at the Savoy be a sufficient penance?'

She cocked her head, considering. 'Very well . . . and I shall bore you by telling you all about my *Lady* interview.'

'I shall not in the least be bored. Did it go well?'

'I think so. At least I had an opportunity to air my views. Whether they wished to hear them may be quite another matter!'

'Ah, then that probably means you are quietly confident. When will you hear the result?'

'Within a few days.'

'Splendid!' Morton said. 'Your life seems suddenly full of excitement. And here we are, sitting like medieval monks, trying to divine the transcendental significance of a phrase like "misled ever so daintily". Truly the future belongs to women!'

' "Misled ever so daintily"?' Catherine repeated. 'What an extraordinary phrase!'

'It was in Chisnall's play. It must have some significance, because he underlined it. A similar underlined phrase was interpreted by Theo Smith as referring to his bank. He denied that it had any significance, but we are not so sure.'

Bragg interposed grumpily. 'When you two have finished, I would like to ask a favour of you, miss.'

'Of course. What is it?'

'You may not be aware of it, but you left a brown paper parcel on an underground train, on Wednesday.'

'I am certainly unaware of it, since I have not travelled by train for weeks!'

'Ah, but it must be yours. It has "Miss Catherine Marsden" on it. "To be called for". We reckon you picked up the parcel from some shop or other, then left it on the train.'

Catherine frowned. 'So I am to be ignored by the constable and exploited by the sergeant. Wherever did the myth about solid and trustworthy policemen come from?'

'It is important, miss,' Bragg said lamely. 'To tell you the truth, we have got ourselves into a bit of a hole.'

'But you had the foresight to ensure that I would be able to get you out of it.' She smiled. 'Well, I accept that it is the citizen's duty to help the police, however disreputable they may be.'

'It is about the size of . . . well, of a book I suppose,' Bragg said. 'Will you pick it up for us, Miss? It will be in the lost property office, at Mansion House station.'

Catherine glanced at her fob watch. 'I might. But since you have at the very least maligned my reputation for reliability, I shall require a big favour from you in exchange.'

'What might that be?'

She smiled. 'I cannot decide at the moment. You will have to credit it to my account.'

'You know you only have to ask,' Bragg said in an injured tone.

'So you say. . . Very well. I take it that neither of you will volunteer to give me a police escort.'

Bragg hesitated. 'Better not, miss. As things stand, it is just an innocent parcel.'

'I see. . . Then I will state my terms. If there is a journalistic scoop in the case, that journalist must be me!'

'You will be editor of *The Lady* by then,' Morton said cheerfully.

She smiled. 'Yes, perhaps I will. Then you will not be able to exploit me!'

Catherine looked in vain for a cab. An empty growler was coming down Old Jewry as she reached the street; but she knew from experience that she would plead in vain for the driver to turn his vehicle in that narrow space. As she emerged into Poultry, a hansom was discharging its passengers, but already a couple was hovering to take their place. Once over that street it was hardly worth taking a cab. Anyway, she was quite enjoying the walk, and she was too excited to want to sit still. Even James was confident that she would become editor of *The Lady*; was apparently looking forward to it. Perhaps it could be the catalyst that would bring the elements of their separate lives together. She skipped down the steps to the underground station and tried to compose her features into a mask of gauche incompetence. She knocked at the door of the lost property office and went in.

'I wonder if you can help me,' she said. 'I think I left a parcel on a train last Wednesday.'

The counter clerk lifted his head from the newspaper he was reading. 'Oh yes?' he said. 'Where were you going?'

'I was going home.'

'And where might home be?'

'Well, Park Lane.'

His brows wrinkled as he looked at her more closely. 'You live in Park Lane?' he asked.

'Yes.'

'And where were you coming from?'

'I. . . I cannot remember.'

'Ah. . . You understand, it helps us if we know what line you were travelling on.'

'I am sorry, I do not know.'

'I see. Would you recognise this parcel?' he asked indulgently.

'Well, it is wrapped in brown paper, and has my name on it.'

'And what might that be?'

'Miss Catherine Marsden. . . Oh, and it had "To be called for" written on it. You see I had called for it, at the shop.' By now Catherine was almost enjoying the role of near-imbecile that he was thrusting on her.

'Well, miss, what size would it be?'

'Oh, the size of a book.'

'Hmn. . . Would that be a big book, a little book, a medium-sized book?'

'I. . . I do not know. You see, I never opened the parcel to find out.'

The man lifted an eyebrow. 'I suppose that makes sense,' he said doubtfully. 'Well, miss, if you will come round behind the counter, we will see if we can find it.' He pushed up the flap and she passed through.

There was rack upon rack of parcels, umbrellas, handbags – even a bicycle. The man walked her slowly down the aisles, turning over the parcels, pulling them out for her inspection even though they patently did not match her description. Then he gave a grunt. 'Here we are, miss,' he exclaimed, holding one out to her. 'This has your name on it . . . a moderately big book, I would say.'

She opened her purse and gave him a shilling. 'I have been such a nuisance to you, I know,' she said sweetly. 'Thank you for being so helpful.'

She walked back to Old Jewry, trying to curb her exuberance of spirit. She felt like smiling at everyone, passing the time of day with complete strangers. She dropped her head demurely as she went into the courtyard of the police headquarters.

'Ah, Miss . . . er. . .' Sir William Sumner was coming out of the doorway. He raised his hat and stood aside as she approached.

'Good morning!' she said brightly, trying to conceal the parcel behind the fullness of her skirt. 'What a lovely day it is!'

'Yes . . . just like India.' He stood irresolute for a moment, then marched off towards the street.

Catherine skipped up the stairs and darted into Bragg's room. 'Goodness me,' she said breathlessly. 'I have had such adventures! I was taken for a half-witted nincompoop by the railway clerk, and now I have just avoided capture by the Commissioner, under full sail for luncheon.'

A look of alarm crossed Bragg's face. 'He didn't see the parcel, I hope.'

'I do not think so. . . Well, here it is.'

'Lock the door, lad.' Bragg placed the parcel on his desk, cut the string and ripped off the brown paper.

'Options?' Catherine exclaimed. 'Since when have you been interested in high finance?'

'You know about them do you, miss?'

'Hardly. I have heard Charles Anstruther mention them, in passing.'

Morton's eyes narrowed, but he said nothing. Bragg turned to the most recent pages, his blunt finger following the entries.

'There is a lot of money to be made in this game, by the look of it,' he murmured. 'Yeulett was right. . . They deal in millions of pounds . . . and not just now and again – day after day they do it.'

He checked and gave a whistle. 'Bloody hell! . . . Sorry, miss. . . Just look at these, lad. They are more in your line than mine. It looks as if they have had it both ways here.'

Morton looked over his shoulder. 'They had closed two contracts on the very morning we . . . the book went missing,' he said.

'Yes. But look at the dates they were made. I don't know what is usual, but, if you look back, a month is a very short time for an option contract. From what Yeulett said, they would be looking further ahead than that. Anyway, you would not expect share values to move much in a month; you might as well make up your mind one way or another at that distance.'

'They certainly made a great deal of profit in those two instances,' Morton said. 'And the interesting thing is that they were contrary deals. The first is a put option with the Hamburg Bank, to have the right to sell it a block of shares in the Imperial Fire Insurance Company.'

'They have the whip hand there, because they need not complete the bargain,' Bragg said. 'Though obviously it paid them to.'

'Yes. They have the whip hand in the second contract also. This is a call option with Bishopsgate Securities for them to acquire a block of shares in Selig Sonnenthal (Bullion Smelters) Ltd.'

'Hmn. . .' Bragg pondered. 'I am uneasy about this, lad. You would think Theo would know what he was doing; but it isn't logical to have two contrary deals, at precisely the same dates, and make money on both of them.'

'Did you say Theo?' Catherine asked in surprise.

'What, miss? Oh yes. . . Theodopolous, that's his name.' He turned back to Morton. 'Both these options had to be exercised on Wednesday the eleventh of July. Both were entered into on the eleventh of June. . . What is the significance of the eleventh of June, lad?'

'None that I am aware of. I cannot see how it could affect our enquiries.'

'Just wait a bit. . . Chisnall had known since the 7th of May that he was not going to last long. I reckon he planned his revenge as long ago as that. You cannot write a play in five minutes, even one as bad as his – and he had to arrange for it to be staged. Yes, it makes a sort of sense.'

'Are you saying that Chisnall's illness and these option contracts are connected?' Morton asked in puzzlement.

'Not directly, no. But I think Chisnall could not resist putting the screws on the people he was going to mention in the play. Perhaps he was trying to blackmail them into giving him money – money to finance their own disgrace. Who knows? But I think our friend Theodopolous got to know of it, and realised what effect it would have on the market.'

'You need not continue with this silly Theodopolous pretence,' Catherine said crossly. 'I am perfectly well aware that you are referring to Theodore Smith!'

'You will never learn discretion, will you, miss?' Bragg chided her. 'There are some things it is best not to acknowledge. You have to learn to protect yourself, as you go through life.'

'Protect myself? You sound like a Salvationist nanny! I have a perfect right to know the truth!'

'You have no right whatever,' Bragg said soberly. 'All you have done is make things more difficult for yourself. Yes, Theo Smith is a suspect in the Chisnall case – as are several other people.'

Catherine's eyes widened in alarm. 'But James, how can you take this so calmly?' she cried. 'Emily is to be married to Reuben in a week!'

'Because he is a good policeman, miss. That's how. I am sorry I involved you in this, but you have always been trustworthy up to now. I thought you were mature enough not to act stupidly.'

'It is not stupid to be concerned about people one is fond of!' Catherine said acidly.

'Maybe not. But there is a higher concern, and it affects you just as much as us – the concern that wrongdoers should be caught and punished, whoever they are.'

'That is typical of a priggish, self-satisfied male!' Catherine cried. 'We are talking about people's whole lives!'

'Yes . . . starting with Chisnall's, worthless as it seems to have been. Now, if you want to go on helping, put your mind to this. If not, you had best go now.'

Catherine glared at him. 'That book before you shows that I have every right to stay,' she said fiercely.

'Right.' Bragg suddenly grinned. 'Only keep your voice down. The Commissioner would have a blue fit, if he found out we have it! Now, where were we?'

'You were just speculating about Theo's reaction, if he had learned about Chisnall's play,' Morton said. 'I imagine the first thought of any City man would be: "How is this going to affect the market?" And his second would be: "How can I make money out of the situation?"'

'That seems fair. Would you agree, miss?'

'Yes,' Catherine said reluctantly. 'And he would no doubt anticipate what did in fact happen, that the market would drop like a stone.'

'It is not quite so simple as that,' Morton said. 'Of these two bargains, Smith's made money on one because the value of the shares dropped, but on the other because their value rose.'

'Rose?' she echoed. 'But Charles Anstruther said absolutely everything fell.'

Morton stared at the ceiling. 'Then at least we can demonstrate that he is not infallible!'

'If he made money both ways – and in such big amounts – I reckon he knew something nobody else in the market knew,' Bragg said soberly. 'If I were you, lad, I would go along to Lloyd's and find out if you can insure against the cancellation of a wedding.'

That afternoon Bragg and Morton took a train to St Albans, where Cotton's complainant in the electric lamp bulb case lived. The house was near to the abbey. It was an ancient, rambling building of old mellow stone, surrounded by lawns and clipped yew hedges. No shortage of money there, Bragg thought. But there was a lively sense of its value, to react so quickly when the Aurora interim dividend was passed. Morton rang the bell. After some moments the door was opened by a slim young maid, in starched apron and cap.

'Is Major Boyes in?' he asked.

'He was a few moments ago, sir. I will go and see. Who is it wants him?'

'Just tell him the City of London police,' Bragg said gruffly.

Her eyes widened. 'Ooh!' she exclaimed, then turned and scuttled out of sight.

They waited in growing impatience for some minutes. Then a short, erect man with close-cropped grey hair came striding towards them from the side of the house.

'Sorry! I was dead-heading the roses,' he said in a clipped voice. 'Come round the back, and I will get Elsie to bring us beer.'

He led them into a formal rose-garden, where curved beds separated by narrow stretches of lawn made an elaborate circular display. Beside it there was a gravelled area, with a table and benches. The major gestured towards them and disappeared into the house. 'I expect you miss this sort of thing, lad, living in London,' Bragg remarked.

'Indeed I do! Particularly so at the moment, when it is so hot, and London reeks of horse droppings and stale urine. I am sure that we were not meant to live like bees in a hive.'

'It's all right for nobs like you,' Bragg retorted. 'For us country clods, life is all piss and muck, winter and summer.'

'Ah! But in the country it smells sweet!'

Major Boyes emerged from the house followed by the young maid. She placed a tray of foaming tankards on the table, bobbed a curtsy and was gone.

Boyes drank deeply from his tankard, then wiped the foam from his moustache with the back of his hand. 'I take it that you have come about Aurora Electric,' he said.

'That is correct, sir.'

'Hmn. . . Took your time, didn't you?'

Bragg was taken aback. Yet he had certainly seen no note of an interview with Boyes on the file. 'Oh, we have not been inactive, sir. Far from it,' he said unctuously. 'There seemed little point in coming to see you, before we had acquainted ourselves with the background to your complaint.'

'So what are you doing about it?'

'I can tell you, sir, that in our opinion you do have grounds for concern.'

'What the devil are you talking about?' Boyes barked. 'I know damn well there is something wrong. The whole thing was a hocus-pocus from the start!'

'But you did buy shares in it,' Bragg said quietly.

'Yes, well. . . I was taken in, and that's a fact. But I was not the only one. Not that it is any comfort.'

'Did you invest a great deal, sir?' Bragg asked.

Boyes glared at him. 'It all depends on how you define it. I put in less than would break me, but more than I could afford to lose.'

'How did you hear of Aurora, sir?'

The major frowned. 'Why, I got an article through the post, back in March – in a kind of financial circular. It seemed to be saying the Aurora was a damned good bet.'

'Did you send for the circular?'

'No, I did not! I normally keep my money in the bank.'

'How do you think the sender got your name?'

'Damned if I know. The Army List, probably. Old Chukka Penbury, down the road, got one as well. He is in it for twice as much as me!'

'In Aurora?'

'In the shit, as like as not! What the devil is happening?'

'The situation is not fully resolved, sir. But it looks at the moment as if the promoters of the company were too optimistic.'

'Optimistic?' Boyes echoed wrathfully. 'What the devil do you mean?'

'I would prefer not to be more precise than that, sir,' Bragg said stolidly. 'We are doing all we can to retrieve the position. . . Did you consult your stockbroker before making the investment?'

'I do not have a stockbroker as such. As I told you, the bank looks after my affairs. When I received the circular, I popped down to see the bank wallah. He said it looked interesting, and might be worth a flutter. I said he could go ahead, so he subscribed for the shares on my behalf.'

'And how much are you in for?'

'Five hundred pounds – which was virtually all my free cash. Good God! I could have repaired the abbey tower for that!'

'Presumably you got a share certificate.'

Boyes snorted. 'Oh, yes. I got one all right. Very impressive it looked, too. Now it seems it is worth damn all! I think I will frame it, and hang it in the privy!'

The following morning saw Bragg walking under leaden skies towards the Temple. He ought to have brought his top-coat, he thought, but the very idea of carrying it made him sweat. He would have liked to undo his collar stud. The tie could keep the collar in place, after a fashion, and it did not rub your neck so much. But it did look a bit of a mess, and Sir Rufus would give him stick about it.

Behind the gothic pinnacles of the new law courts, the sky had turned a deep violet. The storm would not be long in coming. He turned into the Temple and walked round its green lawns, past the Temple church and into Pump Court, where Sir Rufus Stone had his chambers. Since it was a Saturday morning, the corridor outside the clerk's room was virtually deserted. One or two pupil barristers huddled by a window, smoking furtively. A personage in a silk gown came billowing down the corridor, looking neither to right nor to left, imperious in the conviction of his own infallibility. The pupils hid their cigarettes behind their backs, but he took no heed of them. He marched into the clerk's room, and Bragg heard his hectoring voice demanding attention. Then he emerged and stalked back down the corridor.

Bragg went into the clerk's room. 'Sir Rufus sent for me,' he said. 'Is he in yet?'

The clerk gave a grimace. 'Oh, yes. He is in all right. . . I cannot think what has got into everyone, shouting and arguing. The sooner it rains the better!'

'Has he anyone with him?'

'No. He came in to work on a complicated brief. You will do none of us any favours, if you cross him.'

Bragg went along the corridor, knocked on Sir Rufus's door and went quietly in. The coroner raised a hand to acknowledge his presence, then went on reading. When he reached the final page of his brief he gave a grunt of satisfaction and looked up.

'That one is as good as in the bag, is it, sir?' Bragg asked.

'There is no certitude in these matters, Bragg,' Sir Rufus said expansively. 'No certitude until judgement has been delivered. However, it promises to be interesting. . . And why are you afflicting me with your presence?'

'You sent for me, sir.'

'Ah yes.' The coroner rose from his desk, and took up his favourite pose in front of the empty fireplace. He grasped the lapel of his coat in his left hand, and threw back his leonine head. 'The Chisnall case, Bragg,' he declaimed. 'It is now almost two weeks since the wretched man was murdered, and you appear to have done nothing!'

'I would hardly say that, sir,' Bragg said quietly.

Sir Rufus brushed aside his interruption. 'I have an inquest open; adjourned *sine die*. But that does not mean it can remain so at your pleasure. . . I see that you do not have your acolyte with you. Is there any significance in that?'

'As you know, sir, Constable Morton is supposed to be something special in the cricket line,' Bragg said sourly. 'Because he condescends to come down to my level in his working life, he has to have some official recompense. He will be on his way to Chelmsford now, with the cricket team of the Blackheath club.'

'And perfectly reasonable too,' Sir Rufus said sharply. 'We shall need him for the winter tour of Australia. There are other things in life beside grubbing around for criminals, you know. You should be proud to have him! Now stop wasting my time, it is far too valuable.'

'We are on the telephone system, you know, sir. You could easily have talked to me on it. That would have saved us both time.'

'Nonsense, Bragg! I prefer to see the person I am addressing. If they are shifty-eyed and evasive, I learn something about them – and you are frequently both.'

'If it is only the inquest that concerns you, sir, why not bring in a verdict of person or persons unknown? We could all relax then.'

'Relax? What a monstrous suggestion! This is not a Sunday school outing, it is a murder case – and a particularly repellent one. No, Bragg. I want results! I want the murderer named!'

'You may regret it, sir,' Bragg said pointedly.

'Regret it? . . . Why? What is the case about?'

Bragg mused. 'Failure, I would say.'

'Hah! When has that been an excuse for murder? I have known failure myself, Bragg. But when I was not awarded the oratory prize, at Oxford, I did not go around wreaking vengeance on all and sundry!'

'You have hit the nail on the head though, sir. It was a warped sort of vengeance, we think.'

'Then cease proceeding by hint and innuendo, and tell me what you suspect.'

'Names and all, sir?'

'Indeed, Bragg! In this noble country of ours the rich and the poor, the great and the powerful, bend the knee alike before the majesty of the law.'

'Yes, sir.'

'Then proceed.'

'I think it all started over thirty years ago,' Bragg began slowly, 'when Chisnall left school. His father seems not to have had a lot of money; but he had enough influence to get his son started on a City career. The parents went to live in Bristol, so Chisnall was on his own in London. He took lodgings in Monkwell Street.'

'Where exactly is that? I do not recognise the name.'

'It's in the City. Behind the Barbers' Hall.'

'I see.'

'Chisnall seems to have been a very attractive person, outgoing and humorous; and he soon made friends. Before long two other young men joined him in his diggings, John Teverson and Theodore Smith.'

'Teverson? I seem to know that name.'

'The family are stockbrokers in Tokenhouse Yard, sir. As for Theodore Smith, he is now the principal of Smith Payne & Smith's, the bankers in Lombard Street.'

'Ah.' The coroner's eyes narrowed. 'Are you saying that these two gentlemen are under suspicion of having committed this diabolical crime?'

'Among others, yes. I do not know if you have discussed the case in any great depth with the pathologist, but Dr Burney says that Chisnall had a very thin skull. It would have been quite possible for those injuries to have been inflicted by a woman.'

'Good God! You are surely not suggesting . . .'

'It would be unwise at this stage to rule anything out, sir; particularly as a woman is involved.'

Sir Rufus threw back his head. 'Knowing your devious methods as I do, Bragg,' he declaimed, 'you now anticipate that I shall wish to resile from the forthright position I have taken. But you are wrong. I am not susceptible to the potency of rank, or the influence of wealth. I am answerable to the realm – in the person of our gracious Queen – and above her to my own conscience!'

'Yes, sir.'

'Well, go on. You were saying that a woman is involved.'

'Her name was Adelaide Hollyer; the daughter of a wealthy family of merchants. She had just come out in society, was doing the rounds of the parties and such. She met The Three Musketeers there.'

'Three Musketeers? Good God! This becomes more of a fairy story by the minute.'

Bragg smiled. 'Yes, it does seem silly. But these young men became known as The Three Musketeers to the society hostesses, and they seem to have played up to it to some extent. Anyway, Miss Hollyer formed an attachment to Chisnall . . . a close attachment.'

'There is no need to be coy, man,' Sir Rufus said irritably. 'If she became his mistress, then out with it!'

'That would not quite be right. From her letters we – '

'Letters?' the coroner interrupted. 'What letters? Why was I not told of them?'

Bragg looked at him gravely. 'Since you are an important public figure, sir, and inevitably come up against these people on normal society occasions, I hardly feel that you would want to be made aware of details that may not be strictly relevant to our investigation.'

Sir Rufus glared at him. 'If you are attempting to deceive me, Bragg, there will be retribution!'

'Of course I am not, sir. It would be foolish to try. But I suggest that, for the moment, you should draw the line at actually reading the letters. In fact, because of the present situation, I have not allowed Constable Morton to read more than two.'

'Damn you, Bragg!' the coroner burst out. 'Stop talking in riddles!'

'Adelaide sent about forty letters to Chisnall over the years – very warm, very explicit letters.'

'Had her parents stopped their meeting?'

'Oh no. They used to meet regularly, at balls and such. It seems they used to escape up to the bedrooms, for a bit of –'

'I can imagine,' Sir Rufus interrupted. 'You have no need to spell it out!'

'Very well, sir. . . Then, when she got home she would write a letter to him, saying how much she had enjoyed it, and what they might try next time.'

The coroner frowned incredulously. 'I knew that there were women like that, of course,' he said. 'But to find them in that circle . . .'

'Exactly, sir. I found it a bit of a shaker. Anyway, this affair went on for around three years, and then it stopped. But Chisnall kept every line she wrote.'

'And why did the correspondence terminate? Because she grew tired of him?'

'No, for I don't believe she did. It was worse than that. She decided it would be safer if she married someone richer.'

'Hmm. . . Well, that is hardly surprising, if he was in straitened circumstances.'

'Maybe. Where I come from, they have a saying that the devil always shits on the biggest heap. Adelaide Hollyer is now Mrs Theodore Smith.'

'Great heavens! I understand your reticence, Bragg.'

'Yes, sir. There is evidence that, over the years, Chisnall might have been blackmailing both of them. Adelaide has admitted it. And both she and Theo are capable of murdering him. They would swat him like a pestering fly.'

Sir Rufus drew himself up to his full height. 'Well, I applaud your caution, Bragg,' he said. 'But I assure you that my attitude is unchanged. You have my total support in this investigation, whoever the malefactors might prove to be!'

10

Bragg was already at his desk when Morton came in the following Monday morning.

'Did you have a good game of pat-ball on Saturday?' he asked grudgingly.

Morton smiled cheerfully. 'In fact, sir, bat was never laid to ball. The Chelmsford opening pair were just walking to the wicket – in Stygian gloom, I might add – when the heavens opened and deluged the ground! Such spectators as there were promptly departed. We sat in the pavilion for an hour, by which time the wicket was under water, then we came home.'

'So it was a total waste of time?'

'I could never stigmatise our great national game in those terms, sir!'

'No, I bet you couldn't. According to Sir Rufus, they will be asking for you to take four months off, to go to Australia and see if you can beat their team at watching the rain!'

'I hope to have that honour! . . . And is the coroner satisfied with our progress?' Morton asked slyly.

Bragg glowered at him. 'He is intent on stringing up the murderer, if it was Queen Victoria herself! Right, lad. I am going out for a bit. I want you to look through Inspector Cotton's Aurora file again; make a summary of all the information we have. We might try to twist a few tails after lunch.'

He picked up his Gladstone bag and sauntered out into Old Jewry. The weekend storm had cleared away the stifling, humid weather. There were still a few ragged clouds in the sky, but there was a pleasant breeze blowing up-river from the east. It was a day on which to be optimistic. He waited with the crowd at the Bank crossing, until a gap appeared in the clattering stream of hay-carts, hansoms and vans, then strode over to Lombard Street. He went into the great hall of Smith's bank, and crossed over to a grille in the counter.

'I would like to see Mr Reuben Smith,' he said quietly.

The clerk looked at him cautiously. 'You are the policeman who came last week, are you not?' he asked.

'That's right, son. Just go and tell him I am here.'

The young man locked up his cash-drawer and disappeared. Bragg stood back and gazed sourly at the mosaics round the dome, then he felt a touch on his arm.

'Sergeant Bragg, is it not?'

Reuben Smith was of medium height, well-built and with dark good looks. 'I understand that you wish to see me,' he said.

'That is so, sir.'

'Then, come to my monastic cell!'

He led the way to a tiny room, off the back corridor that Bragg and Morton had burst along a week before. The office held a small desk and chair, a few moralistic pictures on the wall and a chair for a visitor. Opposite the window stood a large wooden press. Through the half-open door Bragg could see the spines of great ledgers.

Bragg took the chair in front of the desk. 'You are to be married this Saturday,' he said soberly.

'Indeed! I understand that you have been invited to the ceremony, sir.'

'Yes.'

'Then, may I say that I am happy it should be so, despite our recent contretemps!' Reuben had the confidence and affability of someone whose future had been secure since his first breath. Bragg was tempted to chop him down to size, but there was little point.

'I have come to see you,' he said, 'because I believe that your father has no knowledge of what I wish to discuss.'

'I see.' Reuben's look was wary.

'I am told that your mother recently borrowed a large sum of money from you.'

Reuben was startled. 'Well . . . yes, that is so.'

'How much was it?'

'One thousand pounds.'

'And when did you lend it to her?'

Reuben gazed up at the ceiling. 'It was early last month.' He reached out and flipped back through his diary. 'Yes, it was on Tuesday the fifth of June.'

'When did she tell you she needed the money?'

'On the previous day.'

'Did she say why she needed it?'

Reuben frowned. 'No. Nor did I enquire why. She has her own funds, she is not accountable to me.'

'But the trouble was, she didn't have that amount of pocket-money around,' Bragg said sardonically.

'No. My father has placed virtually all her money in term investments, and none was due to mature at that precise time.'

'Did she say why she had approached you, rather than your father?'

'No. I assumed it was for some purpose that she did not yet wish him to be aware of – a present, perhaps.'

'Quite a present – a thousand quid's worth!'

Reuben shrugged. 'Anyway, it was none of my business.'

'All the same, you saw she got it.'

'I advanced one thousand pounds from my own funds, and recouped the money when one of her bonds matured at the end of June.'

'So you were not out of pocket for long?'

A sneer touched Reuben's lips, and he did not reply.

'You know,' Bragg said ruminatively, 'I cannot believe that she would come up to you and say, all offhand, "Get me a thousand pounds, will you, Reuben?' and you give it her without even a mention of why.'

'Can you give me any reason why I need to be concerned about what you believe?' Reuben said coolly.

'Well, yes. You see, it doesn't chime with what your mother told us. So I know that you were lying just now.'

'You have been to see my mother?' Reuben exclaimed angrily.

'Oh yes. We have no time for games about propriety. What did she say, when she asked you for it?'

Reuben took a deep breath, and exhaled in a petulant sigh. 'She said that she needed it urgently, to make a payment.'

'What kind of payment?'

'She did not say precisely – but I gathered that it was to some acquaintance of my father.'

'Did she say why she was having to make a payment of that size, to such a person?'

Reuben hesitated. 'She was being badgered by some disreputable man from the past. She was afraid that, were the payment not made, some attempt might be made to spoil my wedding.'

'Blackmail, then?'

Reuben shrugged. 'If you say so. . . I suppose that even someone as upright and strait-laced as my father must accumulate enemies during the course of his career.'

'You think it was something he did in the past that gave the blackmailer his leverage?'

'Not in those terms, sergeant. I cannot think that my father would ever have done anything dishonest. But some deals are exceedingly complicated and might, to a partial comprehension, perhaps appear dubious. My understanding of my mother's anxiety was that an untruthful assertion would be disseminated just before my marriage, leaving no time to rebut it. To her, a thousand pounds seemed a small price to pay to avert it.'

'I see. . . And why was the approach made to your mother, instead of to Theo himself?'

'Oh, my father would never bow to such a demand. Were he ever to do so, there would be no end to it.'

'And the rumour would have ruined your wedding?'

'So my mother believed, at any rate.'

'I see. So you handed her an envelope with a thousand pounds inside, and that was the last you saw of it?'

Reuben dropped his head. 'Not quite, sergeant. She asked me to deliver the envelope on her behalf.'

'Where did you take it?'

'To a house in Petticoat Square – number seven.'

'Did you see anyone?'

'No. I pushed it through the letter-box and left.'

'And when was this?'

'On the evening of Tuesday the fifth of June.'

'Did she write any name on the envelope?'

Reuben looked challengingly at Bragg. 'No. But I subsequently became aware that the occupier of the house was a Mr Alan Chisnall.'

'Who was subsequently battered to death. . . Can you tell me, sir, where you were around six o'clock on the evening of Monday the second of July?'

Reuben's eyes narrowed. 'I see that I have already been too frank with you, sergeant. I shall answer no more of your questions, unless I have a lawyer present.'

Bragg got to his feet. 'Very well, sir,' he said amiably. 'Thank you for being so helpful.'

He went back into the main banking-hall, and almost bumped into Theo Smith.

'Do you always have to come in through the rear door, sergeant?' Theo asked pettishly.

Bragg smiled. 'I would have thought you would prefer it that way, sir,' he said. 'Can you spare me a few minutes?'

Theo frowned. 'Very well,' he said. 'If you will excuse me for a moment.' He went over to the man with the pince-nez and gave him a folder. Then he beckoned to Bragg and went into his office.

Bragg followed him and put his Gladstone bag on the desk. 'I understand that you saw fit to accuse me of stealing your options book,' he said brusquely.

Theo looked up at the policeman towering above him. 'I did,' he said spiritedly. 'And I have no reason to regret that action.'

'I don't know about that,' Bragg said. 'To me it seems unwise in retrospect. You see, it has only served to draw our attention to the book. If you had let us examine it in our amateurish way, you might have been better off.'

'I have not the faintest idea of what you are referring to.'

'After you made all that fuss, we thought we ought to make an effort to find it. It seemed that it could not be still here, or your staff would think there was something odd going on. And, in the circumstances, it was not likely that you would take it home. Still we did our best. . . And do you know where it turned up? In a railway lost property office!'

'Lost property?' Theo exclaimed.

'Yes. Safe as a bank, when you come to think of it, sir. . . And I expect a banker would think of it.'

'Absolute rubbish, sergeant! You took it, as well you know!'

Bragg sighed tolerantly. 'I was hoping that you would not take that line, sir,' he said. 'There is usually only one reason for a suspect to start blackguarding the police. And we are trying hard to keep an open mind.'

He opened his bag and took out the options book. 'Now, if you will look at the two bargains that matured on the eleventh of July, you may understand why we think you wanted it safely out of the way before we could see it.'

Theo frowned irritably and took the book. He flicked through the pages quickly.

'I understand that you personally do all the options business, sir,' Bragg remarked.

Theo looked up. 'That is so,' he said. 'As for the contracts you refer to, I see nothing whatever requiring explanation.'

'Well, you will appreciate that we are not by any stretch of the imagination experts in these things; but it seemed very odd that, in the normal course, you could make money both ways – by a put option and a call option – over precisely the same period.'

Theo looked down at the page. 'Are you referring to the Imperial Fire and the Sonnenthal contracts?' he asked.

'Those are the two, sir.'

'And what is suspicious about them?'

'Well, they were both entered into on the same day, to mature in a month. That seemed a rather short length of time, compared to other options contracts you had entered into.'

'The term depends on market conditions, and one's judgement on likely movements,' Theo said tersely.

'Yes. . . The trouble is, you seem to have been able to back it both ways. I mean, one contract is to sell, the other is to purchase, yet you make a fortune on each. And it seemed to us they were out of the general run.'

'Not a bit of it! Any self-respecting bank man should be able to make a profit, when the market is on the slide.' Theo glanced down at the book again.

'Particularly when you have seen that you get the whip hand in each.'

'I do not understand your point, sergeant.'

'The bargain in the Imperial shares was a put option, and the smelting company was a call option.'

'Ah, I see your problem. In fact there is nothing in the point. The Hamburg Bank initially proposed a call option, but I preferred a put option. I always wish to retain the initiative in a bargain, even if it means paying a consideration for the option instead of receiving it.'

'Yes. . . You will have to bear with me,' Bragg said earnestly. 'I soon get out of my depth with money, as you can imagine. But what strikes me as queer is that in one case you are buying, in another case you are selling, yet you manage to make a thumping profit on both.'

Theo smiled. 'I am sure that such would be the view of the generally intelligent yet uninstructed public. Probably one has to be an insider to fully understand the workings of the stock market.'

'I am willing to be instructed, sir.'

Theo sighed. 'Very well. You must understand that the market value of the shares of a company only bears a loose relationship to the actual asset value of the concern. There is an element of sentiment involved – optimism or pessimism regarding the company's future, confidence or doubt about the ability of its managers. That is why even an unsubstantiated rumour can bring the shares of a company clattering down.'

'I can understand that, sir.'

'Well, the same principle operates in relation to the market as a whole. There can be a loss of confidence in shares as a desirable form of investment. In such a situation the whole market can collapse.'

'That is precisely the point I am making,' Bragg said in a puzzled voice. 'And yet you can still make money.'

Theo smiled. 'It is not magic, sergeant, but good judgement. If you think for a moment, you will realise that a great part of any insurance company's reserves are invested in shares. So when there is a general loss of confidence in shares, there will be an even greater reluctance to hold the shares of insurance companies.'

'I see. So the bargain you made with the Hamburg Bank meant that you could compel them to buy the Fire Insurance shares at a price that was a great deal more than you could have sold them for in the market, at that time.'

'Exactly, sergeant.' Theo gave a self-satisfied smirk. 'The difference was of the order of twenty per cent, as I remember it.'

'Yes. . . But the smelting company went the other way. How do you explain that?'

'There is no difficulty, sergeant. Where there is a loss of confidence in shares generally, people want to hold their funds in something as unexciting and immutable as gold. Selig Sonnenthal are gold bullion smelters. There will be a great surge in their activities. For the next year or so, their profits will increase markedly – as will those of any concern involved in gold bullion.'

'So you are buying shares that are really worth more because of the crash?'

'That is true. . . And you make a valid point, sergeant. The profit shown on the Fire Insurance shares derives from the difference between the option price and the purchase price long ago. It has nothing to do with the difference between the option price and the current market.'

'It is still a real profit.'

'Yes. But one we would have lost, had it not been for the option contract.'

'And what about the profit on the bullion smelting shares?'

'It is notional and fortuitous. It could be wiped out overnight, if confidence in general shares revived. . . I really ought to be thinking of a put option to get rid of them at today's value!'

Bragg pondered awhile then: 'I think I have got all that straight, sir,' he said. 'But you still have not explained how you got it right, and no one else did. It seems as if you knew the market was going to drop.'

'I would have been the only person in the City, in that event!'

'Yes. But you see, I think that you were. I have talked to a lot of people, you understand, and you are the only one coming out of the crash smiling.'

'I would certainly not say that we are smiling. But we may have been less badly affected than others.'

'Yes. And I know why. It is generally believed that the crash was brought about by fear of what Chisnall was going to make public in his play. Even the Prime Minister cried off going to the Guildhall banquet, in case his name was tarnished.'

'I think that was merely a political gesture,' Theo interjected.

'Everybody else was caught on the hop,' Bragg went on. 'Everybody but Smith's bank. And that was because you knew in advance the trouble Chisnall's play would cause.'

'Rubbish, sergeant!'

'Oh, no. Chisnall was a methodical man, and he kept the vital papers well away from his house. We know, you see, who he was blackmailing, how much he got from each. We have an embarrassment of riches, as they say. But we think that only one of his victims murdered him. . . I reckon the person who goes on denying everything to the bitter end will swing for it.'

An unhealthy pallor had spread across Theo's face. 'So you have been amusing yourself at my expense,' he said with an edge of contempt in his voice.

'How long had he been blackmailing you, sir?'

'Blackmail? It was hardly that, at first – merely an urgent request for a loan that we both knew would never be repaid.'

'And later?'

'Why yes, there were threats of disclosures. . . Nothing relating to my business dealings. . . But some years ago, Chisnall and I went on a boating holiday. As a charitable gesture we took some unfortunate boys from the East End. . . There were photographs. No doubt you have seen them. I assure you, sergeant, that there was nothing in it – they merely look, well, indecent. But I could not run the risk of their being handed around the City. So I paid up – over and over again. . .'

'And when did you kick against the pricks, sir?'

Theo looked up dazedly. 'It was in the spring, I suppose. I became irritated beyond bearing at being manipulated by such a disreputable individual. I told him that by the autumn he must find another way of life. I said that unless he did so, I would see that he was put out of harm's way... It was a foolish threat, and one that I would have been unable to carry out, but I was desperate. I thought that, once Reuben was safely married, I could retire from the bank and Chisnall would then be effectively powerless. Then he told me that he was going to write a play, that nothing I could do would prevent it.'

'But we have read the play. It said nothing about going with little boys.'

'Oh?' Theo looked at him, relief flooding over his face. 'Thank God for that! So he was merely torturing me, after all!'

'No. I would not say that, sir. As you know, there was the line about integrity being optional in Smith's bank. And here you are, making a killing out of option contracts just because Chisnall's play has brought the market crashing down.'

'I may have mentioned it to him,' Theo muttered. 'One does one's best to distract such people from their devilish concerns.'

Bragg got to his feet. 'It won't do, will it, sir? You knew the market was going to drop like a stone, when you made those option contracts in June. Nobody had heard anything about Chisnall's play then.'

Theo looked up wearily. 'Chisnall had said that he would make public my alleged peccadilloes before my son's wedding. Believe you me, that would have shaken the market just as much as any play!'

Bragg looked down contemptuously. 'I reckon you would try and make a shilling out of the rape of your own mother,' he said. 'But I can well understand why you beat him to death.'

'I did not!' Theo shouted, his face flushed. 'Had I been capable of that, I would have done it years and years ago!'

'It is not that I mind a man lying to us,' Bragg said, laying the flaming match across the bowl of his pipe. 'In a sense we rely on them twisting the facts, so that we can catch them out.' He puffed until the air was blue with smoke around him, then grunted with satisfaction. 'No, it's the self-righteous airs they put on that get up my nose. Old Theo has the brass neck to march over here, creating a fuss, and all the time he is being blackmailed!'

'In fact, he sent his solicitor to complain,' Morton remarked.

'That's even worse! All high and mighty; cannot spare the time to complain himself. But you know what it is, lad. If he had come himself, we would have taken him apart; that was what he was afraid of.'

'You still have not told me what hold Chisnall had over him, sir.'

'Best not to know, since you still might be family... Some people might think it was nothing, shrug their shoulders at it. I expect you would. But the City has its own rules. I expect most of them are no different from Theo, by the way they go on. But everybody has to seem pure as the driven snow, or they are kicked out. This precious reputation of the City has to be preserved, whoever suffers.'

'I still think that it might be useful to show the play to my friend Pargiter – in the strictest confidence. He could well pick up allusions to other City luminaries, which have gone over our heads.'

Bragg pondered. 'No, best not,' he said at length. 'That way a lot of people might be harmed who had nothing to do with Chisnall's death. We will stay with the red underlinings.'

Morton smiled. 'I had a fantasy, thinking about it last night, of a line of Chisnall's victims queuing up for their turn with the poker; each allowed one blow... I am sure that Sherlock Holmes would have been able to deduce, from a fragment of rare tobacco ash, which of them actually struck the fatal blow!'

'Huh! We'll leave that rubbish to the magazines... No, I think the people involved have been close to Chisnall all along.'

'Our Musketeers?'

'And their nearest and dearest. If you are not careful, three of them will have married into your own family.'

'Three of them?'

'Oh yes. Did I not tell you? Adelaide said that she took the thousand pounds to Chisnall's house herself. But Reuben just told me that he took it. It's much more likely, if you think about it. Adelaide would never set foot in Petticoat Square. If she had, somebody would have remembered her.'

'I see. Certainly Reuben will not attempt to produce witnesses as to his whereabouts at the time of the murder,' Morton said.

'Dear Lord! And the wedding is in five days' time!'

'Then we had better get off our arses. Have you got all the Aurora stuff sorted out?'

'I think that I have managed to decipher the notes.'

'Anything interesting?'

'Inspector Cotton interviewed the chairman of the board, a certain Major-General George Hamilton-White. He said the underlying cause of insolvency was that the public did not subscribe for enough shares.'

'I would have thought that was obvious!'

'The company bought its factory and plant, but there was very little money left over to provide working capital. He said that some electric lamp bulbs were produced, but they had not been marketed when the money ran out. I should remind you that my information is derived from some scrappy and occasionally cryptic jottings.'

'Cotton is like that,' Bragg said darkly. 'He can play it either way then. What about Aurora's bankers? Would they not support the company?'

'It seems that Hamilton-White was himself involved, with the manager Binswanger, in discussions with several banks about further finance. At one point prospects seemed bright; then Binswanger disappeared and the whole project collapsed.'

'Stinks a bit, doesn't it? Why don't we go and see the liquidator of the company? He should have the facts at his fingertips.'

Morton referred to his notes. 'He is an accountant; Frederick Wormold of Francis Child & Co.'

'Ah! Is the child with Francis, or Francis with child, do you think?' Bragg said with ponderous mirth.

Morton made a grimace. 'Their office is in Poultry.'

'Just around the corner. Right, let us pop in and see this Mr Wormold.'

In fact it was not an easy matter. After labouring up a steep flight of stairs, to offices over a shop, they were told that Wormold was in conference. On being informed that the meeting was not expected to last much longer, Bragg elected to wait. They were shown into a small room, with bentwood chairs and lino on the floor. Dusty curtains were gathered into uneven swags at the window, a faded etching of a stag at bay hung over the empty fireplace. Bragg strode over to the window and stared grimly out. Morton picked up a copy of that day's *Financial News* and glanced through it. All was still gloom in the City, it appeared. The efforts of the Lord Mayor to placate the Prime Minister and rescue the Guildhall banquet seemed to have failed.

The door opened and a youth's pimply face peered in. 'Mr Wormold will see you now,' he said.

They followed him up a further flight of stairs to a room at the back of the building. A slight, prematurely bald man rose from his desk as they entered.

'Good afternoon, gentlemen,' he said with a smile. 'I am Wormold. I gather that you are police officers.'

'Yes, sir. I am Sergeant Bragg and this is Constable Morton. I wonder if you can help us.'

'If I can, I will,' Wormold said, gesturing them to chairs.

'I understand that you are the liquidator of Aurora Electric Lighting Company Limited.'

'That is so.'

'Can you tell me when it was put into liquidation?'

Wormold went over to the window-sill and brought a bundle of files to his desk. He opened one. 'On the fifteenth of June, sergeant,' he said.

'Did the court order its liquidation?'

'No, it was voluntary – by special resolution of its members.'

'But there have to be two general meetings to pass a special resolution,' Morton said.

'Indeed.' Wormold consulted his file again. 'The first took place on the first of June, the second on the fifteenth.'

'Am I right in thinking', Bragg interposed, 'that the shares were only issued in March?'

'It was before that, I think.' The bald head bobbed from one folder to another. 'Ah! Here is the summary I was looking for,' Wormold said triumphantly. 'The company was registered in November 'ninety-three. I see that some shares were issued in January of this year – to get a stock exchange quotation presumably.'

'So there would be some dealing at that stage?' Bragg asked.

Wormold looked at him quizzically. 'Presumably so,' he said.

'And, when was the bulk of the shares issued?'

'In March, sergeant.'

'On the back of the quotation, I suppose.'

Wormold frowned. 'I am not quite sure what you are implying,' he said with an edge to his voice.

'Aurora seems to have followed a pattern we are familiar with, sir. First a limited issue of shares, which are manipulated on the Stock Exchange by sham deals to put the price up. Then comes a big issue, which is highly recommended in dubious financial news-sheets and circulars. The money floods in from the gullible public, then suddenly it has vanished, and the company is in liquidation.'

Wormold had flushed to the top of his shining pate. 'I am sure that is an altogether unwarranted slur on the promoters of the company,' he said angrily. 'If you took the trouble to make enquiries, instead of wild assumptions, you would see that the money was spent on freehold factory premises, and machinery. There is no question of a penny's having been siphoned off illicitly.'

'I see,' Bragg said airily. 'Can you tell me anything about this Binswanger man?'

With a frown Wormold turned the pages of his file. 'He was a Dutch citizen, who had been engaged in employment at the Philips Incandescent Lamp works in Eindhoven.'

'Yes, we know that. Did you ever meet him?'

'No. There was never any occasion to do so. I had been appointed auditor to the company, but that did not bring me into contact with the employees.'

'And in June you were appointed its liquidator. . . Would you like to comment on the propriety of that, sir? Aurora was a publicly quoted company, after all.'

Wormold almost bounced out of his chair with indignation. 'I trust that you are not impugning the integrity of Francis Child & Co.,' he cried. 'I would have you know that we act for some of the most prestigious concerns in London!'

'And you thought it quite proper to be both Aurora's auditors and their liquidators, did you?' Bragg asked mildly.

'Indeed! It is not as if any trading activities had taken place!'

'No.' Bragg allowed a pause to develop, then: 'Did you ever meet the promoters?' he asked.

'Of course. I had several meetings with Major-General Hamilton-White – who is a very distinguished soldier, as you no doubt know.'

'Anyone else?'

'There was a Mr Burns at one of the meetings, but he contributed very little to the discussion.'

'Could you jot the general's address down for me, please?'

Wormold scribbled briefly on a piece of paper and passed it to Bragg.

'Thank you, sir... So what stage are you at now in the liquidation?'

'Since there has been no real trading, the creditors are few and the debtors non-existent. It is merely a matter of realising the assets, and returning the surplus to the shareholders.'

'So they have no need to be worried at all?'

Wormold hesitated. 'They have certainly less reason to be concerned than shareholders of a company which has been trading while insolvent.'

'Hmm... You say that no trading had been done, sir, yet they had bought machinery.'

'Oh, yes. The machinery was actually installed – they had to prepare a special concrete floor for the purpose. And some bulbs were manufactured. I believe that it is termed "commissioning the plant". All seemed to bode well for the project, until Mr Binswanger disappeared.'

'And when was that?'

Wormold went back to his files. 'On the twenty-ninth of May this year,' he said.

'And a fortnight later the company was put into liquidation. That was a bit quick, wasn't it, sir?'

'It was done on advice.'

'Oh, whose?'

'Largely mine, sergeant. There seemed no prospect of receiving adequate capital to sustain manufacturing, at that point; and the only man who could have run the plant had withdrawn. I saw it as the clear duty of the directors to realise the assets and return as much as possible to the shareholders.'

'And they took your advice.'

'Naturally.'

'Have you been successful in realising the assets?'

Wormold frowned. 'Not exactly,' he said. 'The machinery was very specialised, I gather. It has been placed with some dealers in second-hand plant; which was the best course of action. No doubt they will obtain the best price available.'

'No doubt,' Bragg said sardonically. 'And what about the freehold premises?'

'They are being sold by Prickett & Venables, the commercial property agents.'

'Ah, yes. I know of them. . . Where is this factory?'

'On the river at Castle Baynard Wharf, next to the Carron warehouse.'

'Good. Tell me, have you seen it yourself?'

'No, I have not, sergeant! I have more important things to do with my time!'

Bragg and Morton took a hansom to St Paul's churchyard. Then they walked down Godliman Street towards the river. This area had been at the heart of London's prosperity in the old days. Then the wharves would have been clogged with lighters, laden with cargo from ships moored below London Bridge. The streets would have been jammed with carts and vans, with straining horses and cursing drivers. Now it was deserted and near-derelict. The construction of the great enclosed docks, downstream at Millwall, had rendered these wharves obsolete. For forty years this neighbourhood had quietly mouldered, become a haunt of vagrants and criminals. There were some workshops, a few lock-up stores, but they were of no consequence. The City corporation ought to be ashamed, Bragg thought, to have such delapidated property within its bounds. But they were not. Real trade, like shipping, was a thing of the past. Now it was all money – shares, insurance and banking – with a few furs and diamonds to keep their womenfolk sweet.

'There is the Carron warehouse,' Morton said. 'Presumably the building we seek is on the left, by the river.'

They went down a narrow alley, towards St Paul's pier. Many of the buildings along it were roofless, the walls encircling their yards crumbling. What a place to start a new factory!

'This must be it,' Morton said. 'There is the estate agent's board.'

'Prickett & Venables. . . I'll tell you what, lad, I wouldn't like to work here. It looks as if a half-decent fart would bring the lot down.'

They pushed through a gate hanging drunkenly on its hinges and approached the soot-blackened warehouse. The doors had been nailed shut with timber battens, but they were able to peer through the grimy windows. The walls inside had once been whitewashed, now they were dirty and hung with cobwebs. In some areas of the wooden floor, planks were missing and the joists rotten.

'It makes you wonder if these accountants and suchlike ever condescend to come down to the real world,' Bragg said. 'Look at this shambles! And that sod Wormold is too satisfied with his own importance to realise that scores of people – hundred maybe – have been cheated rotten!'

'There is certainly no sign of their special concrete floor,' Morton said.

'No. . . But who stood to benefit? Let's go and have a chat with the chairman of Aurora, shall we?'

They took a hansom to Chelsea, where they found Major-General Hamilton-White in a gracious house overlooking the grounds of the Royal Hospital. He was a tall, grizzled man, with erect bearing. He received them affably, and took them into a sitting-room cluttered with native spears, tiger-skin rugs and outlandish musical instruments. He waved them to a settee.

'How can I help you, sergeant?' he asked.

'We have been asked to look into the affairs of Aurora Electric.'

Hamilton-White frowned. 'I saw one of your chappies some weeks back,' he said sharply. 'I thought it was all tied up.'

'There are one or two loose ends,' Bragg said mildly.

'I see. I doubt if I can help. I told everything I knew to the other johnny.'

'Can you tell us how you became appointed as chairman of Aurora, sir?'

'I was asked. Got a letter, I think. It is always happening. Not that I often accept – one doesn't like to be used merely to decorate the board.'

'Why did you accept this one?'

'Oh, it was interesting; scientific advance, you know. I was in the Engineers, so I have a slant that way.'

'And you did not feel that you were being used, on this occasion?'

'Good God, no! I insisted on being a working chairman.'

'Hmn. . . Did you buy any shares?'

'No. But they made me a present of five hundred – I had said that I would not take any remuneration until the enterprise was trading profitably.'

'Very proper, sir. And how did you exercise your function as a working chairman?'

'I suppose, mainly in conjunction with Burns, the secretary, and that Binswanger fellow.'

'Ah yes. Binswanger was to be the manager.'

'Yes. Dutchman. Knew his stuff, too. Jolly good chap! Dashed around organising everything.'

'He selected the factory and plant, did he?'

'Yes. Everything was going splendidly. Pity he went. He must have received a very tempting offer, to turn his back on his position with us.'

'Did he discuss the possibility of leaving Aurora with you?'

'No.' Hamilton-White looked mildly affronted. 'One day he was there, the next he was gone.'

'Did that not seem odd to you?'

'Well, where I learned my trade, if a fellow deserted you had him shot. But in civilian life you just shrug your shoulders and look for someone else.'

'And why did you not do just that?'

'I was all for it; but Burns said that Binswanger was unique. In the end I accepted – reluctantly, mind you – that the only course was to liquidate the company.'

Morton intervened. 'Am I right in thinking that the shares were only half-paid, sir?'

'Hamilton-White seemed surprised at his cultured accent. 'Yes. . . That was another odd thing,' he said. 'Just before Binswanger hopped it, there was a proposal put before the board to make a call for the unpaid money on the shares.'

'Who proposed that?' Morton asked.

'Well, Burns put the resolution to the board, as secretary. I do not know who originated it – perhaps that accountant chappie, Worm . . . something.'

'The effect of that resolution, if passed, would have been to double the money in the company's coffers?'

'Exactly so, young man. I frankly could not see the need for it, at that time. The factory had been bought, machinery installed and working satisfactorily. I felt that the sales of bulbs would generate the additional working capital. After all, they were going to be a sure-fire success. So I refused to countenance a further call on the shares.'

'And thereupon Binswanger disappeared?'

Hamilton-White frowned. 'I would not link the two happenings, as you seem to do. However, he certainly went immediately afterwards.'

'What view did the other directors take?'

'Apart from Burns and me, you mean?'

'Yes.'

'They never said much at directors' meetings. They seemed to follow Burn's lead, in the main.'

'How often did the board meet?'

'Hardly ever. Burns would chat over problems with me. When we had talked the matter through, he would sound out the other directors informally.'

There was a pause, then Bragg asked, 'Did you ever see the factory, sir?'

'See it? No. Burns and another of the directors did, and reported back that it was ideal for the purpose.'

'So, in your view, it was just bad luck that it all fell apart.'

'Damn bad luck, sergeant! It would have been of enormous benefit to millions of people. Now no one benefits.'

'And the shareholders have lost their money.'

'By no means! They will get it back from the sale of the factory. At least I did ensure that!'

On the journey back to Old Jewry, Bragg maintained a glum silence. From time to time he frowned or muttered to himself, but he did not share his thoughts with Morton. They had climbed the sweeping staircase, and were on the point of entering Bragg's room, when Inspector Cotton came storming along the corridor.

'What the bloody hell do you think you are up to, Bragg?' he shouted.

Bragg turned courteously. 'I am still working on the Chisnall case, sir,' he said.

'Then what did you draw my Aurora file for?' The inspector was puce with rage.

'There is a side of the Chisnall investigation which touches on the setting up of new companies, sir. Someone mentioned the Aurora case, and I thought I might learn something from it. . . I will tell Constable Morton to put the papers back with the closed cases,' he added mildly.

Inspector Cotton glared at him. 'If I find you have been reworking that sodding case behind my back, I will tear your balls off and boil them in your own piss!'

Bragg maintained a straight face. 'Very good, sir,' he said. 'Will that be all?'

11

Catherine Marsden sat at her dressing-table in the unforgiving morning light, and scrutinised her face. She was barely twenty-three, and already there were frown marks between her eyebrows. They made her look positively disagreeable, she thought. She smoothed a little cream over them, but they refused to disappear. . . The skin of her cheeks seemed coarse and rough, too. Those wretched hothouse society girls seemed able to keep their complexions for ever. Well, she would not wish to be like them – mere decorations, men's playthings! Poor creatures, they did not have a single moment of true freedom in their whole lives. From being dependent on their parents, they passed to a similar dependence on their husbands. Really, they were to be pitied rather than envied. Catherine suppressed the uncomfortable knowledge that her earnings at the *City Press* barely covered her expenditure on fares and the more ordinary items in her wardrobe. After all, her father was only too willing to have her still living at home; took delight in giving her presents of ball-gowns and expensive frippery. In the direst necessity, she told herself, she could have existed on what she earned. Her male colleagues actually brought up families on similar salaries. . . That was the really significant fact. She was holding down a real job, earning the same as a man would do, held in the highest regard by her fellow journalists. As James had said, the future belonged to women; and they had to meet the challenge, crow's feet and all!

Yet he had said it in his usual rallying way. In all probability he had meant no more than that the next generation was inevitably in the keeping of women. . . He could be so infuriating! He was very attentive when they were together; indeed they spent more time in each other's company than most couples who were engaged. Yet he still held back. . . She began to regret having teased him about Charles Anstruther, particularly when she mildly despised the man. James was such a gentleman that he was probably standing back, giving Charles his innings!

She sighed. How unfashionable her face was, she thought. Women considered beautiful had rounded china-doll faces. Hers was somewhat too long, the mouth was uncompromisingly firm, the chin positively jutted. True, the portrait that her father painted of her had been widely admired. When it was hung in the Royal Academy's summer exhibition, the art critic of *The Times* had described her as a self-assured beauty. And, indeed, they had been compelled to put rails round the portrait, to keep off the press of people wanting to see it. But that was two years ago. Perhaps the beauty was beginning to fade, the assurance becoming arrogance. . . She stood up impatiently. If James continued to be so indecisive, she still had her career. New vistas were opening up for her. She dabbed a little eau-de-Cologne behind her ears, then went downstairs.

Since her father had been away, her mother had allowed the servants to become lax. She much preferred to sit with the latest novel, rather than run her house efficiently. Her father would insist on having a full range of dishes at breakfast, from bacon and eggs to kedgeree. In his absence, her mother was willing to settle for a boiled egg and toast. Catherine vowed that she would never allow such slackness in any establishment of hers.

Her mother looked up as she entered. 'Ah, there you are, dear,' she said, putting aside the newspaper. 'A rather important-looking letter has come for you.'

Catherine's heart leapt. 'Where is it?' she asked excitedly.

'On the sideboard.'

Catherine bounded across and picked it up. The envelope was of crisp marbled parchment, the address had been typewritten. It must be! She caressed the paper with the tips of her fingers. At last! This was going to change her whole life. The solution to every problem lay within. She picked up a table knife to open it. No! That would be a desecration. Nothing but her father's silver paper-knife would suffice! Trying to contain her bubbling excitement she walked into the study. Like a surgeon she gently inserted the point under the flap and cut. As she drew out the letter she could see an embossed heading. *The Lady*! Her dreams had come true! She carefully unfolded the letter and read it.

> Dear Madam,
> I have the honour to inform you that, following your attendance at this office on the eleventh inst., full consideration was given to your suitability for the post of editor.

Catherine's heart was thumping, she could hardly contain her growing elation. Already the phrases of her letter of acceptance were forming in her brain, becoming entangled with the sentences in the letter. She took a deep breath and read on.

> After an extensive discussion, it was concluded that, although your credentials are impressive, the board should appoint someone with actual experience of editing a magazine.
> I am instructed to thank you for your interest, and to wish you well.
> Yours faithfully

Catherine subsided into a chair, then incredulously began to read the letter again. If only the Prince of Wales had not interfered! That must have been at the instigation of Lady Lanesborough. . . If her godmother had only known how much it meant to her! . . . Catherine blinked away her tears, and went back to her breakfast.

Bragg and Morton climbed the stairs to the office of Francis Child & Co., the liquidators of Aurora. After a short sojourn in the gloomy waiting-room, they were shown up to Wormold's office.

'Good morning, sir,' Bragg said affably. 'I just want a quick word about Aurora.'

Wormold's bald head bobbed irritably. 'If you must,' he said.

'I think you told us that you had never been down to the factory.'

Wormold frowned. 'That is so, sergeant. I am an accountant, not an engineer!'

'So you accepted everything that Binswanger told you.'

'Naturally. He was the only person with the knowledge and skill to run the plant.'

'That is a great pity,' Bragg said sarcastically.

'A pity?' Wormold's hackles were raised. 'I demand to know what you are insinuating!' he cried.

'So you shall, sir,' Bragg said mildly. 'The so-called factory is nothing more than a derelict warehouse. It is not even weatherproof. Further, you were apparently told that a special concrete floor had been laid, and machinery installed. There is not a square inch of concrete near the place, and the floor boards would give way if a rat landed on them.'

Wormold looked flabbergasted. 'You are not serious?' he said in alarm.

'Oh yes, sir. I would be surprised if any machinery has been near the place.'

'But . . . but I trusted them!'

'Yes. Well, you will know better than me how far it was wise to do that. Who was the factory bought from?'

'I do not know.'

'Was it you that arranged for it to be sold?'

'Yes. I instructed Prickett & Venables personally.'

'What about the machinery?'

'I left that to Burns.'

'I see. . . Do you have an address for Mr Burns?'

Wormold fumbled about in his files. 'Ah, here it is,' he exclaimed in some relief. 'Mr David Burns, eleven Harper Road, SE.'

'That is near the Elephant and Castle, isn't it?'

'It could well be.'

'I take it', Morton said, 'that you still have the deeds of the factory in your possession. It was freehold, after all.'

Wormold looked across at him defensively. 'Not actually in my possession, but under my control, certainly.'

'Where can we see them?'

'They are in the offices of my own solicitors. Yappe & Maunder of Finsbury Square.'

Morton smiled encouragingly. 'Would you please give us a note for them, authorising them to let us examine the deeds?'

Wormold hesitated, then took a piece of paper from his desk and scribbled briefly. He held it out to Bragg. 'I hope that there will be no trouble in this connection,' he said ingratiatingly.

'No more than you are in already,' Bragg said roughly. 'I expect we shall want to see you again.'

They set out for the solicitors' office on foot. The weather had recovered from the weekend storm, the sun shone, a cooling breeze blew from the west. Bragg almost felt like whistling.

'It should be a perfect day for the wedding on Saturday,' he said.

'I think you may be making some unwarranted assumptions,' Morton said sombrely.

'Maybe. But we will do our damnedest to sort it out. . . It is queer that we are in Finsbury Square, not all that far from Yeulett's house. This case seems to go round in circles.'

'I only hope that we are not wasting valuable time in pursuing the Aurora strand.'

'Can you think of anything else we could be doing?' Bragg asked curtly.

'Short of arresting Theo, Reuben and Adelaide, no.'

'Right.' He turned into a doorway embellished with the brass plates of companies' registered offices, and rang the bell in the reception office. A gangling youth appeared.

'I have a letter here, authorising us to see some deeds you hold,' Bragg said.

The youth scanned the letter. 'I will have to take this to Mr Parkinson,' he said. 'Just a moment.'

After a wait of ten minutes or so, Bragg was getting restive. Then the youth reappeared. 'I have cleared a little office at the back, so that you can examine them in peace,' he said. 'You understand that we cannot actually give you physical possession of them.'

'We know that, sir,' Bragg said testily. 'We shall only be half an hour.'

The youth gave him an uncertain smile and led them to the back of the building, where a door stood ajar. On a desk was a large bundle of documents. 'Those are the deeds you want,' he said, and backed out.

'Hmn. . . Quite a pile for one building,' Bragg remarked. 'But it must go back a good few years.'

'They seem to be in chronological order,' Morton said. 'I suggest that we work backwards. The early deeds are unlikely to be of more than passing interest to us.'

'Right.' Bragg settled in a chair near the window. 'The property seems to have been called the Paul's Wharf Warehouse. . . It was bought by Aurora on the second of April this year, though the purchase was not completed for three weeks or so.'

'I suppose that the subscription money for the shares did not cover the cost until then,' Morton remarked. 'What was the purchase price?'

Bragg turned a page. 'Bloody hell!' he exclaimed. 'One hundred and twenty thousand pounds!'

'That is a fortune! No one can remotely have thought that the building and its site could be worth even a fraction of that! Who was the vendor?'

'A man called Jonathan Bailey.' Bragg glanced at the deed beneath it in the pile. 'You are wrong, you know. Bailey had paid a hundred and ten thousand for it himself. . . Hullo, he only bought it in December last year! . . . And who do you think sold it to him?'

'I have no idea.'

'John Teverson of Finsbury Circus, EC.'

'Teverson!'

'Yes. Bailey was no more than a screen.'

'But did the chain go further back?'

Bragg turned over the deeds. 'No, Teverson inherited it from his father.'

'It will be interesting to hear Teverson's explanation of these transactions,' Morton said.

'Yes. But first I want a word with Mr Bailey. His address is . . . eleven Harper Road, SE! Interesting, isn't it?'

'That was the address of David Burns, the Aurora director.'

'It's unravelling with a vengeance now, lad. Come on!'

The journey in the growler to the Elephant and Castle was agony for Bragg. He perched uncomfortably on the edge of the seat, peering out at the traffic. The slightest check and he was muttering imprecations under his breath. When they became involved in a jam of traffic on Waterloo Bridge, he leapt out and tried to clear a path for them. Even when the tangle had eased, he kept his head out of the window, as if that gesture would prevent them from becoming embroiled again. As soon as they arrived at Harper Road he jumped out, telling the cab driver to wait.

The house was one of a terrace of small Georgian houses. They looked dingy, with their smoke-blackened yellow bricks and brown paint. Not the residence of a man of substance, Morton thought grimly. The door opened, and a fleshy middle-aged man stood on the threshold.

'Mr Burns?' Bragg enquired unctuously.

The man looked startled. 'Er . . . yes,' he said.

'We would like a quick word about Aurora Electric. May we come in?'

'Are you from Francis Child?' he asked.

'No. We are police officers.'

The blood drained from the man's face. He took hold of the door jamb to steady himself. 'I, er. . . Yes, I suppose so.'

He turned and led them into an over-furnished parlour at the front of the house. He seated himself by the fireplace, staring vacantly in front of him.

Bragg sat down opposite him, and for some moments there was an almost companionable silence. Then Bragg spoke.

'Why did you do it, sir?' he asked quietly.

'Do it?' For a moment Morton sensed a last flicker of hope in him, a spark of resistance.

'Your real name is Bailey, is it not?' Bragg said. 'You sold that derelict warehouse to Aurora for a factory. Most of the money subscribed by the shareholders went through your hands.'

'Through them, yes. But I was not the instigator of it.'

'We know that, sir. You were just a pawn. But you broke the law, nevertheless.'

'I would dispute that, officer.'

A friendly smile crossed Bragg's lips. 'I am sure that in due course, you will pay some barrister a great deal of money to do just that,' he said.

'I have not got a great deal of money,' Bailey said irritably.

'I don't know. Ten thousand pounds managed to stick to your

hands. Some folk would call that a great deal of money.'

'You do not understand, officer. That was my wife's money.'

'Hmn... You are right there, sir. I don't understand.'

'My wife was a Teverson. When the old man died, he left comparatively little – the business and the warehouse. All my wife got was this furniture and one hundred pounds. It was unfair! Even my brother-in-law agreed to that. He said that he could not dispose of the practice, for obvious reasons. But he promised that, when the warehouse was sold, she should get a share of the profit.'

'I see, sir. Have you seen the warehouse?'

Bailey's head dropped. 'Yes.'

'I wouldn't give you a fill of tobacco for it... Who worked out the scam?'

'Scam?' He looked up defiantly.

'The scheme to defraud the public, if you want it in plain English.'

'Well, I did not! All I wanted was to get the money due to my wife.'

'So it was Teverson?'

'Yes. He planned it all. He found the nominee directors, he prepared the prospectus.'

'It was all down to him was it?'

'Yes, it was!'

Bragg paused, as if in thought. Then he shook his head. 'It won't do, will it, sir? You had meetings with the chairman of the company and Binswanger. You led old Hamilton-White by the nose for a long time.'

Bailey gazed at Bragg and said nothing.

'Who was Binswanger, by the way?' Bragg asked.

'A Dutch engineer that my brother-in-law brought in. He could talk very persuasively in engineering terms.'

'But it was you who proposed that the unpaid portion of the company's capital should be called. If it had not been for the pig-headedness of Hamilton-White, you would have had another hundred and fifty thousand pounds to share between you... Is your wife at home?'

Bailey looked up dully. 'No. She died last year.'

'I see... Very well. Jonathan Bailey, I am arresting you for conspiracy and false pretences. We shall take you to the City of London police station at Moor Lane, where in due course you will be formally charged. If you wish to instruct lawyers to act for you, you will be able to do so at that stage. Do you understand?'

Bailey's head was in his hands; he was sobbing quietly. Bragg touched his shoulder. 'Come along, sir,' he said. 'There is no help for it.'

After they had left Bailey in the charge room at Moor Lane, Bragg and Morton walked to Tokenhouse Yard. They sat patiently in the waiting-room, until Teverson had finished his business with a client. When they were shown into his room he greeted them affably. Bragg ignored his proffered hand, and took a chair opposite him without a word. In the silence Teverson's pained expression turned into apprehension.

'We have just seen your brother-in-law,' Bragg said finally. 'He has been charged with conspiracy and false pretences. I must inform you that you need not say anything. If you do, it will be recorded by Constable Morton, and may be used in evidence.'

Teverson's face went white. In a daze he opened his mouth. 'I. . .' He swallowed painfully.

'Do you want to tell us about it, sir?' Bragg said encouragingly. 'When did you first get the idea for the scam? After all, the factory had been yours for many years already.'

'It was all Chisnall's fault,' Teverson babbled. 'He suggested it. He told me how to go about it. He is the real criminal!'

'Was, I think you mean, sir. . . Did you never spare a thought for all the people you intended to defraud?'

'They could all afford it, I took care of that. We got the names from the Navy List, the Army List, Crockford's Clerical Directory. . . All people who were comfortably retired. We did no real harm.'

'If I were on the bench, that plea in mitigation would not go down well with me,' Bragg remarked. 'But what on earth made you do it?'

Teverson looked up defiantly. 'I needed the money,' he said. 'When I took over the business it was at a low ebb. My father had kept all the worthwhile clients for himself. He was in poor health for a long time before he died, and in that period his clients had drifted elsewhere. It was all that I could do to keep the firm going.'

'But you inherited the warehouse,' Bragg said.

'Huh! As you must know, it is nothing better than derelict. It was utterly useless for any purpose, even then.'

'But it stood on freehold land.'

'Yes. At any other time one might have turned it to advantage. But the whole area is decayed. No one wished to set up a business there. I have had the premises with various agents – for sale, or to rent – for fifteen years. Not one serious enquiry have I had. It would require a wholesale clearance scheme to put that part of the City on its feet again. I have tried several times to interest the Common Council in such a project, but they always had other irons in the fire. . . It is a public disgrace, so close to St Paul's Cathedral!'

'No doubt,' Bragg said drily. 'But surely this firm gave you enough to live on? I mean, you were on your own from your late twenties.'

'Were it not for Chisnall, I would have been able to manage,' Teverson said in a self-pitying voice. 'For years I have been paying him more than I spent on myself.'

'Why was that, sir?'

'An incident, long ago. I have no intention of augmenting the number of accusations you will no doubt throw at me.'

'And if he had made the matter public, you would have been ruined, eh?'

'That is the essence of blackmail, sergeant,' Teverson said angrily.

'You helped him with some sort of scam, did you, sir? Is that how you learned your trade?'

Teverson compressed his lips and glared mutely at Bragg.

'And, of course, he was involved in Aurora, wasn't he?' Bragg asked.

'Only to the extent that he wrote the circular and sent it out.'

'Was he due to get a share of the loot, or did you just pay him a fee?'

'A fee. . . Though my share would have mostly found its way to him, in time.'

'I see. . . Can you tell me why Chisnall put you in his play?'

Teverson looked at Bragg stonily. 'I do not know what you are talking about,' he said.

'Chisnall told the producer that the actors had to emphasise certain phrases. One of them was "profitable enlightenment", which, of course, meant Aurora. Now, why would he want that, if you had plenty of money to pay him with?'

'I just do not know, sergeant. At one stage he was pressing to be a full partner in the scheme. I refused, and he became very angry. But latterly he no longer seemed to care.'

'It is all quite simple really,' Bragg said mildly. 'He knew he had not long to live. We think he was planning an obscure kind of vengeance, in the play, on all the people from his youth who had done better than he had. So you see, you had no need to kill him.'

'Kill him?' Teverson's voice rose to a hysterical shriek. 'I did not kill him! I may be a fraudsman, God help me; but I am not a murderer!'

'Let us hope He does.' Bragg rose to his feet. 'John Teverson, I must ask you to accompany us to Moor Lane police station, where in due course you will be charged with conspiracy and false pretences in connection with Aurora Electric Lighting Company Limited. Other charges may follow.'

Bragg tapped on the door of Inspector Cotton's room and went inside. Cotton raised his head, then went on reading the file on his desk. Bragg stood for almost five minutes in front of him, before he closed the folder and looked up.

'What do you want?' he asked unpleasantly.

'I am sorry to say, sir, that it has proved impossible to keep the Chisnall investigation and your Aurora case apart.'

Cotton flushed angrily. 'What the bloody hell do you mean, "proved impossible"?'

'Chisnall was blackmailing Teverson, the stockbroker. Teverson could well have murdered Chisnall.'

'I don't give a tuppenny bugger about Chisnall! I told you to keep away from Aurora.'

'We tried,' Bragg said blandly. 'But Chisnall was involved in that scam too.'

'Scam? What scam?'

'Teverson owned a derelict warehouse near St Paul's pier. With a bit of help, he got it sold to Aurora for a hundred and ten thousand pounds. I reckon it is worth no more than a thousand, in its present state. His brother-in-law, Bailey, fronted for him. They are both in Moor Lane police station.' He dropped a bundle of papers on Cotton's desk. 'These are the interview notes, sir. We have not charged either Teverson or Bailey. I thought you would like to do that bit.'

Bragg turned on his heel and left Cotton spluttering with anger. Smiling smugly he bounced into his room, only to find the Commissioner staring gloomily out of the window.

'Ah, Bragg.' Sir William turned and wandered over to the fireplace. 'Constable Morton has been telling me that you may be getting closer to solving the Chisnall case,' he said diffidently.

'It is a big may, sir.'

'Hmn. . . I was hoping we could at least take some kind of action – as a demonstration that we are actively engaged in pursuing the culprit.'

'Action based on evidence, you mean?'

'Er . . . yes, of course,' Sir William said sheepishly.

Bragg sat down at his desk, and stared at the gas-bracket hanging from the ceiling. 'Well, sir, we could certainly make out a case for arresting one or two people. Inspector Cotton has Teverson in custody on a fraud charge. We know that Chisnall was involved in a scam with him. We also know that Chisnall was blackmailing Teverson.'

'A clear motive for murder.' The Commissioner's face was struggling to look optimistic. 'What a pity that Inspector Cotton has got him already.'

'Yes, sir,' Bragg said drily.

'Are there no others that you can arrest? I am under the most extreme pressure from the police committee to be seen to do something. They tell me that, until the Chisnall case is dead and buried, the market will remain in the doldrums. I know it sounds absurd to us, but it is apparently a matter of confidence.'

'You mean, sir, that until we arrest one rogue, all the others will be uneasy?'

'No. I do not mean that, Bragg!' Sir William cleared his throat uncertainly. 'But some decisive action is undoubtedly called for.'

Bragg sat up briskly. 'Well, sir, the other clear suspects are as follows. Firstly Theodore Smith, principal of Smith Payne & Smith's bank; secondly Adelaide Smith, wife of the said Theodore Smith; thirdly Reuben Smith, son of the said Theodore and Adelaide Smith. . . I think that's the lot. We probably have enough evidence to get warrants. Would that be enough to restore confidence to the stock market?'

'You know perfectly well it would be disastrous, Bragg!' The Commissioner looked up suspiciously. 'You are not bulling me by any chance, are you?'

'No, sir. I would not dream of such a thing.'

'Hmn. . . And do you really think that this Teverson man will turn out to be the murderer?'

Bragg appeared to ponder the question. 'Well, he is certainly a fraudsman. . . I suppose he might well be resolute enough to kill his blackmailer. Though there was precious little to link him with Chisnall, when we started out. I expect you ought to discuss that with Inspector Cotton, sir. He has a kind of prior claim, now that he is charging Teverson with fraud.'

The Commissioner sighed dejectedly. 'Yes. . . I suppose that is the best course.' He wandered slowly out of the room.

Morton chuckled. 'Are you not in danger of giving too many hostages to fortune, sir?' he asked.

'Me?' Bragg said incredulously. 'I am the most dutiful subordinate a Commissioner could ever wish for. . . And he is such a nice fellow, at bottom.'

'You could become even more subordinate, if Inspector Cotton ever found an opening.'

'Yes. . . You are right. I have no ambition to rise higher, but it would be a real sickener if I were reduced to constable again. . . Right, lad, we must go through all the evidence again, to make sure that we have not missed anything. You take Teverson, since you have that side in your head. I will do the Smiths.'

Bragg lit his pipe and they settled to their work in silence. After a time there was a knock at the door and Catherine Marsden came in.

'I hope that I am not disturbing anything vital,' she said diffidently.

Morton looked at her closely. 'You seem very subdued this morning,' he said lightly.

'Do I?' She hesitated. 'Well, as a matter of fact I have had some mildly disappointing news.'

'Oh dear! What is that?'

Catherine took a deep breath. 'I have not been appointed editor of *The Lady*,' she blurted out.

'Ah. Then I am most sorry. You would have brought a breath of new life to it.'

'New life was the last thing they wanted!' Catherine exclaimed angrily. 'I have since learned that they appointed the existing deputy editor to the post! The interviews were an utterly sterile gesture. The succession must have been settled even before they began!'

'Then they are the losers. . . Though I am not at all certain that you would have enjoyed the work.'

'But it would have solved so many difficulties!'

Morton put a brotherly arm round her shoulders. 'You would have come to hate it,' he said gently. 'You could never have borne their snobbish attitudes to life.'

Catherine sniffed and pushed away his arm. 'Well, I did not intend to bring my problems to you,' she said. 'I have come with the solution to one of your problems!'

Morton grinned. 'That is more like the Catherine we all know and . . . admire. Were we aware of this problem?'

'Oh yes. It is the third phrase underlined in Chisnall's play. Do you remember it – "misled ever so daintily"?'

'Of course.'

'I have been thinking about it, you know! Last night I took the Stock Exchange year-book home, and went through it.'

'With Charles Anstruther?' Morton said acidly.

'Of course not,' Catherine said airily. 'I have not seen him for . . . oh, for some days.'

'Well, you might have realised that I have already been through the year-book,' Morton said nettled. 'There is no mention of a Dainty on the Exchange.'

'Not in London, perhaps,' she said loftily. 'But if you had been thorough, you would have realised that there is an appendix at the back of the book, which names the members of provincial Stock Exchanges!' She paused provocatively.

'Go on, miss,' Bragg said urgently.

'There is a firm on the Birmingham Stock Exchange named Norrington Dainty & Co.'

Bragg leapt to his feet. 'Norrington?' he exclaimed. 'It must be connected to Yeulett Norrington!' he cried. 'Well done, miss! Here, lad, get the Bradshaw and find the time of the next train to Birmingham!'

12

'I think you may be proved right over our fascination with *The Three Musketeers*, sir.'

The express train slackened speed, as the suburbs of Birmingham came into sight.

'Why is that, lad?' Bragg asked. 'It was me thought they were making a game of it.'

'You said that it might mislead us, and that may indeed have been the case.'

'How can that be? We know that Teverson was Porthos; and Adelaide herself said that Theo was Athos.'

'Yes. But we assumed that Chisnall must therefore be Aramis. We looked only at the three lodgers in Monkwell street. Yet the hero of the book is D'Artagnan. He was the outsider, the youth with no patronage or influence. He made his way in the world by his courage and effrontery; he won the secret love of the fair heroine. I believe that Chisnall saw himself as D'Artagnan.'

'Hmn. . . So on that basis Aramis could be Yeulett, eh?'

'One could make out a case for it.'

'Well, we will give it a run. Where did you say the main police station is here?'

'Steelhouse Lane, according to our records, though they may well be out of date.'

The train coasted to a stop at the platform, and they hurried out of the station. There was a small crowd by the cab rank, and they waited for fifteen minutes before their turn came. When they secured their growler, it took them a mere quarter-mile before depositing them at police headquarters. They could have walked it in half the time, Bragg thought grumpily. After negotiating with a brisk duty sergeant, they were shown to the office of the head of the criminal investigation department. Inspector Parkinson was a bluff north-countryman; he received them with thinly veiled hostility.

'Why are you interested in what goes on up here?' he asked brusquely. 'Haven't you got enough rogues in London?'

Bragg smiled. 'I cannot think we have a monopoly of swindlers, anyway. The trouble is, they are getting cleverer all the time.'

'And what do you mean by that?'

'Well, if they plan their villainy in one city, carry it out in a second, and dispose of the loot in a third, they might think they can get away with it.'

'You are one of those who want an army-style police force, like the Frogs, are you?' Parkinson said with a sneer.

'No, sir. I am all for local forces,' Bragg said meekly. 'But I think London can learn a lot from the provinces, if it did but know it.'

The inspector looked at him coldly. 'And what do you hope to learn from me?' he asked.

'We have some bond-brokers in the City called Yeulett Norrington & Co. The proprietor of the firm – Robin Yeulett – is on the fringe of a murder enquiry. The victim was blackmailing all and sundry, so he got what was coming to him. What we have to sort out is who bashed his head in.'

'And why should we know?'

'We gather there is a firm of stockbrokers in Birmingham called Norrington Dainty & Co. It is a bit of a long shot, but it seemed to be too much of a coincidence that there should be two Norringtons in the same line of business.'

Parkinson looked at them suspiciously, then he pulled an index-book from his drawer. He turned the pages, then grunted. 'We had a complaint that involved Norrington Dainty & Co.,' he said. 'We should have a file somewhere.' He replaced the book in the drawer, ostentatiously locked it, then went out.

'I think that your vision of a patchwork of separate forces, all co-operating with each other, is somewhat Utopian, sir,' Morton said with a smile.

'Never mind, lad. We are getting somewhere; I can feel it in my bones.'

Parkinson came back into the room with a slim folder in his hand. He sat down at his desk and went through it in silence. Then he looked up. 'Not much here for you,' he said. 'We had a complaint, last year, about a company that Norrington Dainty handled. A Rear-Admiral Thompson wrote in. He had expected big dividends from some shares he bought. When they didn't come, the silly bugger complained to us; as if we could pay them out!'

'What was the name of the company, sir?' Morton asked.

Parkinson looked down at his folder. 'Rand Gold Mines Limited,' he said.

'Ah, yes. I have seen a financial circular relating to the company,' Morton said.

'What action did you take, sir?' Bragg asked.

'We went to see old Arthur Norrington. He was not a well man, even then. . . As far as I could see, there was nothing for us. It was a public company, with a general and a magistrate on the board. Everything seemed to have been done properly. The prospectus made it clear that it was a speculation. People should not put money they cannot afford to lose, into risky ventures.'

'What was the upshot of your investigation, sir?' Bragg asked mildly.

Parkinson gave him a hostile stare. 'I've told you, sergeant. There was nothing we could do then, and there is still less anyone can do now. Arthur Norrington died just before New year.'

'Is the firm still continuing?' Morton asked.

'It may be. You could go and see. They were in Albert Street. But you will be wasting your time!'

Bragg thanked Parkinson with an irony that was lost on him, then led the way to the offices of Norrington Dainty & Co. They were in a rather dejected building, in a dark side-street. They went into the general office, where a white-haired clerk was poring over a rent-book. He looked up.

'Can I help you, gentlemen?' he asked.

Bragg showed his warrant-card. 'We just want a quick word about Rand Gold Mines,' he said.

'Well, there is not a great deal I can tell you,' the clerk replied. 'We were acting on behalf of our associated firm in London.'

'Yeulett Norrington & Co., you mean?'

'Yes. We have not handled a new issue of shares for forty years. Mr Arthur was content to plod along quietly, with the same old clients. . . The trouble was that man is mortal, and our business was beginning to dwindle.'

'Did Mr Yeulett show you what to do?'

'Yes. Of course, he knew he would inherit this firm when his uncle died. I suppose he had become concerned that there might be nothing left, if he did not intervene.'

'Are you saying that he gave you the necessary instructions, without consulting Mr Norrington?'

'That is so. I am sure that Mr Arthur knew all about it, but he was so ill at the time.'

'When precisely was this?'

'Precisely? Oh, you will have to wait while I get the papers.' He went shakily out of the room.

'Not the most thriving of concerns,' Morton remarked flippantly.

'What was this Rand Gold Mines circular you mentioned?' Bragg asked.

'One of Chisnall's. If I remember aright, it was not with the Aurora circular; but the papers have become so mixed up over the last few days. . . I am certain, however, that it did not have "Aramis" written on it.'

'What made you notice it, then?'

'My trustees were considering a similar, though I trust a more reputable investment. President Kruger is releasing large tracts of the Rand for mineral exploration. South African gold mines are currently the favoured financial gamble. There is certainly gold in the area, perhaps in great quantity. But whether the particular patch of land in your mineral lease contains any is indeterminable until you drill. And you cannot drill without having first raised considerable capital resources.'

'Are you saying these gold shares can be a good investment?'

'Not in the sense of being safe, I think. Certainly my trustees abandoned the idea, after a brief dalliance with it. No, I would say that at best they would be a lottery.'

'And at worst?'

'Why, they are a fraudman's dream! No one would travel out to Johannesburg and trek out into the veld to find their little plot of land. If they did so, and managed to identify it, they would see merely a part of a vast expanse of grassland. They would have to make test drillings, before they could pronounce on the likelihood of finding gold. Even if there were no gold-bearing rock, they would not be able to complain.'

'So a villain could invent a so-called exploration lease, sell it to a company and push the shares on to a gullible public?'

The clerk came into the room with a large bundle of files. He put them on the desk, and undid the strap that held them. He took the top folder and went slowly through its contents. Morton could see that Bragg was fuming with impatience. Finally the clerk looked up.

'I see that the circulars began to be sent out in February of eighteen ninety-three,' he said. 'We posted them in batches, from the seventh to the twenty-fifth.'

'Who did you send them to?' Bragg asked quietly.

'People around Birmingham, Coventry, the Potteries.'

'Fairly well-to-do people, then?'

The clerk turned to another folder and extracted several sheets of paper, containing columns of names and addresses. 'There were a lot of military and naval officers,' he said, 'and clergymen.'

'Did you decide who to send them to?'

'No. These lists were prepared in the offices of our associate firm in London.'

'Have you a copy of the circular?' Morton asked.

The clerk opened yet another file, and handed him a document. Morton scrutinised it. 'Yes, this is the one.' He handed it to Bragg, then turned back to the clerk.

'The company you were floating claimed that it had options on several mineral leases, in an area where large deposits of gold-bearing rock have been located,' he said. 'Did you take any steps to verify that statement?'

The clerk looked at him apprehensively. 'No. It is not the function of a flotation house to verify the contents of the prospectus. The directors of the company are alone responsible for that.'

'But you did get complaints from the public?'

'Well, yes. Many people seem to have interpreted the prospectus as promising them a guaranteed interim dividend in September. If they had thought about it at all deeply, they would have realised that in no way could an exploration company buy the leases, complete the drilling programme, sink a mine shaft and extract the gold, all in six months. The only way they could have been paid a dividend would have been out of the share subscription money. . . That would have been illegal!' he added self-righteously.

'Yes. . . So what is the position now?'

'Well, the police came, because someone had complained to them. They found nothing wrong. And I do not believe there is anything wrong.'

'Of course.' Morton said reassuringly. 'The subscription money came to you, I suppose.'

'Yes, and we sent out the share certificates. I can show you one, if you like.'

'That is not necessary, thank you. What were your instructions regarding the cheques?'

'Mr Yeulett used to come up and get them.'

'I see. Why did you not pay them into a bank in Birmingham?'

'Mr Yeulett said not to. The company's account was with a bank I have never heard of.'

Bragg intervened. 'Try and remember, will you, sir?' he said encouragingly.

The clerk frowned. 'It was three names . . . quite ordinary names, I think. But they do not have any branches up here.'

'Would it have been Smith Payne & Smith's, by any chance, sir?' Bragg asked.

The man's face cleared. 'Yes, that is it!' he exclaimed. 'Smith Payne & Smith's! Fancy you guessing that!'

By half-past four Bragg and Morton were at the office of Yeulett Norrington & Co., in the Strand.

'Where is Mr Yeulett?' Bragg demanded of a startled typewriter.

'He is in his office.'

'Right! We will go through.'

He pushed past the protesting girl, and down the corridor to the back of the building. He crashed through the door of Yeulett's room. The bond-broker was standing by an open press, a file in his hand. He looked round startled. There was a flicker of fear across his face. He placed the file in the press and closed the door.

'Good afternoon, gentlemen,' he said calmly. 'Please take a seat.'

They sat opposite him in silence for a space, until it seemed that a deliberate effort would be needed to shatter it. Then Bragg spoke.

'We have just come from Norrington Dainty's,' he said quietly. 'We know all about Rand Gold Mines.'

Yeulett looked at him steadily. 'I see,' he said.

'Why did you do it?'

Yeulett gave a harsh bark of a laugh. 'For the money, of course,' he said. 'Why else does one do anything?'

'How far was Chisnall involved in it?'

'Chisnall?' Yeulett's eyes were wary.

'We know he prepared the circular.'

Yeulett let out a long breath. 'In effect he devised the whole scheme,' he said. 'He came to me with the suggestion of a gold exploration scheme. I had no doubt at all about the bona fides of the company . . . it seemed to point the way to the future, to be the salvation of this firm.'

'But Norrington Dainty did all the work, way up in Birmingham,' Bragg said quietly.

'Naturally, they are stockbrokers. I wished to take the temperature of the water, before committing this firm to a change of direction. In any case, they did not do all the work.'

'How do you mean, sir?'

Yeulett gave a ghost of a smile. 'A week after each batch of circulars had been sent out, Chisnall arranged for canvassers to go to the houses of the recipients, ostensibly by chance. They would be singing the praises of other investments, but would ensure that gold mines were mentioned. On being told that a circular relating to Rand Gold Mines Limited had been received, they would acknowledge with some reluctance that it was a much more attractive investment than anything they could offer themselves. We always got a second flush of applications from that.'

'By then, of course, you knew it was a scam.'

Yeulett hesitated. 'I did become aware that it was a dishonest scheme.'

'Was Theo Smith involved in it?'

'Theo? No.'

'But Rand Gold Mines banked with Smith's.'

'Chisnall insisted. He said it would look better in the prospectus than a joint stock bank.'

'So Theo got nothing out of this?'

'Nothing except the normal banker's turn.'

'Do you think Chisnall might have had a further fetch to it?'

'I do not understand.'

'He has struck me as a man who did nothing without a reason. I wondered if he saw a possible opportunity for blackmailing Theo.'

Yeulett gave a grimace. 'There you have it. Blackmail was his trade. . . I did not realise the fact until it was too late. I had accepted all the documentation of Rand Gold Mines from him in good faith. I was acting purely as an issuing broker.'

'But not in the way one would normally float a public company.'

Yeulett considered. 'Only in the marketing of the shares was there a significant difference,' he said.

Bragg shook his head. 'I wasn't born yesterday,' he said in mild reproof. 'You first issued a small number of shares – possibly to yourselves – then you put through a lot of sham deals, which made it look as if there was a tremendous demand for Rand Gold Mines, and forced the price up. They would not be likely to spot that sort of thing, up there on the Birmingham Stock Exchange. It was on the basis of that inflated price that you issued Chisnall's puffing circular.'

Yeulett slumped back in his chair. 'What does it matter?' he said. 'Chisnall had done it before, no doubt he would have done it again.'

'If you had not killed him.'

Yeulett ignored Bragg's remark. 'I had no sooner banked the proceeds of the share flotation than I discovered the precariousness of my position with a vengeance,' he said. 'Chisnall pointed out that I and Norrington Dainty had strayed over the line into criminality. He himself was in the clear. He demanded money. I had none of my own. I said he could take it from the commission owed to my firm for the flotation. He laughed at me! He said he was going to write a play; that I would be in it. Unless I paid up, I would be ruined.'

'When was this, sir?' Bragg asked.

'I don't know; in the spring.' Yeulett's voice was becoming petulant. 'He took the commission, and more. And he always came back again. . . I had not very much left in life, but he was destroying it. . . He pushed me too hard, sergeant. He pushed me too hard . . .'

'What did he want, the night you killed him?' Bragg asked gently.

'More money. . . A final application. The play was in rehearsal, my name would be blackened unless. . . He even showed me what he proposed his character should say. He gloated. . . I did not mean to kill him. I had to give vent to the rage inside me. . . He taunted me, said I was a feeble old woman. I lost control. I must have picked up the poker and hit him. When my mind cleared I had the poker in my hand and he was lying on the floor.' He stopped speaking, his eyes staring into the distance.

'And then?' Bragg prompted him.

'Then? . . . Why, I took the script of the play and burned it.'

'And you tried to burn down Gatti's Music Hall.'

'It was the only way. I knew, you see, that they must have another copy.'

'What else?'

Yeulett shook his head uncomprehendingly.

'You cleared out the desk, and the volumes from the bookcase.'

'Ah. I had written him a letter of protest, which attempted to show that he was morally just as involved in Rand Gold Mines as I was myself . . . I failed to find it.'

'So you had another go with the poker to make sure he was dead.'

Yeulett looked at Bragg, as at a dull-witted child. 'But he was an animal! . . . He would have left me with nothing . . . and all to wager on stupid racehorses. I could not allow it to happen. I could not allow it . . .'

Bragg got to his feet. 'Come along, sir,' he said. 'Get your hat. It's all over now.'

EPILOGUE

Catherine Marsden could not sleep. She tossed and turned in the little monastic cell she had been given at The Priory. Her mind was full of brilliant patterns, like a kaleidoscope. If she tried to shake it empty, different patterns would form. It was so hot in the room; even with the tiny window open. Although the humid heat had gone, the stone seemed still to radiate warmth.

Why had she been given this room? Clearly The Priory was bursting at the seams, with people converging on Hollingbourne from every point of the compass. The whole village was full of wedding guests. At least she was in the house. . . But why her? Had she been put in this tiny room because she was unregarded, or because she was someone they did not need to impress? Was she unimportant, or virtually one of the family?

She wrenched her mind from that self-flagellating course. The aura of monastic asceticism must be infecting her mind. She wondered impiously how the monks would have reacted, had they seen her as she now was – stretched naked on top of the bedclothes. In a very human way, if their reported conduct was anything to go by! Of more immediate concern, what would she do if James tiptoed in? In her present mood she would not want to send him away. She gently drew the tips of her fingers along her belly and down her thighs. She had a good, strong body; body and mind should act in conjunction, not be at war with each other . . . She wondered what the moral equivalent of a cold bath was! Of course, Emily and Reuben would be in bed in Dover, *en route* to their honeymoon in Venice. Their first night together. Emily would be fully a woman by now . . .

On the verge of sleep, Catherine had a sudden vision of James – in Violet's bed! She jerked awake. That predatory bitch! Why did Americans think they had a right to come over to England and take all the best men? She had made a set for him right from the beginning; straightening his tie in the church porch, and pawing at him. . . Perhaps it was a last desperate attempt to get him. Once he went back to London, he would not see Violet again on this visit. And he would be going back to London with her! . . . All the same, Violet had quite spoiled her enjoyment of the wedding. In the space of three years, since she had been persuaded to stay at The Priory while a badly sprained ankle healed, she and Emily had become very close. It still rankled that Violet had been the principal bridesmaid; the more so because James, as principal groomsman, had processed back down the aisle with Violet on his arm. She had unworthily wished that Violet would catch her heel in the hem of her dress, and go sprawling. But that might have been worse. James would have caught her in his arms, and fussed over her . . .

Catherine tried to force her mind on to a happier track. It had been a beautiful wedding. The little church had been full of flowers and greenery. White flowers for a chastity soon to be surrendered. It seemed a quaint conceit. During the interminable photography afterwards, Emily had seemed serene and somehow complete, on her husband's arm. . . And it had been a joyous wedding! Sergeant Bragg had prowled about, before the reception, like a great self-satisfied bear. She had seen Theo Smith shaking his hand, Reuben had sought him out. There was a sense of elation, even of carnival about. Adelaide had seemed almost skittish. She wondered why . . .

The meal in the Great Hall had been a wondrous affair. As a bridesmaid she had been on the top table, looking down on the company seated at the great walnut table which was said to have been brought back by the crusaders from the Holy Land. The many-branched chandeliers had cast a warm light over the guests. When the house was being electrified, Lady Morton had decreed that the Great Hall should remain inviolate. She was undoubtedly right, though Sir Henry had grumbled about self-conscious archaism.

Catherine got up and went to the window. She drew back the curtain; already it was daylight. She gazed over the deer-park, with its great trees and misty hollows. The Priory was an enchanted place, an oasis in the frenetic clamour of modern life. It had to be kept just as it was. . . It was strange that Lady Morton, born and brought up in the New World, should have such an instinctive affinity with its ancient buildings. She had been an honourable custodian; but who would succeed her? . . . Catherine was painfully aware that, from now on, her own status would be different. She had been able to come down to The Priory when she wished; was welcomed as Emily's friend. There had been no need to insinuate herself as an intimate of James. But now Emily would no longer be here. . . No matter! She would find a way; her destiny seemed to be bound up with this untidy sprawl of ancient buildings.

Her mind at last in repose, Catherine lay down on her bed again, and drifted into sleep.